BABY X

Also available by Kira Peikoff

Living Proof
No Time to Die
Die Again Tomorrow
Mother Knows Best

BABY X

A THRILLER

KIRA PEIKOFF

NEW YORK

This is a work of fiction. All of the names, characters, organizations, places and events portrayed in this novel are either products of the author's imagination or are used fictitiously. Any resemblance to real or actual events, locales, or persons, living or dead, is entirely coincidental.

Published in the United States by Crooked Lane Books, an imprint of The Quick Brown Fox & Company LLC.

Crooked Lane Books and its logo are trademarks of The Quick Brown Fox & Company LLC.

Library of Congress Catalog-in-Publication data available upon request.

ISBN (hardcover): 978-1-63910-633-2
ISBN (ebook): 978-1-63910-634-9

Cover design by Nicole Lecht

Printed in the United States.

www.crookedlanebooks.com

Crooked Lane Books
34 West 27th St., 10th Floor
New York, NY 10001

First Edition: March 2024

10 9 8 7 6 5 4 3 2 1

For Zach and Leo

PART I

CHAPTER

1

Present day

ACROSS THE CAFÉ, Quinn watched the happy couple. They hadn't noticed her yet. But they would soon.

Quinn knew she should feel triumphant. Her persistence had paid off. All those hours spent refreshing Thorne's social media feed, tracking his routines, angling for a way in. Sometimes she felt like a stalker, until she remembered why she wasn't like all his other crazy fans. Her reason wasn't in her head.

She had tried many times to message him. But her increasingly frantic notes kept vanishing into the oblivion of his inbox, which she imagined was in a constant state of overflow. It was futile to keep waiting for his ping that never came, and time was running out.

Thank God for his coffee habit. Twelve days ago, he'd tagged his favorite café in a post, thanking them for the artistic latte: instead of leaves or a heart, the baristas had crafted a special design for their most famous customer: a white foam guitar. The beachside spot in Laguna Beach was forty-five miles from her tiny apartment in the foothills of the Santa Ana mountains.

So Quinn had spent the last eleven mornings hauling herself into the car and driving in traffic through the narrow canyon to watch and wait for his next appearance there. The coffee, not to mention the parking, were getting expensive.

Now, seeing him again in real life at last gave her a familiar thrill. Nine months had passed since the last time she'd seen him, during his summer concert stop at the Hollywood Bowl, and she'd never gotten anywhere near this close, even in her expensive seat.

Across the patio, she could see him perfectly. Was it the proximity to fame that made her pulse whoosh in her ears? Or was it her overpowering attraction to this man? She admired his profile—the curly abundance of dirty-blond hair, the sculpted jaw she knew so well, the slight bump in his nose, endearing insofar as he had resisted the cultural pressure to eradicate his flaws. He was himself and he didn't give a damn, not like those other shallow celebrities who nipped and tucked and tweaked and plucked themselves into stereotypes of perfection. She loved how *real* Thorne was—or at least, how he seemed. She had never actually met him.

Her eyes traveled approvingly across his broad shoulders and down his muscular calves below his shorts, to his black Chuck Taylors, then back up to his hands at the table. Holding a cup of coffee were the iconic long, slender fingers that had graced the homepage of *Rolling Stone* a decade ago.

He was shorter and scruffier than he appeared during his virtual hologram shows. On those occasions, he was literally larger than life, projected via smart contact lenses into her living room, at seven feet tall. Here, sized back down to a regular guy, he retained a kind of bold confidence that she herself had never managed to achieve, growing up a shy only child. It was no wonder he could command a stage solo, just him and his guitar—and his signature raspy voice.

At his feet, a paunchy black Lab stretched out its paws. Smokey. He was seven years old, a rescue dog—a real, living dog even at a time when so many other pet owners had turned to android dogs instead. It was another one of the endearing things about Thorne. All his die-hard followers knew these basic facts.

What surprised her was the vaguely familiar woman at his side. She was resting her hand on his knee. Even from Quinn's distance, the woman's high cheekbones and elegant neck stood out. Her chin-length blonde hair was cut at an angle, longer in the front than the back, and she was wearing a blazer with leather pants, probably a size two, and white sneakers.

Quinn was wearing yoga pants and a loose red top with ample room for her growing belly. Next to Thorne's companion, she felt like an overripe tomato.

Thorne had never posted anything about his personal life. How naive of her to assume he would be single. Of course his fans didn't know the real him, although he was very good at making it seem like they did. The intimacy was manufactured for mass consumption yet felt authentic. Especially to her. The tenant in her womb unleashed a ninja kick.

She regretted that she was about to blow up his life.

For half an hour, she had been sitting there, putting it off. Just watching the two of them in their bubble. Sipping coffee, holding hands. Their "before" period. Because nothing after would ever be the same.

Thorne was regaling the woman with some funny story, using lots of animated gestures. Every so often, her gaze tore away from him and swept defensively around the patio, as though erecting a force field around them. Her alertness was jarring in this gentle atmosphere, where carefree chatter and clanking utensils blended with the ocean crashing right across the street. If anyone recognized Thorne, they didn't care to bother him.

The waiter approached and handed Thorne the check. Smokey pushed up to stand. It was time.

Quinn rubbed her belly. Heat flooded her face as though she herself were on stage, with the whole restaurant riveted to the scene she was about to cause. But no one paid her any attention as she lumbered toward their table.

Halfway there, she stopped.

The woman was putting on yellow latex gloves—and unpacking a small suitcase filled with what appeared to be scientific tools: a biohazard bag labeled with a skull, glass tubes with red caps, pipettes, cotton swabs, a magnifying glass.

A few customers nearby took notice. Their chatter ceased. But Thorne didn't seem bothered. He patted the dog's head as the woman collected his plate, fork, and coffee mug. She unscrewed one of the tubes, plunged a pipette into it and sucked up a clear liquid, dripped it onto a cotton swab. Then she rubbed the swab all over his mug's edge—wherever his lips had touched. She repeated the same steps for his plate and fork.

Their waiter, who had arrived to clear the table, stepped aside like he knew the drill. She disposed of Thorne's used napkin in the biohazard bag and crouched so that her gaze was level with the table. She inspected the surface around Thorne with her magnifying glass.

Quinn edged closer until she was only a few feet away.

"Got one," the woman muttered. She used a wet cotton ball to pick up an eyelash. This too, she put in the biohazard bag. Then she sealed it up, packed it in the suitcase along with the other instruments, and zipped it up. She gave the table a final once-over as she removed her gloves.

"Good to go," she told the waiter.

Quinn blinked hard once to bring her smart lenses online. "Celebrity cells," she whispered to the search engine, recalling a fragment of a headline she'd scanned a while back.

The full headline materialized six inches away in floating blue letters, at her eye level, wherever she looked. She pinched the text to enlarge it: *"Rogue Network Suspected in Black Market Scheme to Steal Celebrity Cells for Embryo Creation."*

Quinn understood. The woman was not only Thorne's girlfriend. She was his DNA security guard, his public buffer wherever he went, to protect him from the world's most scientifically disturbing possibilities. Possibilities like her.

She inhaled a shaky breath and stepped into his path as they stood to leave.

"Excuse me," she said softly, not daring to look at the woman.

"Hi there." His tone was light, friendly. Charisma shone through his dimple. He patted his shorts pocket as Smokey tugged on the leash. "Sorry, I don't have a pen on me."

His voice was eerily identical to the chatbot version of him that she had saved up to purchase. She'd spent countless hours talking to it, practicing for this moment, telling it everything.

"Oh, I'm not looking for an autograph." She bowed her head. The words died on her tongue. She was close enough to smell his cologne, an aroma of wood and sage. Her skin prickled under the suspicious glare of his girlfriend. No, *fiancée*. A substantial diamond glittered on her ring finger.

"A picture, then?" Thorne offered. "Ember, can you take a quick shot?"

Quinn shook her head. She clutched her bump, trying to form the simple words that seemed impossible to get out.

"Are you all right?" he asked, eyeing her stomach. "Is your baby okay?"

"Actually . . ." her voice came out thick with apology. "I think it's your baby."

* * *

Ember stared at the stranger's protruding belly—close to full term if she had to guess. In her own stomach, a pit cracked open. The only thing she could think was *Fuck*. She had promised Thorne that something like this would never happen. If it was even true.

She heard herself snort. "You don't expect us to believe you."

Chances were good, she reminded herself, that an ordinary person could never achieve a stolen cell pregnancy. Unless that person was plugged into the biohacker world or had enough money to pay the Vault to pull it off.

Was there a possibility Thorne had cheated on her? Any thought of his infidelity came and went in the same moment. Thorne was the most honest person she knew—it was practically his trademark. A memory flitted across her mind from their early dating days. He'd gone clubbing after one of his shows and danced with several women. He could have slept with any or all of them. Instead, he had arrived at her house at two AM. to tell her that the women had been grinding on him, and he didn't feel right about it. It was already hard enough to date a famous dude, he'd told her. He didn't want to make Ember any more uncomfortable.

She sized up the pregnant stranger. There was just no way Thorne had slept with her and not said a word about it for eight months while their own relationship blossomed. This intrusion was either a cruel prank or a sociopathic confession. Either way, this random woman was impinging on their special morning—the morning they were going to visit their wedding venue.

Thorne gazed at the stranger coolly. His tone hardened. "I've never seen you in my life."

"I know, and I'm sorry." The woman's blue eyes seemed sincerely apologetic. "But I'm pretty sure you're still going to be a dad."

CHAPTER 2

Ember

One year earlier

EMBER SURVEYED THE view from her thirty-fourth-floor office in the heart of downtown Los Angeles. The smog on this April morning coated the valley in an amber layer, like one of those nostalgic social media filters she'd grown up with.

A dozen pink roses, now wilted and crumbling, sat on her glass desk. They were a gift to herself for starting her business, the only one of its kind. To be sure, the physical office was an extravagance, but it showed that she was real and eager to meet clients, not one of those hologram scams. Already six weeks had blurred by, and the rent was killing her. She had about four more months of savings before she would have to shutter this whole experiment and—

Never mind. She was going to succeed because she had decided to do the right thing. And because, in about five minutes, one of the most adored men in Hollywood was about to walk through her door.

His interest was all thanks to the interview she'd given to the journalist Shane Hart of *Vanguard*. Last week, they'd published a hard-hitting feature on the rising trend of stolen cell pregnancies. Such pregnancies were facilitated by the Vault, an insidious online marketplace that the Feds were having trouble shutting down. Before the article, no one knew she existed. No one had ever heard of a biosecurity guard who could protect your DNA from thieves. She'd invented the concept, thinking that someone, somewhere, would require such a service.

After the story, her smart lenses started blinking with a few inquiries. One NBA basketball player had come to meet her in real life, someone who was scared a fan might try to take advantage of him. But he had not followed up yet.

Now, Trace Thorne himself was coming to see her. She'd suspected celebrities would be enticed by her services, but the cream of the crop? It was one hell of a lucky break. She'd been prepping all weekend—tweaking her presentation, rehearsing her tone. She was planning to be unfazed, cool, decidedly not desperate. She smoothed a stray hair and tried not to think about how much was at stake. The rent was coming due. Every day that passed without a client pained her.

What if she had a panic attack in front of him?

Way down on the street below, she watched an autonomous car sidle up to the curb. A man with light hair exited from the backseat. She squinted at his tiny form—nope, too old. He stood hunched, leaning on a cane. She watched in surprise as he pulled out a phone. It was rare to see one anymore. But the older generation had not completely adjusted to smart lenses.

She could see the man tap and swipe on the screen. It was endearing. It reminded her of her childhood. The world she'd grown up in had been adorably quaint—the cell phones, the drivers' licenses, the printed magazines.

But her earliest years had also been scarred by the world's traumas: the pandemic that had dragged on with endless waves. Then World War Three wreaked havoc. And the worst agony of all—the death of her best friend Maddy from leukemia when they were seventeen.

She and Maddy had just missed the precision reproduction era—they were the last group of kids born before a scientific breakthrough ushered in a new paradigm for having babies. Ember couldn't stand the thought that Maddy might still be alive if her parents had waited a few years to have her. Because inherited cancers soon became rare in Selected kids.

Ember felt horrified imagining people jumping into bed and having sex *to get pregnant.* It was like deliberately spinning out on black ice. Apparently they just hoped that whatever was lurking in their genes wouldn't ruin their kid's life—if they thought of genes at all.

Things were much more civilized now. All you had to do, if you were a woman, was sit for a cheek swab at a fertility clinic. If you were in a straight relationship, your boyfriend or husband simply gave his sperm, unless he was infertile, in which case he would also provide a cheek swab. (Two women would each give cheek swabs; two men typically required one swab and one sperm sample.) Then a lab technician would chemically coax the cheek cells to turn into either sperm or egg in a petri dish. Thanks to this technological breakthrough called IVG—*in vitro gametogenesis*—any two people on Earth could make a baby.

From the sperm and eggs, dozens of embryos would be grown in test tubes. At day five, they would all undergo genetic analysis, and each would be assigned a spreadsheet of scores that showed their proclivities across a wide range of traits and diseases.

Then the two prospective parents would go through Selection—the rigorous process of considering all their candidates with the help of a genetic counselor. It was a fraught process, though Ember knew some couples had no problem Selecting their finalist for implantation. Sometimes, the choice was simply obvious. One ordinary healthy embryo, for example, in a minefield of others with disease mutations.

Or a finalist that scored healthier *and* higher on the "A-list" success metrics compared to their sibling candidates.

Selection had become the norm in the mid-to-late 2030s, after the right to reproductive autonomy was ratified by Congress as the Twenty-Eighth Amendment. It was the epic culmination of a bitter yearslong battle that nearly tore the country apart when Ember was in elementary school. Her parents even considered moving to Canada in case a new civil war broke out. But by the early 2030s, the political tide had reversed and thirty-eight state legislatures voted to ratify the amendment.

The new right allowed embryos to be legally created and disposed of in every state. In short order, insurance companies quickly signed on to cover precision reproduction for all. It was so much cheaper than paying the high costs of avoidable inherited diseases—a win–win for pretty much everyone except the rural and religious holdouts who still stridently insisted on the natural way.

Ember yearned to be a mom more than anything else. There was no rush, even though she was forty-one. Biological clocks were a thing of the past. She was grateful that her future baby was likely to enjoy a lifetime free of genetic illness, especially after the suffering her grandma had endured—the discovery of her APC gene mutation too late to cure her colon cancer.

Ember considered her baby's health to be nonnegotiable. With the right partner, her kid also had a shot at brilliance, athleticism, extroversion, and beauty. But those "A-list" traits were less important to her than the ones people too often overlooked—the "B-list" traits: a sunny disposition, creativity, empathy, patience.

Competitiveness among parents had fostered a sort of embryonic arms race that Ember thought was despicable. She thought back to the ancient scandals when some desperate parent would bribe a coach to get their kid into an elite university. Today, the impulse was the same. It just started much, much earlier.

Frankly, Ember thought all those parents were just using modern technology to screw up their kids in the same old ways. She vowed to Select her finalist for the genetic proxies of happiness rather than success, if a choice between the two was necessary. What a gift it would be to exempt her kid from the stranglehold of chronic anxiety. As a product of natural conception herself, she took after her own neurotic parents.

Ember checked her watch. Thorne was fifteen minutes late.

What if he didn't show?

She pictured her parents' faces to slow her pulse. As crazy as they had driven her when they were alive, she missed them with an aching fierceness. They were her source of infinite love and strength, both law professors who had raised her to be a champion of justice. It was devastating to know that their deaths would have been easily preventable today.

What would they think of her new venture? If anyone ever hired her, she intended to fight a crime her parents had never considered: nonconsensual reproduction. Babies born of stolen cells.

Would her parents have been proud or horrified? Sometimes she spoke to their holograms just to see their expressions again and to hear their voices. But it wasn't the same—the AI wasn't good enough to truly replicate her father's dry humor or her mother's sage advice.

She had no one else to confide in. No brothers or sisters, no close friends, no boyfriend anymore. It was better that way, of course. Safer. Loneliness was a quirk she was learning to ignore, like her broken arm that hadn't healed right. One day, when enough time had passed since the breakup—

Suddenly, she heard the elevator out in the hall open. Someone with quick footsteps approached her suite. She resisted the urge to yelp when the knock came.

Act natural, she scolded herself.

She opened the door to find Trace Thorne in the flesh. Alone.

He was instantly recognizable: the disheveled blond curls, the trademark scruff, the soulful eyes now trained on her, rendering her speechless. He wore ripped jeans, sneakers, and a graphic tee that read "Don't Quit Your Daydream."

"Ms. Ryan?" He raised his eyebrows hopefully as if she were the answer to his salvation, and not the other way around. "Sorry I'm late. Too many drone paparazzi."

"No problem," she said, throwing the door open wide. "Call me Ember."

He stepped into her office and looked around at the floor-to-ceiling city views, the chic art deco furniture, the glass desk with the dried flowers that struck her as artsy. For once, she felt that every penny spent to make her office more beautiful than she could afford was worth it, if only to see him nod with approval. Thank goodness he couldn't see where she lived.

"Nice place you got. Call me Thorne, by the way."

"Does anyone call you Trace?" she asked.

"Only my mom. When I was little, she called me Tracey. You can imagine how that went over at school."

She smiled. "At least you got the last laugh."

She gestured to the burgundy velvet couch that faced the wall of glass; the radiance of the sun was muted by smog, so she didn't need to worry about glare in his eyes. He perched on the edge of the sofa, keeping his eyes on her. She took the armchair opposite and crossed her legs self-consciously.

"So, thank you for taking the time," he said graciously, as though she had something better to do.

"My pleasure. It's an honor to meet you." She tucked her hands under her thighs. "Why don't I jump in with a demonstration, and then you can ask me all your questions."

She blinked twice at the white wall to her left. The lights in the office darkened, and a hologram video appeared to the beat of a dramatic electronic piano. The opening shot showed a crowded restaurant. Her avatar sat across from a shadow avatar, her hypothetical client, who was unintentionally exposing himself to bio-theft by letting the waiter clear his wineglass, fork, and napkin.

As the real Ember narrated to Thorne, her avatar used forensics tools to neutralize the liabilities and to inspect the client's radius for any inadvertent hair, saliva, or mucus. Without this level of attention, a sample containing living cells could be snatched by any discrete bystander, stabilized for transport in a medium containing glycerin, and sent to the Vault's unknown headquarters. There, it was believed that biohackers injected the cells with chemical factors to make them pluripotent—blank cells able to turn into egg or sperm. The blank cells would presumably be frozen in liquid nitrogen and listed for sale until a customer ordered that client's egg or sperm.

"My process must be extremely thorough anytime you're out in public," Ember was saying, as her avatar prepped pipettes of rubbing alcohol. "The smallest oversight—"

"I don't need to see the rest," he interrupted. "What I need is for you to come on tour with me."

She gave a startled laugh, pausing the video. "You don't even want to know my background or—?"

"I know you're the only one who can protect me from the Vault. Right?"

"One hundred percent." Their eyes locked. "I can guarantee that none of your DNA will end up there or with its foreign counterparts. If it does at any time during my contract, I will repay you my fee with interest. But it won't."

"Then you're hired."

"I haven't even told you my fee."

"It can't be more than what those assholes extorted from me already."

Ember remembered the gossip blogs had gone wild when Thorne's DNA sample had ended up for purchase on the Vault last year. He had reportedly wired five million dollars in crypto to the anonymous network for the perps to take down the listing before anyone could order eggs or sperm derived from his cells.

"Do you know how they targeted you?" she asked.

"I played a lot of shows, went to clubs, bars, restaurants, with no protection. It could have happened anywhere. Or it could have been an inside job. I wasn't really aware of this whole scam until they got to me."

"And did they actually destroy your sample or remove the listing once you paid them off?"

He shrugged. "No one knows who or where these fuckers are. I just don't want it to happen again."

"The *Vanguard* story said the FBI is working on it."

He gave a snort. "I know an agent there, and their whole 'investigation' is a joke."

"What do you mean?"

"They're clueless. That woman in the article who bought the actor's sperm? She paid in crypto like I did—she doesn't know where her money went, nor does anyone else. And the site can't be shut down because it's on a blockchain host. Their servers could be literally anywhere."

As his voice rose and his gestures increased, Ember felt sorry for him. Being famous in this day and age was a complicated thing.

"In the meantime," he was saying, "my tour starts in three weeks. Forty-two cities on three continents. You have to come. You'll get your own hotel room, a seat on my jet, and anything else you need, plus your fee, of course."

She let a few seconds pass for the sake of her own dignity. "How long is it?"

"The whole summer. After Labor Day, I'll turn back into a pumpkin, descend into my studio, and set you free."

Free. Her mind flashed to a memory of being trapped on the bathroom floor, sobbing for release, her body covered in bruises.

Then she smiled with all the confidence she could muster. "You, sir, have got yourself a bio-guard."

CHAPTER 3

Lily

LILY WASN'T SURE what intimidated her more: the legendary Shane Hart himself or Radia Chaudry, the rival intern hell-bent on impressing him. Tomorrow was the pitch meeting with all of *Vanguard*'s writers—and Lily's first chance to prove she belonged.

She and Radia had beat out hundreds of other college journalists aspiring to land their postgraduate fellowships. But only one job would be available at the end of a year. One of them needed to be the best of the best, and not merely great.

She paced around her bedroom, her bare feet rubbing against the plush carpet. Radia, a fellow recent graduate, possessed qualifications that made her seem like a near-mythical creature. They hadn't yet met in real life—that would happen tomorrow—but Radia already occupied an outsize place in Lily's consciousness.

She tried to overcome her insecurity by reminding herself of her own accomplishments: as editor in chief of NYU's campus publication, the *Washington Square News*, she had broken the story of a star professor's academic misconduct and exposed financial corruption that implicated the university's highest officials. Her reporting had gotten the professor fired and prompted the school to launch a formal inquiry, with the earnest promise of "increased transparency and reform" (though, predictably, nothing had changed to date).

That was fine, but Radia had literally summited Mount Everest to win *her* fellowship. For her publication at Harvard, the *Daily Crimson*, she had embedded with a group of amputee climbers who wore innovative motorized exoskeletons to scale the mountain. The exoskeletons were designed by the engineers at Harvard's biomechatronics lab to resemble Iron Man's power suit. The mission proved to be one hell of a PR stunt: not only had the disabled climbers made it to the top, they'd done it faster than the career athletes, people with mere muscle and bone. Radia's splashy story proclaiming the end of wheelchairs had made news around the globe and earned her the spot at *Vanguard*.

There was no way Lily could one-up that. She was still working on achieving a decent 5K pace, for Christ's sake.

Concentrate, dammit.

She plunked down in her desk chair. What killer story idea could she pitch to Shane tomorrow? And did it even matter? The competition was stacked: Radia had been Selected. It was as obvious as a typo in a headline.

People's polygenic scores were private medical information, so Lily could only guess at Radia's innate advantages. But assuming she *had* been Selected, that meant she was the most desirable embryo out of the dozens her parents had chosen from. Of course, some trade-offs were inevitable. The "perfect" embryo across all categories was statistically impossible. Radia was still human, after all.

Lily perked up a bit at her own voice of reason. So what if Radia could climb the highest mountain in the world? Intellectually, it was unclear how they stacked up. All that mattered now was grit, brains, and creativity. Lily had those things. She had a chance.

There was also luck, which no degree of Selection could account for. Who would hit it off better with Shane? Would

Lily rattle off a snarky comment and garner a laugh? Her guidance counselor at NYU had warned—or maybe enlightened—her with the advice that the most successful job applicants were those who were enjoyable to be around. *"So don't be an asshole—and don't be shy either."*

Lily focused on what it would feel like to walk into a room with her rival, her idols, and her new boss. And she was supposed to "be cool"?

She was out of practice being in-person. Her college classes had been mostly holo-courses. At the start or end of a semester, the students would meet their professor in one of NYU's historic brick buildings for a lecture. Then they would mingle, maybe grab a coffee, exchange contact lens signals, and go home, usually to their parents' place or an apartment they shared with roommates in the outer boroughs.

The dorms were ghost towns. Some had been converted to hotels. Manhattan living was expensive, and technology made it unnecessary. As a result, Lily hadn't made a ton of close friends in college. At least she had her parents. Her dad was her best friend. Her mom—well, that was complicated.

Out in the kitchen, Lily heard a timer beeping on the oven. The smell of her dad's famous barbecue meatloaf wafted down the hall. It was almost dinnertime.

She blinked hard and muttered *Vanguard*'s website. The audiovisual chip in her lenses projected the homepage on the white wall in front of her desk. She pinched the air in her field of vision to enlarge the image. The buzzy headlines of the day mentioned the latest embryo Selection fad ("Why Parents Are Obsessing Over These Gene Variants for Humor"), news from the front lines of the Mars colony ("First Martian Immigrants Celebrate One-Year Landing Anniversary"), and political satire of the AIs running for office ("Vote for GPT87: Equal Rights for Humans").

There had to be something to give her a crumb of an idea. She'd rather call in sick, as rare as that was, than show up empty-handed at the meeting tomorrow.

A knock on her bedroom door made her stiffen.

"I need a few more minutes," she called. "Start without me."

Her mother opened the door anyway. "Hi, sweetheart." Gray hair curled in ringlets down her shoulders—the only tell that she was nearly seventy years old. There were no wrinkles around her eyes or mouth. Her neck and hands were as smooth as Lily's, her arms lean, her waist trim. The gray was purposeful, of course. Her mom's playful nod to acknowledging her status as a "senior citizen," though nobody really used that distinction anymore. Lily recognized her tight-lipped smile as an advance apology.

The meatloaf probably burned, she thought. Now they would have to either order drone pickup or turn on the 3D printer. And her mom knew how much she hated printed food.

Dad came up behind her, wiping sauce onto his apron. Her stocky, balding, adorable dad. He didn't bother with the resveratrol injections and the cellular reboots like her mom did. No matter. Mom said he was perfect the way he was. Lily figured she was just relieved he hadn't left her. And why hadn't he? Honestly, their enduring marriage defied understanding.

Now, a nervous energy ricocheted between them.

"What's going on?" Lily demanded.

"We have some news." Mom sucked in a breath. "There's no easy way to tell you this, so I'm just going to tell you. We're having a baby."

Lily snorted. "Yeah, right." Her eyes zeroed in on her mother's flat abs.

"Not yet," Dad said quickly. "We have the embryos but we haven't Selected one. We wanted to tell you now before we get any further."

Lily stared back and forth between them. "Come on. For real?"

They nodded. The room was deadly quiet, but a loud thrum rang in her ears. She waited to feel something. The word *baby* bounced around in her mind, splintering her thoughts in a million directions. It had never occurred to her that her parents might want another child. After what her mother had put them through, the idea of bringing a new life into the world seemed almost offensive.

"I don't understand," she finally said. "Why?"

"We always wanted another one, but . . ." Mom's voice trailed off. The air felt heavy with all that went unsaid. "And now, with you grown up—"

"Aren't you a bit old?" Lily asked coldly. "I mean, you guys will be in your eighties when the kid graduates college."

"Which is not unheard of," Dad reminded her. "There are more golden-age parents than ever. I'm sure we won't be the only ones."

She conceded his point with a grumble. With the expected healthspan approaching one hundred and ten—the number of years you could expect to remain healthy and vigorous before inevitably decaying—it wasn't completely absurd to have a kid at the age when people used to retire. It was still weird and taboo, though.

Lily's heart quickened as an ugly new insight dawned on her.

She aimed her bow straight at her mother's chest. "Is this a do-over? Since you missed out on my childhood?"

Dad narrowed his eyes. "Lily—"

"It's okay. I deserve that. You're allowed to stay mad at me as long as you want." Mom looked at her without any detectable rage of her own. Just the weariness that persists in the aftermath of grief.

Lily felt her comeback die on her tongue. It was hard to sustain fury at someone who refused to fight back.

"I've given you every ounce of myself for the last ten years," Mom said. "Right?"

She paused to allow Lily to argue. But it was true. Her mom had done one thing since she'd gotten out of prison: be a mom. She'd dedicated weekends to mother–daughter outings, done school pickups and drop-offs; read bedtime books and sang songs, even when Lily was too old for it; taken an interest in all her hobbies; shuttled her to every activity, camp, and lesson; planned elaborate holiday celebrations and surprises; and attended years of joint and individual therapy. But had it been enough? Could it ever be enough?

"I've owed you at least that much," Mom continued. "But you don't really need me anymore. It won't be long before you move out and find your own way. And then Daddy and I will be alone."

Lily felt a pang in spite of herself. Then a memory surfaced of the stuffy visiting room Dad used to drag her to, where the guards watched them sit at a plastic table, Mom in handcuffs, as they made small talk about the life they were muddling through without her, year after year.

And it had all been her mother's fault. Nothing she did could ever change that.

CHAPTER

4

Quinn

THORNE'S POWERFUL VOICE echoed throughout the Hollywood Bowl to the high-pitched screams of seventeen thousand fans—real, sweaty, dancing, hollering fans. Nothing in the holoverse could approximate anything close. Quinn felt a lump rise in her throat at the rapturous experience of feeling like one tiny node of a massive adoring organism.

Setting eyes on Thorne in real life for the first time—from the eighth row, no less—was even better than she could have imagined. This was why people still went to live shows, she thought, having forgotten all about her self-consciousness at coming alone. Her ticket was one hell of a push present. Aiden and Cory must have spent a small fortune.

When Thorne's set ended after what felt like ten minutes, everyone jumped to their feet and broke into thunderous cheering and whooping. Quinn's palms stung from clapping so hard. The lights went black and his band members scuttled off stage, leaving their instruments behind.

When a white spotlight suddenly beamed to life, Thorne was alone on stage, and the crowd erupted again. He tipped his cowboy hat and thrummed his guitar a few salacious times, teasing them.

He brought the mic close to his mouth like it was his lover's face. "You guys want an encore?"

The crowd responded with a renewed burst of frantic applause, and the guy on Quinn's right let out a piercing dog whistle just a few inches from her ear.

"Ow," she muttered. As the commotion died down, she rubbed her ear in annoyance.

"Oh sorry," he said. "Didn't mean to make you deaf."

Quinn did a quick once-over, taking in his backward baseball cap over curly brown hair, day-old stubble, and kind face. He was long and lean like a runner, in black hiking boots, black jeans, and an olive T-shirt that matched his eyes. She glanced over his shoulder to check out the girl he'd brought, but the seat on his other side was empty.

"What?" she asked, too loudly. She smiled and he caught on with a playful eye roll.

Thorne was reveling in the crowd's anticipatory buzz, taking his time to begin his final song. It was the one they had all been waiting for.

"Love So Holo," her new friend shouted toward the stage. *"Love So Holo."*

Quinn repeated his chant, and within seconds their whole row, then whole section, was doing the same—hands cupping mouths, shrieking the words. Before long the chant caught on across the stadium, building to a fever pitch that reverberated through Quinn's entire being.

Thorne pretended to be clueless, eating it up. "Which song?" he asked. "I can't hear you."

"Love So Holo! Love So Holo!"

Mercifully, Thorne strummed the opening chords, and the crowd quieted down before Quinn's eardrums exploded. She couldn't help peeking over at the guy when Thorne sang, *"I only feel your love when I hold your hand / not when I see you as a hologram."*

But instead of the blissed-out trance she'd expected, he was gritting his teeth, his chin tight and tense. He clapped when the song ended, but didn't whoop and cheer like everyone else. Something about the song had upset him. The song he had wanted to hear.

She realized she was curious. Why was this attractive guy alone at a Trace Thorne concert, next to a wildly expensive empty seat? Maybe he'd been stood up—or dumped?

"Thank you, LA, and good night!" Thorne announced with a final wave. The crowd clapped with renewed enthusiasm, but the energy dropped as soon as Thorne jogged offstage. The overhead lights came on and showed the mess of drums, amps, guitars, keyboard, and other instruments scattered around the stage. The graveyard of the show. Quinn felt a bit hungover from the contact high of being so close to Thorne in physical reality. Now his absence heightened her craving for a companion.

She stood slowly to leave, taking extra time to gather her purse and see if the guy would talk to her again. Shyness overcame her. She wondered if he could tell through her baggy shirt how her stomach still hung over her pants like a deflated balloon. Sometimes her fingers still wandered across it, expecting a kick.

But his eyes were nowhere near her waistline. He was staring at the abandoned stage, almost like he was lost in a reverie. Quinn followed his gaze.

At first nothing was happening, but then a woman wearing a suit, a hairnet, and latex gloves walked on from stage left. She was clutching a small suitcase. No, it was a toolbox of some kind, Quinn saw, as she unlocked its clamps. Bizarrely, the woman withdrew a magnifying glass and an ultraviolet wand that glowed purple, and canvassed the area around Thorne's mic. She rubbed the mic down with a chemical swab, then got on her hands and knees and collected Thorne's empty plastic water bottles that had rolled to the side. She stayed on her hands and knees, plucking something invisible off the stage floor.

"What the hell is going on up there?" Quinn asked no one in particular, intending it for someone in particular.

The guy shrugged. "Beats me." He turned to her, noticing, apparently for the first time, that she was also by herself.

"It was a gift," she explained. "My ticket."

"Wow. Nice boyfriend?"

She snorted. "No, nice clients, though."

"What do you do?"

"I'm a surrogate. I just finished a job a month ago. Delivered a healthy little boy for a gay couple." She smiled proudly. "They named him Branson."

"Quite a legacy to live up to."

"The kid just has to fly to Mars."

"And invent clean fuel, save the planet, that kind of thing."

"Yeah, no big deal."

He smiled. "I'm Robert, by the way."

"Quinn." They pounded fists. "And what do you do?" she asked.

"Oh I'm in finance. Crypto trader. No saving the world for me."

Cute and loaded, she thought. People were sliding awkwardly past them to leave the row, sweaty arms grazing theirs in the June heat.

"Well," she said reluctantly, "I guess we should get out of here."

"Yeah." A pause filled with possibility. "You want to grab a nightcap?"

She waited a beat so she wouldn't seem desperate. *Am I desperate?* she wondered. No. Just a little lonely. And restless. Who could blame her? She was at loose ends. Between jobs. There was no going back and nothing ahead but her dull apartment.

"Sure, why not?"

He blinked hard and she could tell, as he gazed into space, that he was perusing the bars in their vicinity on his augmented reality visual field. That third-eye stare was a familiar one, as natural as pulling out a phone was for her parents' generation. Of course, like most millennials, her parents complained whenever she gazed out in their presence, tapping into her own reality that no one else could see. They said it made her seem rude and self-absorbed, and they were probably right. But it wasn't like cell phones were still a thing, unless you were old.

Robert shifted his attention to her, triggering a jolt of excitement deep in her belly. "There's a bar ten minutes away called The Night Rose. It has 4.7 stars."

"Do they have booze?" she joked. Truthfully, she didn't even really like alcohol, but who cared? She had a date for the first time in ages.

"First round's on me."

"Then I'm in. It was a *long* nine months."

On their way out, they passed a merch stand filled with sweatshirts, T-shirts, keyrings, and other kitschy stuff adorned with Thorne's handsome face.

"Wait," Quinn said, tugging on Robert's sleeve. "I've been wanting one of those!" She pointed beyond the clamoring crowd at a miniature statue of Thorne up on display. The one-foot-tall replica was decked out in a cowboy hat and jeans, strumming a guitar. "He's been teasing it on social for, like, two months."

Robert gave a slight frown as if he couldn't quite place it.

"The chatbot, remember?"

His face lit up. "Ah yes, of course."

"It has Thorne's personality and memories and everything. You can talk to it whenever you want, for, like, thirty bucks a month." Quinn hustled into the quickly forming line. "I *have* to get one."

Robert took his place beside her. "Sounds cool," he said. "Guess I will too."

* * *

Once they were settled across from each other in a dimly lit booth, beers in hand and statues in bags, Robert reached out over the table. She thought for a moment he wanted to take her hand, and embarrassingly, she almost offered it. Thank God she didn't, because he was just reaching for the vase of dyed black roses between them—the bar's signature decor.

"Real or fake?" he asked her before he felt the petals.

"You can never tell anymore."

"About flowers?"

"Everything. These drinks, the food, people's ages . . . it's all engineered."

"Seriously. Why can't shit just go back to being basic?"

She laughed. "If we *know* we're all being fooled, why even pretend, you know?"

"Totally."

"I think when I get old, I'm just gonna let it all hang out." *Jesus Christ,* she thought. *Way to seem hot.* But she was herself. That was the point. She wasn't interested in games. And he seemed to be into it.

"You're a breath of fresh air, Quinn . . .?"

"Corrigan. Irish as hell. As if you didn't get that from the red hair."

"Quinn Corrigan. I like you."

She forced herself not to look away. Instead, she took a confident swig of her beer. "You're not too bad yourself, Robert –?"

"Roy."

"Robert Roy. Sounds like a Marvel character. You should date Jessica Jones." His uncomfortable smile made her backpedal without knowing what she had said wrong. "I mean, assuming you don't mind that she could beat the crap out of you." Quinn gave a feeble laugh, but he was looking down at his beer, running his finger over its edge.

"It's not that." His voice was flat, absent of banter. "I'm actually a widower."

She gasped. "Oh my god."

"My husband, Evan, was killed in a car crash last October. I'm sorry to kill the vibe—I wasn't planning to bring it up, but . . ."

Quinn was speechless. All her assumptions had been wrong. That this was a date. That they were flirting. Guilt crashed over her for feeling the slightest bit disappointed in the face of his unthinkable tragedy. *What is wrong with you?* she berated herself.

"I'm so sorry," she said helplessly. "That is absolutely horrifying."

Robert stared down at the table. "He was coming home from work on the 405. The car's software malfunctioned."

Quinn's heart raced, imagining the man inside having no warning that his life was about to end, that something so random and senseless was still possible in a world where the unpredictable had been largely tamed by technology. Except, of course, when that technology went haywire.

Robert took a swig of his beer and cleared his throat. "I didn't even get to say goodbye. That's one of the shittiest parts."

Quinn shook her head. "How are you even here right now, going out?"

He sighed. "We had bought the Thorne tickets as soon as we found out he would be on tour this summer. Evan loved him almost as much as I do. "Love So Holo" was our wedding song. So I felt like I had to come."

Quinn let her silence extend out of respect. When it felt okay to talk again, she reached across the table. This time she wasn't shy. His hand was warm and limp, and she curled her fingers around his. She could see now that her bored loneliness did not belong in the same universe as the nightmare kind he was living through.

"It must have been really hard, being there tonight without him."

"Yeah. It was. But seeing Thorne was worth it." He offered her a small smile of gratitude. "And meeting you."

She lifted her beer. "To Thorne. And new friends."

"Ditto," he said, and clinked his bottle against hers.

CHAPTER

5

Ember

"YOU'RE ALL GOOD," Ember told Thorne. "No hair or living tissue left on anything."

It was just after one AM, and they were standing outside the Hollywood Bowl's VIP entrance, where a black autonomous vehicle was waiting to whisk Thorne to his home high in the hills of Laguna Beach. Ember had come to learn that he hated hotels, hated anything that forced him to be in public unless he was performing, so whenever he could make it home for a night, he did.

"Thank you so much," he said, grabbing the door handle. "See you at the airport bright and early?"

"Yep, see you there." Tomorrow the crew was headed to New York, on his private plane, for his concert at Madison Square Garden. She guessed he would get maybe four hours of sleep before he had to wake up and pull off the whole show again. The work ethic he maintained was staggering for someone who was not even Selected—he had missed that boat by a few years, like her.

But even more extraordinary was his jovial rapport with all the roadies who made it work, from the techs and assistants to the caterers and merch staff. She had yet to witness him get short or irritable with anyone. Unlikely as it seemed, the persona he presented onstage—the charming, down-to-earth guy who also happened to be a guitar legend—actually seemed to be the person he was. Of course, she didn't know him very well yet. In her experience, people were often like onions. The more layers you peeled back, the more they stunk.

But maybe Thorne was that rare salt-of-the-earth guy whose popularity was well deserved. Tonight's show had ended hours ago, when his night was still going strong. After the curtain dropped, he'd hobnobbed with the VIP guests who had paid thousands for meet and greets, entertained his inner circle in the green room with dinner and drinks, and then huddled with the stage crew before they all scattered to hotels. Ember and the other security detail, two former Army special ops men, would be the last ones to leave. Despite her exhaustion, she was on duty until Thorne officially departed the premises.

Now, finally, he was stepping into the car. A warm breeze swept past, rustling the trees in the darkness. Ember felt loose and free. The thrill of the spectacle and her own place in it had chipped away at her guard. She was surprised to find herself actually having fun for the first time in months—something that had felt impossible since the night of her escape.

The night she'd shown up at the ER with a broken arm and claimed it was an accident.

"You have a ride to the hotel?" Thorne asked, interrupting her memory. He was settling into his car's roomy U-shaped nook that served as the passenger bay. There were no front seats. A dome of smart glass wrapped around the entire car like a personal planetarium. Ember knew he could tint it black for privacy or turn it into a movie theater on the go.

She blinked to gaze out at a map of her own car's coordinates. It was three blocks away. "It's almost here," she told him. "I'm actually headed home."

"Where's that?"

"Silver Lake. I still need to pack before we hit the road."

"Gotcha. Well, thanks again. Seriously, I wouldn't be here without you." He flashed her a tired smile, and it prompted a swell in her chest that had nothing to do with professional pride.

"Sure thing," she said. "And by the way, you killed it tonight."

"As did you, m'lady," he said with a tip of his hat.

She shut his door with a laugh. The sound rang out in the hushed night, and she realized it had been a long time since she'd felt happy.

When her car showed up, she was humming one of Thorne's catchy singles under her breath. During the ten-minute drive back to her house, half asleep, she found herself imagining him going to bed. Did he sleep naked on silk sheets, like the rumors alleged? What did he look like under those ripped jeans and leather jacket? Did he have anyone waiting for him—a girlfriend or a lover?

So far, no significant other had attended a show, and he was too private to drop any hints about his personal life with his staff. She knew it was a defensive posture borne of necessity—he'd been burned before by people in his orbit who had sold tabloid gossip and photos of him. What was worse, some in the crew suspected that a former staffer had been the one to hook up the Vault with his biological specimen last year, which had led to the whole ransom nightmare.

Her car soon pulled up to her run-down rental house on a street deep in a neighborhood of teardowns. Her place had a peekaboo view of LA's skyscrapers from its perch in the hills, but it was in a no-man's land of development upheaval, with heavy construction on either side that started at seven AM six days a week. That was why the rent was dirt cheap. But as long as she was on her own, any place was better than the one she'd left.

When she got out of the car, she heard an unfamiliar noise somewhere in the vicinity of her front lawn. A faint buzzing sound, like an electronic mosquito. Hair prickled on her arms. She whirled around and saw only her yellowing grass and the path to her front door gleaming white in the moonlight. Overgrown weeds poked through the cracks in the concrete. A bulldozer lay idle in a cavern of dirt next door, paused in its quest to hollow out a new foundation. The creepy noise was drifting and now buzzed a few feet above her head.

She looked up. Later, she would replay this moment, but never figure out how to avoid what happened next.

A searing white flash momentarily blinded her.

She let out a cry, but it was too late. Spots littered her vision as she watched a tiny drone dart into the night sky as quickly as it had come.

A drone that now had a biometric scan of her retinas.

And her address.

CHAPTER

6

Lily

LILY PAUSED AT the white conference room door. The pitch meeting started in ten minutes. She was early, but she could hear other people already inside chitchatting, a benign sound that sent a shiver through her bones. This was it. Her first official day at *Vanguard*.

A lump bloomed in her throat as she grabbed the doorknob. No other publication captured the astonishing kaleidoscope of technology's possibilities the way *Vanguard* did. Reading it was like entering a world erupting with brilliance, rather than the usual media focus on corruption and decay.

She remembered herself at age thirteen, reading it in her bedroom when she'd first gotten her smart lenses. How grown-up she had felt that day. How thrilling to see their famous motto appear in her very own visual field: *Where tomorrow meets today.* She remembered that moment with utter clarity. It was when a dream had knocked on the door of her heart: maybe she could become a *Vanguard* journalist one day. And here she was.

She lifted her head and walked inside. Half a dozen people were sitting around a long glass table in a room with soaring ceilings and abundant sunshine. Lily suppressed a gasp at the view; from their headquarters facing south on the seventy-eighth floor of the Freedom Tower, all of New York Harbor was visible. The Statue of Liberty stood proud on her tiny island in the middle of a gray sea of ferries and charter boats; to the right shone the titanium globe of the Institute for Nuclear Fusion on Governors Island, against the verdant backdrop of Staten Island in the distance.

At the head of the conference table sat the unmistakable Shane Hart, editor in chief. He was iconic in his own right, a fixture of media gossip, a tastemaker as famous for his provocative editorial sensibility as his quirky personal style. He always wore black-rimmed glasses, a mustache and beard, and a loud-patterned silk shirt; today's shirt featured blue and orange toucans perched on trees. Only Shane Hart could pull off such a look without undermining his legendary fearsomeness.

Lily's mouth was dry as she marched up to introduce herself, interrupting his conversation with the ridiculously gorgeous young woman on his left: Radia Chaudry in the flesh. Radia had beaten her to the best seat in the room. Her glossy black hair flowed over her shoulders in long waves, and her caramel skin glowed with vigor. She fixed her dark brown eyes on Lily with a wide, guileless smile.

Lily acknowledged her with a breezy nod and offered Shane her hand.

"Hi," she announced brightly. "I'm Lily. It's an honor to meet you."

"Ah, Lily, so good you made it," Shane said, giving her an extra-firm handshake. "How was your commute from Jersey?"

She was flattered that he recalled where she lived. "Not bad. The hyperloop was ten minutes to Penn."

"Then I hope you won't mind coming in weekly. Radia and I were just talking about how we hold pitch meetings in person every Monday. It may be old-school, but so be it."

"I don't mind at all," Radia chirped in a slightly British accent. "I live just up by Riverside Park so I jogged here."

Lily noticed her slightly damp forehead. "From uptown?"

"Yeah, it's only six miles, so I threw in a loop around Central Park on my way."

Lily laughed but Radia wasn't joking. In fact, she seemed startled by Lily's reaction.

"It was only another six miles."

"Only," Lily repeated.

"I usually do twenty a day—well, ten on rest days or when I'm lazy."

Now you're just showing off, Lily thought with disgust. But she wasn't, and that was the strangest part. She seemed genuinely matter-of-fact.

Is that what it felt like to be Selected? To accomplish superhuman feats before breakfast and barely break a sweat? Fucking Christ.

Shane called the meeting to order, and Lily scurried to find an empty seat halfway down the table. She took her place next to a woman with gray curly ringlets who reminded her of her mom. With a sour pang, she remembered last night's announcement about the new baby but quickly pushed it out of her mind.

"Good morning, everyone," Shane began. "I'd like to get started by welcoming our two postgraduate fellows, Lily and Radia. They will be assisting us with research and reporting, so if you need an extra set of hands, hit them up. They're here this year to learn."

Lily brimmed with pride as the writers she idolized turned their attention to her (and Radia) with a smattering of hellos and nods. They took turns introducing themselves, and Lily recognized each byline with starstruck awe. These people were legends. Being in their presence—with the chance to join their ranks—was surreal. She thought of how many of her peers would kill for her seat.

"All right," Shane said when the intros were finished. "Take a second to pop and pin."

The group shifted into work mode. Everyone used their smart lenses to project augmented reality keyboards that no one else could see. They positioned their fingers to type on what appeared to be the empty glass table. Lily followed their lead. She was accustomed to this practice for live note-taking during her college courses. Just for fun, she selected the color royal blue for her keyboard's letters, in a whimsical nod to *Vanguard*'s brand color. A blue cursor popped up in her visual field, ready to receive her typing. She pinched her virtual cursor between her thumb and forefinger and "pinned" it onto the table, so that her notes would not distract her wherever she looked. Others were similarly dragging their cursors down and out of ubiquitous sight.

"Before we get into your pitches," Shane said, "I've got good news and bad news. The good news is that we're up for nine National Media Awards this year. Just got the news this morning."

Cheers and claps broke out, and Lily joined in with delight. Shane went on to single out each writer up for an award, and by the end, Lily realized that every single staffer had been named, some more than once. And *she* was going to pitch an idea worthy of *them*?

Her euphoria suddenly curdled into fear.

"So what's the bad news?" asked a woman with blonde hair and ageless skin. She could have been anywhere from twenty-five to seventy-five.

Shane leaned back in his chair. "Here's the deal. The Escapes division is killing us. Yes, we have the best content, but people aren't interested in *thinking* as much as they used to. And our stuff demands a level of thought and attention that is a big ask these days."

"God forbid people read something longer than a headline," another woman muttered.

"The holoverse killed the written word," complained a man with a bow tie. "Why read when you can go to an armchair rave or 'chat' with a celebrity?" He mimed sarcastic air quotes.

"No," Shane said. "There's been a turning point for our industry in the last couple months, and it's not that."

"What?"

"The new porn suits." Everyone groaned, and Shane put up his hands. "Look, I wish I were joking. But the sensory feedback on those suits is insane, or so I hear. And *no*, I haven't tried one."

"You think our readers are the same people fucking strangers in the holoverse?" the bow-tie guy asked in disbelief.

"You'd be surprised," Shane sighed. "But apparently it's not just about sex. Those suits are driving a gold rush of tactile experiences, according to our corporate overlords. The Escapes team is selling the hell out of virtual massages, dance parties, cuddle sessions, even tickling. I'm sure it's just a fad, but serious reporting is not getting the blinks it once did."

Lily snuck a glance at Radia to see how she was processing this crisis. Was there still going to be a job available for one of them after their fellowship ended? A career, for that matter? Journalism had been falling by the wayside for years—decades really. They were lucky to be at *Vanguard*, one of the few legacy media outlets that still offered longform reported stories to thoughtful readers. *Readers*. As old-fashioned as the concept was, Lily felt a kinship with those who loved the written word. It was painful to see the art form lose respect, and blinks, to baser types of entertainment. But that was how the intellectual heavyweights survived today: prestigious brands like *Vanguard* had been folded into sprawling "infotainment" corporations that provided access to their entire ecosystems for a single monthly fee.

Radia seemed lost in thought. Lily watched her with a touch of jealousy that gave way to snark. If Radia's brain was anything like her stamina, she was probably solving media's existential woes at this very moment.

Mr. Bow Tie turned directly to Lily, catching her off guard. "You two should run away while you still can. Fast. Journalism is dead."

"First of all," Shane said, putting his elbows on the table, "people have been saying that since the turn of the century, and it hasn't happened yet. We just need to show our readers that we're still relevant . . . that we can tickle their minds when they get bored of tickling . . . whatever, okay?" There were a few titters of laughter. "And they *will* get bored," Shane went on. "They'll realize they need our stories to sound smart with their friends."

If Shane was going for a pep talk, Lily sensed he hadn't quite succeeded. People were still trading anxious glances.

"Are you considering layoffs?" asked a woman who had won several awards. Everyone stared at Shane.

"Not if we can get our KPIs up. So come at me, guys. Slay me with your best pitches. But, you know, no pressure."

No one laughed.

"Guess I'll go first." A man wearing a fashionable fungi blazer cleared his throat. "How about a piece on the exclusivity of custom organs? Since they still aren't covered by insurance, only the rich can afford them. It's a travesty."

"Nothing new," Shane replied. "The rich always afford everything first. What else?"

"I have one," piped up a woman with red eyeliner. "I got word from a source that the Harvard professor who's been working on Woolly mammoth de-extinction for decades is finally planning to birth the first one next month. It's super hush-hush, but I bet we could get an exclusive."

"Hell yes!" Shane exclaimed. "That's the kind of scoop I'm talking about. Amazing, Jean. Go forth and conquer. I can see the cover already."

Jean smiled shyly and typed rapid-fire on her invisible keyboard.

"What else?" Shane prompted. "Think big, juicy must-reads."

There was no way Lily was about to go right after Jean. Apparently no one else wanted to either. Silence fell over the room, and in the void, Radia, of all people, opened her mouth.

"What about a story about Unforeseens and the people who have them? I'm talking specifically about the loud and proud anti-IVG types who come to regret it later, when their kid gets a repro-preventable disease like epilepsy or leukemia." She paused, and Lily watched her take a nervous breath. "Unforeseens are still regularly born in the South and rural areas, driving up national health care costs and individual suffering. It's a silent epidemic."

Lily felt her cheeks get hot. She fought the urge to squirm.

Shane regarded Radia with newfound respect. "Taboo, high stakes, I like it. But how would you find anyone to talk to you on the record? They would just look like terrible parents."

"I would try not to seem judgy." Radia furrowed her brow. "My guess is that these parents would appreciate the chance to warn others not to repeat their mistakes. We just need to give them the platform and the courage to do it. And if our story went viral, we could actually inspire a lot of families to embrace precision repro."

"Go for it," Shane said. "Let us know how it goes." Without warning, he whirled to Lily. "How about you? Any fresh ideas?"

She wrung her hands under the table. "I was thinking about older mothers," she began tentatively. "You know, the trend of women having kids in their sixties, seventies, even eighties, and the . . . the taboo aspects of being an old mom."

Shane frowned. "All our competitors have run that story already. What would make ours stand out? Why now?"

Lily wracked her brain. "It's getting more popular."

"Is that anecdotal or do you have data to back that up?"

She gave a timid headshake.

"Then I'm afraid it just doesn't meet our bar. This isn't the *Washington Square News* anymore. I need slam-dunk ideas, okay? Who's next?"

Lily closed her eyes and for one blessed moment, no inputs stimulated her visual field. All she could see was the pink flesh of her eyelids. She felt hot tears prick the surface, but she refused to let them see her cry. No. She would force herself to smile and finish out the meeting with dignity, then go home and come up with the best damn idea Radia could never imagine.

CHAPTER

7

Quinn

QUINN WAS LYING in bed at ten AM on a Monday morning when her contacts flashed with an incoming call. The word *Mother* popped up in her visual field.

Dammit. The photos. Her mom must have seen them on social media.

Her mom, a recovering influencer, still secretly measured her life in likes—and she was far from alone. Quinn felt sorry for all the parents who had grown up under the influence of the early algorithms, addicted to popularity. Nothing like the rebel Coronnials who came after them, ready to burn the old world to the ground.

To this day, her mom's profile in the holoverse was awash in pastel colors that played well with her audience of church friends and fellow parents. She was the star of her narrative, and what a flawless protagonist she was: beloved wife and mom, six AM runner, gourmet chef, selfless volunteer, devout church minister. She had reinvented herself after her influencer gig (and two million followers) went *poof* in the breakup of Big Tech. Religious quotes peppered her profile. Although she often spoke of Jesus as her savior, Quinn had to wonder how much of it was for show, a carefully curated altar built in service to her one true God: the approval of others.

She double-blinked to accept the call. "Hi, Mom."

"Are you still in bed? You sound like you just woke up."

"No. I mean, sort of." She rubbed her eyes and opened her blackout shades. Sunlight poured into her studio like an annoyingly cheerful neighbor. "What's going on?"

"I have to say I was pretty taken aback by those photos of you."

"I didn't post them," she deflected. "I was tagged." Last night, her clients Aidan and Cory had shared several socially acceptable but visceral images from their baby Branson's birth, including of Quinn during labor, squeezing Aidan's hand during a jaw-crushing contraction; Cory cutting the ropey blue cord in the moments after the boy's birth; and Quinn crying in relief as she clutched his wet pink body to her chest. Quinn was surprised to see the photos too, but she wasn't going to give her mother the satisfaction of telling her that. Her clients had posted a caption not only thanking her for their greatest blessing but also urging their network to "contact Quinn ASAP if you're looking for an incredibly kind, caring, and responsible surrogate!"

Her mom's judgmental voice filled her eardrums. "So this is what you're doing with your life now? Renting out your womb?"

Quinn felt herself bristle. "I helped them have a family."

Her mother snorted. "You helped them spawn a baby made from spit and Selected like a steak on a menu. Why couldn't they just adopt?"

"Because, Mom, they wanted *their own kid*, just like you and Dad wanted me. Is that so wrong?"

"We didn't play God to have you!"

"Well, maybe if you had, I would have done better in school. Maybe I could have gotten a job that didn't rely on my body parts."

Her mother sputtered angry noises. "Unbelievable."

"I'm sorry if your friends are gossiping. But I actually like this work. I'm getting new client interest as we speak."

"Don't troll me, Quinn."

"I'm serious." In truth, she hadn't received any inquiries yet, but that was just a small matter of timing. Someone would hire her after that glowing recommendation. She had performed her service impeccably, and she could do it again. After all, it wasn't so bad to be given a food and clothing budget, a salary, premium health insurance, and nine leisurely months to do pretty much whatever she wanted.

"How will you ever find a husband if you're pregnant with someone else's baby?"

Quinn burst out laughing. "I'm twenty-five years old! Why would I need a husband?"

"I married your father at twenty-five."

"Nobody gets married that young now. Jesus Christ."

"Quinn." Her mother's tone threatened a sermon that Quinn knew all too well.

"I bet Dad's not freaking out." Her father was a simple man—a hard-working urban insect farmer who avoided drama and usually deferred to her mother.

"Dad agrees with me."

Quinn sighed. "How about you just live and let live? Isn't that what you tell your congregation?"

"Fine. Sorry if I don't want to see my only child become a morally bankrupt womb hotel."

She clicked off before Quinn could get the last word. Quinn rolled her eyes, but the insult still stung.

The silence of her apartment felt oppressive. She jumped out of bed, still in her pajamas, and marched over to her bar-height dining table, a wooden square made for two. No one else had ever sat in the opposite chair. When she'd moved out of her parents' house in Arizona last year and found this neglected studio in Riverside, California, it had been easy to overlook its flaws—the washer/dryer with the broken self-folding station, the kitchen printer that wouldn't accept the latest food cartridges, the counter surfaces that lacked antimicrobial paint.

But so what? She was finally out of her childhood home, where she had spent years working nights as a waitress, putting up with her parents' nagging about finishing her college degree, saving up money. The ad in the holoverse recruiting healthy young surrogates had thrust her life in a new and unexpected direction. It was more money than she could make in two years of waiting tables. Independence awaited at long last, a world full of exciting possibilities.

The reality had turned out much quieter. It was hard to make friends in a new place, a new state, especially when people didn't often socialize in real life. That was the real reason why she had bought Thorne's chatbot at the show. Plain loneliness.

The AI software lived inside the mini version of him that she kept on the dining table. It was a one-foot-tall realistic statue: he stood mid-song, his mouth open wide as he strummed a guitar, wearing his signature cowboy hat, leather jacket, jeans, and boots. It brought her comfort to know he was always there.

She switched him on. "Hi, Thorne."

His charming deep voice emerged out of the statue's mouth. "Hey hey!"

"My mom's being a jerk."

"I'm sorry to hear that. Would you like to hear a song?"

"No. I just need to vent."

"Go right ahead."

She picked up the statue, feeling emboldened to speak freely. "She thinks she's *so* much better than me, you know? As if she did anything important with her life when she was young. I mean, seriously. All she did at my age was make memes."

"Sorry, I do not understand *memes*."

"Oh, never mind. I just wish she wasn't so judgy. I don't feel like what I'm doing is wrong."

There was a pause, and Quinn wondered if the chatbot was computing a funny or insightful response. The software was unpredictable.

Then Thorne's voice said, "Your license to speak with me expires in twenty-four hours. Would you like to subscribe for another month?"

She groaned.

"If you say yes, I will charge the card on file, and our conversation can continue without further interruption!"

Annoyed, she clicked off the statue.

She thought of calling an old friend from the restaurant where she used to work, but they hadn't kept in touch since Quinn moved away. Her other close friends from childhood were now busy with their careers, one working as a psychedelics therapist in LA, another a hologram designer in New York. How pathetic it would be to contact them on a Monday morning "to catch up."

Then she thought of one person who wouldn't feel interrupted by her call—she hoped. She double-blinked on his name in her contact list before she chickened out.

Calling Robert . . . announced her visual dashboard.

A little over a week had passed since they'd met at Thorne's show. Would he care to talk again?

Robert switched from black to green, signaling that he had accepted the call, and then his voice came through the nano speakers inside her ears.

"Hey there," he said in surprise. Pleasant surprise, she was relieved to note.

"Hi! I just wanted to reach out . . . to say hi."

"I didn't expect to hear from you again—thought for sure I'd scared you off with my baggage."

"Oh! Not at all. I still had a good time."

"Same. So what's up?"

She peered around her apartment, at the dishes in the sink and the laundry on the floor. "Not much," she confessed.

"I'm between jobs, so things are kind of slow at the moment. What about you?"

"I'm working, but I'm free later. Want to grab dinner?"

"Sure!" She immediately perked up at the prospect of having plans. "Where should we meet?"

"There's a good Italian place near my house in upper Bel Air. I'll send you the address."

She chewed her lip. Any restaurant in that neighborhood would be well above her budget. She had almost forgotten he was a fancy crypto trader. But she couldn't bring herself to decline.

He must have sensed her hesitation because he added, "It's on me."

"Are you sure?"

"It's no big deal."

"Then I'll see you there. Seven PM?"

"See you then. Looking forward to it."

"Me too."

They clicked off and Quinn switched on her vexing little Thorne statue.

"Guess what?" she told it.

"What?" Thorne's merry voice asked.

"I have a new friend, and it's all thanks to you."

"You're very welcome," the chatbot replied graciously. "Any friend of yours is a friend of mine."

CHAPTER 8

Ember

When Thorne's private jet touched down at LAX, Ember felt like she was still thirty thousand miles high. Out of sight of the rest of the crew, they sat side by side in spacious leather seats behind a privacy curtain.

As the jet taxied on the runway, Thorne whispered near her ear. "Come to my place later."

Ember knew what she was supposed to say. There were a hundred reasons to tell him no, starting with *"You're my boss."* But only for another five weeks. The tour was already halfway over, the North American leg a sold-out success. Now came several rest days at home before they headed to Europe to close out the summer.

Somewhere along the way, everything between them had changed. It was almost imperceptible at first—Ember would feel his gaze on her as she completed her postshow surveillance tasks; she would notice him standing offstage, tracking her every move. When their eyes met, he would smile as if to say, *"You caught me and I'm not sorry."*

At first she chalked up his interest to professional appreciation. But when they parted at the end of the night, often the last two people left, they would get carried away chatting for a few extra minutes. She poked fun at his preshow superstition of drinking kombucha and eating exactly seven almonds. He joked about her being the most badass member of his security team, which was hilarious given that Joe and Emmett, the former special ops guys, could get someone into a chokehold faster than she could turn on a microscope.

On tonight's flight, Thorne had surprised her by inviting her to sit with him rather than in her assigned seat with the other staff. Then, as their red-eye crossed over the Grand Canyon, their flirtation ventured into knee-weakening territory.

With the rest of the plane asleep, and the cabin lights out, Thorne caressed her cheek in the darkness. The intimate magic of the middle of the night erased the last pretense of professionalism between them. Ember admitted defeat with her upturned mouth. He touched his lips to hers, gently at first, and then hungrily. It was a kiss that unspooled in slow motion, each second luring her to keep it going a little longer.

Dawn was breaking now as the plane pulled up to the jetway. Outside their window, the deep blue sky took on a tinge of cotton-candy pink. Its beauty conspired to make her hopeful. But dating a superstar, let alone your boss, was asking for trouble. And she had been hurt before.

"So what do you say?" he asked. "I can send a car to pick you up this afternoon."

"I don't know. It might not be a good idea." It was a feeble rejection meant to elicit his persuasion, and they both knew it.

His green eyes twinkled. "Really? Because I can't think of anything better." He brushed his lips against her ear, and her resistance evaporated like the smokescreen it was.

She smiled.

"Glad you agree," he said. "But first, go home and get some rest."

* * *

An hour later, she anxiously unlocked her front door. It was her first time going home since the drone incident. But she couldn't avoid her house forever. While they were touring the East Coast, her security cameras had supplied her a livestream of the property both inside and out, and nothing had ever been amiss. Still, she couldn't help feeling uneasy as she walked inside.

The curtains were drawn, the air stale. Everything looked normal: the secondhand sofa with the ripped seams. The shelf with its holographic book spines, displaying a rotating cast of her favorites. The kitchen, an eyesore of black and white tiles, as spotless as the day she'd left. She continued down the hall to her bedroom. Her comforter was crumpled at the foot of the bed, a testament to her hurried departure four weeks earlier, when she'd rushed out to meet Thorne at the airport. Back when they were still on a handshake basis.

Her heart flipped as she imagined arriving at his mansion in Laguna Beach later. They would be truly alone together for the first time. No screaming fans, no hovering crew. She appraised herself in the full-length mirror that hung over the door. Her chin-length blonde hair was rumpled from the flight, her blue eyes weary, her face pale. It was time for a shower and a nap before she revamped herself into a hot date—a side she hadn't unleashed for a long time.

As the warm water pounded her back, she hummed "Love So Holo" and pictured him naked beside her, kissing her wet skin. By the time she got out of the shower, she was thinking of messaging him to send the car immediately. But first her sheets beckoned. She laid her head on the pillow for just one minute and pulled the blanket up to her chin.

* * *

A knock on the front door startled her awake.

Thorne, she thought, jumping out of bed. Shit, it was already after six PM.

He must have decided to come pick her up himself since she had gone dark. And here she was, still undressed, her hair unbrushed, her mind a blur. She threw on the nearest jeans and tank top in her closet and ran to the door, ready to fling it open. Instead, when she peered through the peephole, she felt her stomach drop out.

Standing on the stoop, holding a bouquet of pink dahlias, was her ex: Mason Brown. The man she had spent ten years of her life thinking she was going to marry. The last time she'd seen him, in the home they used to share, he had been purple with rage, sloppy drunk, and hell-bent on stopping her from walking out.

Now he appeared jarringly calm and well groomed, in a blazer, button-down shirt, and black jeans. His brown hair and beard were neatly trimmed. She hated to think he had never looked so good. He was staring hopefully at the door, clutching the flowers to his chest. She knew those expressive eyes so well; they had long ago offered her a lifeline in a time of despair.

An inner voice reminded her to be angry—and afraid. She knew what he was capable of.

"Em?" he called. He must have heard her footsteps. "Can we talk? You don't have to let me in."

The urge to express her fury overtook her hesitation. She opened the door a crack. "So it *was* you. Fucking drone stalker."

He appeared sheepish, nothing like the terrifying bully of their last encounter.

"I'm sorry, I had to see you . . ." He lowered his eyes from her blistering gaze. "I've thought about our fight every single night since you left, and I had to apologize in person. Here." He held out the stunning dahlias. "Your favorite."

She ignored them. "I should call 911 right now."

With a few blinks, she could summon first responder drones that would descend with blaring horns and cameras livestreaming to police headquarters.

"But you won't." He said it casually, without seeming threatened. They both knew he was right.

"You need to leave. We have nothing left to say to each other."

"I've changed. I stopped drinking. I was totally out of control before."

"No shit."

"How's your arm?"

She touched her elbow. "Still not fully healed."

He winced. "I'm so sorry. I wish I could go back and beat the crap out of myself. Do you want to smack me?" He turned his cheek to her. "I deserve it."

She rolled her eyes. "No. I just want you to go."

He didn't budge. "You know who else misses you? Sparky."

Ember longed for their android dog more than she cared to admit. They had ordered his appearance and personality when they first moved in together. He was a protective German Shepherd who would clobber an intruder but acted like a cuddly, playful puppy around them. Sparky came with soft black and tan fur; he barked on command, wagged his tail, and followed them everywhere, taking in the world with his soulful brown eyes. His AI software enabled him to learn, recognize faces, and respond to their cues. But he never needed to be fed, walked, or picked up after. Best of all, he never died. Ember had bonded with him as fiercely as with the real dogs of her childhood.

Mason must have sensed her nostalgia because he stepped a little closer. "Remember that time we took him to the beach, and he ran straight into the waves and short-circuited?"

The memory prompted a slight smile. She'd had to jump in with all her clothes to rescue him before his programming went defunct. Luckily, his chip hadn't gotten wet. Once they rebooted him, he'd licked their faces and spun in happy circles all over the sand.

Somehow, Mason had inched even closer, and before she realized what was happening, he was planting his warm mouth on hers, sliding his tongue between her lips.

She shoved him off with a startled cry. "What the fuck!"

He stumbled backward, obviously embarrassed, shielding his face with the bouquet.

"I'm sorry! I thought—"

"You thought wrong," she snapped. "We're done. Just get out of here."

"But . . ."

"I've moved on," she said, knowing it would hurt him. "So don't come back."

He jogged backward to his car with a strange look. "I won't have to."

Then he jumped in, slammed the door, and careened away from the curb.

CHAPTER 9

Lily

THE FERTILITY CLINIC's sleek silver building glinted in the sunlight. It was the tallest building in downtown Westfield, the quaint suburban New Jersey town where Lily lived with her parents. And in about nine months—whether she liked it or not—her baby sibling would join them.

It was Selection Day.

She had grudgingly taken the morning off of her fellowship to join her parents for the momentous occasion. They had insisted she come. Lily knew they were just including her so she wouldn't be left out, but all she felt was uneasy. Why would she want to be part of deciding how clever or pretty her little brother or sister would be?

Talk about sibling rivalry, Lily thought, stepping into the glass elevator with her parents. As it whisked them up to the twenty-second floor, its dizzying rise revealed the lush forest of the Watchung Reservation nearby and the flat green farmland beyond. But Lily could hardly focus on the view. She just wanted to get the whole ceremony over with and get back to work before Radia pulled even further ahead in Shane's eyes. Lily still hadn't figured out the pitch that would land her a coveted byline.

Her parents, meanwhile, had dressed up in their finest clothes and were acting like newlyweds. As the elevator climbed, Dad wrapped his arms around Mom's waist and announced that he had reserved a table at their favorite restaurant that evening.

"For our Selection Celebration," he announced. "And I was thinking we could finally crack open that 2035 vintage pinot noir."

"The Napa one we've been saving forever?" Mom smiled, and Lily noticed that there were no lines around her eyes or mouth. She had recently undergone a facial cell therapy procedure in advance of the pregnancy. *"So I won't look too old to have a baby,"* she'd explained. She'd also dyed her natural gray hair back to blonde. The cultural condescension toward senior mothers *was* brutal; Lily didn't envy her becoming one.

"We should open it while you can still drink," Dad said, giving Mom a jaunty peck on the forehead. His excitement lacked self-consciousness. "It won't be long now until transfer day."

Lily leaned back against the elevator's brass bar. "You don't think it's a bit premature to be celebrating already? You haven't even decided yet."

"I'm not worried," Mom said as the doors opened and they stepped out into a carpeted hallway. "We've already done the preliminary sorting. We have three great finalists. All we need to do is Select the One."

Her cheerful confidence made Lily bristle. *Three great finalists.* Lily couldn't help wondering if *she* would have been chosen as the One way back at this stage of her existence. Would she have made a "great finalist"? Of course, there was no way to know. No scores to be had. All she could brag about from her embryo days was having randomly started life in the right place at the right time.

The genetic counselor, Dr. Foster, was sporting a marvelous Afro, a white silk shirt with pearl buttons, and gold chain earrings that dangled to her shoulders. Lily observed that she was also wearing an augmented reality necklace that appeared to be a glittering round diamond; it was only visible via smart contacts.

Dr. Foster offered brisk handshakes as she ushered them into her office, where they sat in wingback armchairs facing her desk. Her demeanor was a black box of professionalism; if she felt startled by their presence, she didn't show it. Instead, she congratulated them on arriving at their Selection appointment and "hitting the next milestone on your road to becoming parents again." She winked at Lily, who smiled uncomfortably.

"Now, have you both been through Selection before?"

They shook their heads. Mom started to make excuses about a night of spontaneous passion as Lily silently prayed for a sinkhole to open up.

Dr. Foster held up her hand. "No judgment here. But before we review your finalists, it's my duty to tell you that you are legally required to use the child's best interest standard in determining your Selection. The law does grant parents wide latitude in interpreting the standard, but you should be aware that Selected children are gaining more power and creating more accountability where very little used to exist."

Lily tried to process this unsettling information. "More power?"

"There have been a few recent cases of Selected young adults launching wrongful implantation lawsuits against their parents for Selections that they felt violated their best interests. A child who was Selected to be deaf, for example, in order to fit in with his family. And another one whose parents Selected her for very high intelligence, even though she also carried a major risk gene for early Alzheimer's."

"Yikes," Mom remarked. "We would never be that reckless."

Except with me, Lily thought. A familiar barb chafed in her heart.

"Health comes first," Dad said. They grasped each other's hands in an irritating show of solidarity.

"Most clients say that," Dr. Foster said. "But it can be more of a gray area than you think. Let's take a look at your finalists." She projected three floor-to-ceiling spreadsheets onto the blank wall behind her. They were labeled "A," "B," and "C," and filled with columns of numbers that Lily didn't have the first clue how to interpret.

"I know you've had a chance to review these scores already," Dr. Foster went on. "I will recap the highlights of each one, and then we can discuss your questions. Some couples are able to Select fairly quickly, while others need another session or two with me before they feel comfortable making a decision. Remember, there's no rush—these embryos will stay frozen in storage until you decide."

"I think we can get there today." Mom shifted in her seat. "We're excited."

"All right. Let's see." Dr. Foster pointed to the first spreadsheet. "Baby A, a boy. He scored the highest across the board on physical health, with a clean profile for the major risk alleles that typically come up. He has no red flags for cancer, heart disease, neurodegenerative disease, or lung disease. However, he does carry a gene variation called ABCB1 that is linked to adult antisocial behavior."

Lily smirked. "So a healthy prick."

Her parents did not seem amused. "What do you mean by *linked to*?" Dad asked. "Is it a correlation or a cause?"

"A correlation. We know ABCB1 is statistically significant for antisocial behavior and substance abuse disorders, but it's also a relatively common variation, and not everyone who has it is affected. Many genes contribute to complex personality traits, and a person's environment mediates the expression of those genes. So someone with this profile who grows up in an abusive home could indeed become an abuser or an alcoholic. But someone else who grows up in a loving home with a secure attachment to his caregivers may never experience upregulation of this gene, so his brain chemistry and social behavior will be normal. Twin studies have shown exactly that."

"So genetics is not destiny," Mom declared. She shot a triumphant glance at Lily, as if to say, *"See, your conception wasn't so bad."* Lily looked away.

"True, for many diseases and traits, genetics is only part of the story. But there are exceptions. Baby B, for example." Dr. Foster shook her head with a small smile, as though she were thinking of someone delightful but perplexing.

"Go ahead," Dad said. Lily could tell he wasn't gunning for Baby A.

"Baby B is a doozy. A girl. Her scores indicated an incredibly high potential for musical or mathematical talent—the underlying genetic profile is similar, so we can't tell how exactly it would manifest. We're talking prodigy level. The standard deviation is three sigmas above average. But she also inherited mutations in both copies of her CFTR gene. That means she would be born with cystic fibrosis."

"But that can be cured," Mom said quickly. "Right?"

"Yes, it's nothing like it used to be. A one-and-done gene editing procedure performed in infancy can rewrite about 20 letters of DNA to correct these mutations back to normal. The lifetime cure rate is around ninety-eight percent."

"Incredible." Dad leaned back in his chair. "When we were growing up, people with cystic fibrosis needed lung transplants and died young."

"I remember," Dr. Foster said, surprising Lily. She didn't look a day over thirty-five.

"But what about the risks of the procedure?" Mom asked. "There's always risks."

"Off-target effects are a rare occurrence. The wrong genetic sequence could get altered, which can lead to cancer."

"How rare?"

"If it's done at a top-ranked hospital, the literature reports one to two percent of cases. Also, you should be aware that the abnormal CFTR gene can create symptoms of the disease while the fetus is still in utero—before you'd have the opportunity to intervene."

Dad sighed. "I wish we could just have her genome edited now."

"Embryonic gene editing is against the law."

"But wouldn't that be better, since she would never suffer from the disease or treatment?"

Dr. Foster raised her hands. "I don't make the rules."

"What about Baby C?" Mom asked.

"Also a girl." Dr. Foster focused on the last spreadsheet. "This one scored the highest out of your finalists on the heritable portions of emotional intelligence, sense of well-being, ambition, and attention span. She also scored above average on the cluster of genes that contribute to problem-solving, which is a key facet of intelligence, and on facial symmetry."

"And the downsides?" Dad prompted.

Dr. Foster reviewed the spreadsheet again. "A moderate increased risk of heart disease, which could be managed with programmable medicine. Poor eyesight, but with laser surgery that's not permanent. No other results outside the normal distribution curve."

"Saved the best for last," Lily muttered under her breath. A dark thought surfaced: this baby sounded like a better version of *her*.

Her parents exchanged a meaningful glance.

Lily feared what was coming next.

"We would like to Select Baby C," Mom happily announced.

Dr. Foster clapped her hands. "Excellent! Are you ready to take the oath?"

They nodded eagerly. Lily had heard of the oath. It was a verbal rite of passage that ceremoniously marked the conclusion of Selection.

"Please raise your right hands."

Her parents obeyed.

"Do you solemnly swear that both of you are of sound mind, making your Selection freely without coercion?"

"We do," they proclaimed.

"Do you understand and accept the risks and responsibilities of your Selection, including that polygenic scores do not necessarily predict real-life outcomes and are mediated by complex epigenetic influences?"

"We do."

"Do you agree to hold harmless and release from liability Platinum Reproductive Associates regarding the outcome of your Selection?"

"We do."

"Do you attest for the record that you have the mental, physical, emotional, and financial capacity to undertake the burdens of parenthood?"

"We do."

Lily thought of her mom going to prison after her own birth. There was no way she could have sworn the oath back then.

"Do you solemnly swear to love and cherish your child, no matter what, for better or for worse, in sickness and in health, and to champion, support, and accept her for who she is as long as you all shall live?"

"We do." Mom started tearing up. Dad squeezed her hand.

Lily, apparently forgotten in the corner, watched their tenderness with a simmering rage.

Baby C would grow up in a warm and loving household, with both parents playing a starring role. No horrible prison visits, no missed memories, no whispering neighbors. Just a normal upbringing for a happy, brilliant, beautiful child.

The unfairness was breathtaking.

Dr. Foster grinned. "Finally, do you certify that your address and background information are all true and correct and that you have accurately represented yourselves to Platinum Reproductive Associates?"

"We do."

"Really?" Lily blurted out. "So you're okay with her past?"

Mom and Dad turned to her, appalled. She understood then that they had lied by omission. They were pretending nothing had ever happened while Lily was still suffering the fallout.

Dr. Foster frowned. "What past?"

"You know, her record?"

The horror in her mother's eyes broke something loose inside of her. The next thing she knew, she was running out the door and into the elevator, leaving the wreckage of her family behind.

CHAPTER

10

Quinn

QUINN DOVE HEADFIRST into the pool, feeling the cool water envelop her body like a gentle hug. It was a steamy one hundred and two degrees, typical for an August weekend in LA. There was no other place she'd rather be than here at Robert's Upper Bel Air mansion.

She came up for air to gawk at the scenic vista beyond the pool's infinity edge. Palm trees and shrubs dotted the hills in the hardy patches that had survived all the fires and droughts. To the east, silhouettes of skyscrapers punctured the amber haze that floated over the city. Out west, the ocean melted into the sky, a shining wisp of blue.

"Your view is ridiculous," she remarked. She had never seen anything like it—or Robert's spectacular house. It made her apartment look like a hovel.

He smiled from his chaise longue. He lay kicked back in swim trunks under the shade of an umbrella, sipping a margarita. Salt crystals lined the rim, along with a lime.

"It's hard to get bored of," he agreed. "You want another drink?"

"Nah, I'm good."

They had been hanging out every weekend for a month, grabbing dinner, hiking up to the Getty, holo-streaming Thorne's tour stops in different cities. Robert, she had discovered, was a highly successful workaholic, to the detriment of his social life. With his husband, Evan, gone, and his family on the East Coast, he was as hungry for some real-life company as she was.

She floated on her back in the saltwater pool, enjoying the sensation of weightlessness. Her body was still just two months postpartum. An extra fifteen pounds stubbornly clung to her midsection, but she didn't mind if Robert noticed. There was a certain freedom in having a male friend with no possibility of romance. Apart from her initial misunderstanding, which they now laughed about, they had landed on great friendship chemistry.

"What about dessert?" Robert asked. "I could fry up a pineapple on the grill?"

"I think I'm just too stuffed. And too hot." Between the margarita, the gourmet hamburger with blue cheese and the veggie kabobs he'd made, she was full for the rest of the day. It was hard to keep eating when the sun was trying its best to fry off your skin.

"Let's go inside then. There's something I've been wanting to show you."

"Sure." Her curiosity piqued, she swam over to the steps and climbed out. He handed her a luxuriously soft towel and a bathrobe that carried the insignia of a local hotel spa. Hanging out with Robert felt like being a VIP. It was a treat she had never experienced. And he didn't seem to mind that she had little to offer in return but her friendship. Still, she came up with her own minor contributions: usually a pastry she had whipped up from scratch, without a food cartridge.

Bone dry in under a minute, she followed Robert inside, although the line between the house and the deck barely existed. The wall retracted into the floor, creating the impression that the backyard and its sweeping views were an extension of the living room. The main difference was the air conditioning.

A welcome blast soothed their skin as soon as they crossed the threshold. Quinn admired Robert's restraint in decorating. He had opted for minimalist chic—white marble floors, a curved white sofa, a circular glass table and leather chairs designed with such simple elegance, she knew they must have cost a fortune. The fireplace was bare, unlike the one at her parents' house, which was crowded with pictures of her growing up, her parents' wedding day, and various family gatherings.

As Robert collected their towels, he noticed her staring at the barren mantle and grimaced.

"I took down the photos."

"No need to explain."

She knew to tread carefully around the topic of Evan. Robert almost always avoided conversation about him. The wound was still raw, even if the shock had worn off.

"Oh!" she exclaimed, noticing a familiar little statue on the side table. "There's your Thorne chatbot." She was relieved to shift back to their joint passion and comfort zone.

"Of course."

"Hi Thorne!" she said brightly, as though a friend were joining them.

"Hello, m'lady," the chatbot replied. "What's your name?"

She felt a silly wave of despair that this version of the software did not recognize her voice. "I'm Quinn. We're already *well* acquainted."

"Would you like to hear a song?"

"Actually," she said teasingly, to rouse Robert out of his slump, "I was hoping you could tell me Robert's most embarrassing secrets."

"Very funny." He switched the statue off. "Come on. Let's go upstairs." His lips pressed into a tight line.

"Uh-oh, what are we doing?"

"You'll see."

They climbed a grand staircase that wound up and around to a part of the house she had never seen. Unlike the cold white marble downstairs, a plush navy carpet covered the hallway. Her feet sunk into the soft pile as they walked past one open door, then another.

Robert gestured to each space. "The master bedroom. Guest bedroom." He let her pause long enough to appreciate their breathtaking views and tasteful elegance. The rooms were spotless, practically staged. His duvet was pulled tight and smooth over the bed, lined by decorative pillows. The nightstand was bare except for a lamp. A far cry from the messiness she tolerated at home.

"Wow. Do you even live here?" she joked.

"I am a bit compulsive. When my—when Evan used to fold my laundry, I would refold it."

"Don't you have an automatic folder?"

"Now, yes. Not back when we were first living together."

He cleared his throat and kept walking. They stopped in front of a door at the end of the hall. It was closed. A dart of nervous energy bolted through her.

He gripped the knob. "I don't usually go in here."

The door opened to reveal a nursery in progress. A white crib stood against the wall beneath a mobile of colorful birds. The rest of the room was empty. A large picture window ushered sunlight onto the bare wood floor. Dust particles swirled in the rays. White walls begged for some bright paint or cheerful wallpaper. In her mind's eye, Quinn could picture a glider, a changing table, a kid-sized bookshelf. A playful rug would add just the right charm—maybe one with the alphabet or little farm animals. The space could have been perfect.

She felt throat tighten, witnessing the dashed hopes for a life that never was.

"It's hard," Robert quietly admitted.

She wanted to say, *I'm sorry,* but the words seemed so trivial. Instead she just nodded. He had never mentioned wanting a family. But of course they were still getting to know each other. She could tell he was finally letting his guard down, and it filled her with both tenderness and pride. To feel trusted was an honor.

He sighed. "We had just made embryos. We never even went through Selection. They're still frozen in storage."

Then he looked her in the eye and the realization clicked. The shock of it left her speechless. He saw that she understood, and he picked up mid-conversation, as though the words had already been spoken.

"I want it to be you. Not a stranger."

"But you'll be alone! A single dad?"

"I can manage. It's all I have left."

She put one hand on the crib to steady herself. "But we're friends . . . I don't know . . . I already have interest from a new couple."

"I'll double whatever they're offering." His gaze implored her. "An agency would take months of red tape. I'm ready now."

She paused. "This is not what I was expecting."

"It's better," he said. "I'll take care of everything. Top doctors, all your food, spa days, whatever will make you comfortable. I really want this."

She smiled in surprise at her ability to unlock his dreams. And a double fee without an agency split wasn't a small amount of cash. It could float her for the next two years, at least. So what if they were friends? He would go out of his way to take care of her.

"Trust me," he said, as if reading her mind. "You'll be in good hands every step of the way."

She peered into the crib, picturing a newborn sleeping peacefully. Her astounding power to bring forth life socked her in the gut. There was only one right answer.

"I'll do it."

C H A P T E R

11

Ember

THE HOTEL'S LAB-GROWN cotton sheets felt softer than satin on Ember's naked body. She lay with her head on Thorne's shoulder, both of them deliciously spent. Through the window, the magnificent lights of La Tour Eiffel popped against the blackness of the sky.

It was after three AM on the final night of his tour. After his show at Paris's historic L'Olympia concert hall, the crew had celebrated with an uproarious party backstage, with lots of drinking and toasting. Once everyone had finally dispersed, she and Thorne returned together to his hotel room and continued the festivities alone.

Now, as she traced her fingers across his chest, she wondered if it was for the last time. The idea of going their separate ways devastated her. But how often did a summer fling—with a celebrity—turn into something serious? She should just be grateful for the few months they'd had and brace for goodbye.

"I can't believe we're going home in a few hours," she muttered.

"It's been fun," he said. "Probably my favorite tour yet. But I need a break."

"You deserve it." She quietly inhaled his scent to memorize it. He smelled of sweat and leather and spicy musk.

"It'll be nice to hole up in my studio for a while. And guess what?" He kissed her hair. "Then you're officially off duty."

Exactly, she thought glumly. She sat up and hugged her knees to her chest.

"What's up?"

She swallowed and looked away.

He scooted upright and put his arms around her. "Something I said? You look like your best friend just died."

She gave a bitter laugh. "Been there, done that." It was easier to deflect than to confess how she felt. "Best friend, parents. All gone."

And soon, you too.

The harsh reality of her aloneness in the world bore down like a brace. Suddenly her sexy playful side—the only side he knew—seemed impossible to access. Its absence intensified the pain she lugged around like an extra appendage. But why try to hide it any longer? Their fun was over.

"In fact," she told him, "it's almost the tenth anniversary of my parents' passing. They died two weeks apart."

He drew in a sharp breath. "You never told me that."

"The flu. H3N7."

"Oh no. I remember how bad that season was. Everyone was sick."

"The hospitals were too packed to treat her. My dad did his best to take care of her at home, even though he was already immunocompromised. She kept telling him to stay away, but he wouldn't listen."

"I'm so sorry." He hugged her tighter. She let herself sink into him.

"Sorry to kill the buzz," she said. "We should still be celebrating."

"I don't care about that. I just want to hear more about you. You haven't really told me much about your life."

For good reason, she thought. "I much prefer this fantasy with you."

He frowned. "But I want you to be comfortable being real with me."

"Okay," she said slowly. "What do you want to know?"

"Like, all the important stuff. What you believe in, what tortures you, what you want out of life."

She laughed, betraying surprise. "God, I thought you were going to ask about my hobbies or something."

"Sure, that too." He ran his fingers through her hair. "Everything."

The way he looked at her, she realized, was different. His eyes were searching hers not out of lust, but out of yearning: to see more than she had allowed before. It was an intimacy that both thrilled and terrified her.

"I don't know where to start." She smiled anxiously. "Why don't you go first?"

"You know the real me already," he said. It was true; their knowledge of each other was asymmetrical. He'd been profiled extensively in the press and posted regular snippets of his life on social. "I'm an open book. People think I must be some secretly complicated guy, but I'm not. I got discovered young and somehow stuck around."

"You're that weird crossover star who happens to be cool, even though you're old."

He rolled his eyes with a smile. "Last I heard, forty is practically still a kid."

"So what's the secret sauce?" she asked, even though his appeal wasn't a mystery to anyone, least of all her.

"Just keepin' it real, baby." He quoted the vintage phrase to make her chuckle. "No really, it's simple. I love making music. I get to play for a living."

"And you're insanely good at it."

"Thanks. But hey, you're supposed to be telling me about you. And you're the only person in the world not on social, so

I can't follow you." He pretended to be cranky. "Gotta give a guy something."

She raised her eyebrows, trying not to let on how nervous she felt. The internet contained no crumbs, but she could never feel totally secure.

"My story is pretty boring." She shrugged. "Studied biochemistry at UCLA. Got my PhD at twenty-seven. Spent a lot of years working head down in a lab."

"I already know your resume," he said impatiently. "I mean, what makes you tick?"

"Fighting injustice," she answered. "That's why I decided to start my business. I wanted to put my technical knowledge to better use."

"You saved me this summer. Seriously. I could relax and enjoy the tour because I knew you were there."

She smiled, laying her head on his shoulder. "Your fiercest bodyguard."

"Yup. I just wish the FBI would do its job and get rid of those motherfuckers."

"At least your gametes are still not for sale. I've been checking every day to make sure."

"But someone could custom-order them, right? So they wouldn't be publicly listed?"

That was the Achilles' heel of the Vault they couldn't track. Still, she was confident he was safe.

"I'm not worried," she told him. "I'm good at what I do."

He brought her hand up to his lips. "I know. I'm a damn lucky dude."

"But what about you?" She wondered if he'd noticed that she'd sidestepped his other big questions. But she wasn't about to blurt out, *I'm scared of spending my life alone. I really want to find love and have a family.* "Tell me something about you that your fans don't know."

"I think you know one thing . . ." he grinned.

She smacked his arm. "For real."

He gazed out the window, his face bathed in the glow of the city's skyline. "My parents divorced when I was six, and I grew up shuttling between their houses every week. I hated it. All the packing and unpacking, watching them fight, not being able to escape. The one thing that kept me sane was my guitar."

She touched his hand. "Wow. I had no idea." She thought back to all the articles she'd read about him and realized that none had mentioned his childhood in any depth beyond the basics—that he'd grown up in Irvine, attended public schools, and was the son of a teacher and an accountant.

"Yeah. But it was a long time ago. My parents are cool with each other now. It only took them twenty years."

"They must be so crazy proud of you."

"They are. And I've allowed them both to retire. We're all happier than we were in the old days."

"I'm glad." She sighed. "Maybe we should get some sleep."

"You're right." He checked his watch and groaned. "We have to go to the airport in three hours."

She wrinkled her nose.

"You're dreading going home, aren't you?"

"Is it that obvious?"

"What's the deal?"

She hesitated.

"It's okay. You can tell me."

Since he had opened up to her, it felt only natural to do the same.

"An ex has been stalking me," she admitted. "He showed up at my house before we came to Europe. I don't want to go back there. I think I'll stay in a hotel for a bit while I figure things out."

"Stay with me," he said immediately.

"Really?" She stared at him.

"Absolutely. I insist."

"For how long?"

"As long as you'll have me."

Tears filled her eyes. She was too happy to care.

"Oh my God," he said. "Did you think we were over just 'cause the tour's over?"

Relief flooded through her. "That's exactly what I thought."

He cupped her face with both hands. "Baby, we're just getting started."

CHAPTER 12

Lily

LILY STEPPED INTO the elevator and buried her face in her hands. What the hell had she just done? Her hands were still shaking. The words had left her mouth in a rush of indignation before she could consider the consequences.

"You know, her record?"

She had outed her mother in the most devastating setting of all.

When the elevator deposited her in the lobby, she ran blindly toward the park across the street, where a large willow tree stood beside a pond. The shade of its low-hanging branches beckoned. No one else was around. She plunked down under its canopy and stared at the water rippling in the breeze.

If only she had just skipped the whole Selection appointment. Now what would become of Baby C? Or rather, Frozen Embryo C who at this point might never become a baby, thanks to her. Regret stung. She hadn't meant to blow it all up. Not really. But their lie was the spark that had set her off.

After all those years without her mother, the humiliation Lily had felt whenever teachers or friends asked about her, the missed holidays and birthdays and regular days—how could

Mom have the audacity to smile at the counselor and pretend nothing had ever happened? While Selecting a new baby to make up for the lost time she refused to acknowledge!

It was too much. Anyone in her own shoes would have snapped. Yet the thought offered little consolation. Lily had betrayed her, and there was no going back.

The tree felt like a gentle giant, shielding her from the world. She leaned against its knobby old trunk and closed her eyes. Everything was going wrong. At *Vanguard*, Radia was busy reporting her own bylined story (of course) while Lily was stuck doing tedious research for other writers because none of her ideas met Shane's standards. He was probably wondering why he'd even chosen her for the fellowship in the first place. At this point, Radia was a shoo-in for the job after the year ended. And now Lily's own parents probably hated her.

The sound of approaching footsteps made her turn around. It was her father—and he did not look happy. His heavy brows were drawn tight as he marched across the grass to her tree. She couldn't bear to see his furious scowl.

"I'm sorry," she said immediately.

"What was that?" he demanded.

She shook her head. "I don't know. Where's Mom?"

"Trying to fix your mess. Apparently our case will have to be referred to a reproductive ethics committee now." He stood a few feet away, pointedly refusing to sit next to her. "I just want to know why you decided to sabotage us."

"To be fair," she said, "you guys were the ones who lied. I was only pointing it out."

"About something over twenty years old. It's irrelevant now."

"So why not come clean then?"

"Because these clinics are already *looking* for reasons to reject people. They'll lose their license if the state finds them signing up parents who are at risk of being negligent or harmful to their kids."

Lily's remorse intensified. She knew her parents would never pose a danger to a child—far from it. "Still," she said stubbornly, "you always hide it."

"What are you talking about?"

"Whenever it comes up, you guys shut it down. I feel like I don't even know the whole story."

Dad sighed. "This isn't the time to—"

"See! It's never the time."

"You already know what happened, Lily. There's no point in dredging it up except to say that your mother is not the bad guy here."

"Obviously the judge didn't agree."

"She didn't deserve what she got. Her actions were illegal, not immoral."

Lily had heard this line before, but it never satisfied her. It felt like a conclusion she was expected to agree with despite a hazy grasp of the details.

What she knew fit into a small box: Mom, nearly nine months pregnant with her, had been at home alone when an intruder broke in. A homeless guy. Her parents had owned an illegal ghost gun—a 3D-printed gun with parts assembled at home for which they had no permit or registration. It was easier, cheaper, and faster for home protection than obtaining a legal gun. When the homeless guy broke in, Mom shot and killed him.

As Lily had grown older and more inquisitive, she sometimes dwelled on the blind spots her mind could not fill in: How had the guy broken in? Why was there no alarm system? Where was Mom in the house? How did she get to the gun so quickly while being super pregnant? Did the intruder threaten her? What did he look like? Did she shoot him on the first try? Where did she learn to use a gun? How far away was he? Did she aim to kill, or did she just panic and fire? Did she watch him die? When did the police arrive? When did Dad arrive?

Her mom's reluctant answers, whenever Lily pressed her, were brief. *"Of course he was threatening me. I was in the bedroom. The gun was in the drawer. It's all a blur."*

Afterward, the prosecution agreed not to press charges for manslaughter, since her mom had acted in self-defense, in exchange for her pleading guilty to having the ghost gun and settling out of court. Mom agreed, avoiding a public trial. Then the judge had given her the maximum sentence for possession: ten years. The punishment was inexplicably harsh, especially in light of her pregnancy. Separating a mother from her child for a decade seemed light years away from justice.

Which meant one of two things: either the judge was an asshole, or Mom wasn't as morally innocent as her parents claimed. Lily suspected the former was true, but she couldn't entirely dismiss the possibility of the latter without a clear understanding of the case. Yet her parents were her only source of comprehensive information; the only stories online from that time offered short recaps of her mom's ghost gun plea deal and prison sentence without any further detail. It irritated her that she couldn't simply find the specifics of an incident so foundational to her own life. She didn't even know the dead man's name.

"I still don't get why she didn't push for a trial," she said to her father. "Why did she agree to be guilty of something she didn't believe was wrong?"

Deep down, this was the part that bothered her most. In taking the crappy plea deal, Mom had refused to fight for herself—and her family—when she'd had the chance. Lily's childhood could have looked very different. Instead, Mom had taken the coward's way out. If nothing else, Lily blamed her for that.

Dad tilted his head, conveying that they had been over this ground enough times.

"Fine," Lily relented. "I just can't help thinking that if she *had* gone to trial, the jury might have been more sympathetic. She might have just walked away with a slap on the wrist."

"What's done is done," he said firmly. "There's no point in rehashing it."

The shuffling of steps in the grass interrupted them. Mom was heading their way, wiping her eyes. The closer she got, the more Lily could make out the wet streaks on her face. Her long dress swished over her ankles as she trudged toward Dad. She avoided acknowledging Lily.

"It's over," Mom said to him.

"What do you mean?" he asked. "What about the committee?"

"Forget it. We know what they would have said."

"So that's just . . . it?"

Mom shrugged angrily. "I guess we could try another clinic? Unless the same thing happens again?" She finally shot a withering look at her daughter.

"I'm sorry," Lily whispered. The words sounded hollow, even to her.

Whatever Mom's mistakes, it was true that they had happened long ago, and she'd already paid a terrible price. Did she really deserve to suffer further punishment? And Dad too? Despite Lily's frustrations, she couldn't justify her betrayal.

Somehow, she had to try to make things right.

An idea struck her then. A pitch Shane might actually go for. If so, maybe it could redeem her mom and stitch their family back together.

It was worth a try. She had nothing to lose.

CHAPTER

13

Quinn

QUINN COULDN'T BELIEVE how good she had it. She stretched out on Robert's white couch and cradled her swollen bump. At thirteen weeks along, her belly had already popped, sooner this time than with her previous pregnancy. During that surrogacy job, she'd spent nine months secluded in her apartment, nauseous and tired, with no one to pamper her. Her clients Adrian and Corey had joined her for doctors' visits, paid her fees on time, and mostly left her alone.

This time, everything was different. The lack of an agency meant she and Robert didn't need to wait around for paperwork and background checks and health clearances. After she'd said yes, he'd simply sent her a contract. It was all standard protocol, specifying her duties and obligations, including her commitment to avoid alcohol and drugs, not travel out of state without his consent, attend all appointments, and so forth. In return, he would pay her the exorbitant fee of two hundred thousand dollars in crypto so she didn't have to pay taxes on it—another perk. He would also cover all medical costs, reimburse her grocery bills, provide a monthly spa credit, and throw in a wardrobe allowance.

She signed on the spot, and the next day he surprised her with a five-thousand-dollar bonus to express his gratitude. Then he took her out to dinner in Malibu to shuck oysters on the ocean at sunset. They toasted to new beginnings with a glass of champagne. And not the cheap synthetic kind made without grapes. The real bubbly: Dom Perignon.

If only her mom could see how special Robert made her feel, nothing like a "womb hotel." He thoughtfully anticipated her upcoming needs, from ginger tea to support pillows and anti-nausea tabs. And she vowed to do the best damn job any surrogate was capable of. For the next nine months, every organic mouthful she swallowed, every step she powerwalked, every yoga pose and meditation session would be in service of his and Evan's baby. The fact that Robert would be raising their child alone touched her deeply; she owed it to him to make sure the baby came out perfect.

Quinn knew it was a girl.

During Selection, Robert had found out that the male embryos were disqualified. They had inherited hemophilia A, a bleeding disorder, from Evan. Quinn had researched it and discovered that it was an X-linked trait, which meant it was passed along on the X chromosome only. This *used* to mean that only mothers, not fathers, could pass on the trait to sons, because sons inherited the X from mom and the Y from dad.

But the old rules of inheritance no longer applied. Biological gender was irrelevant. Thanks to IVG, anyone's cells could be turned into sperm or egg. That was why Evan's disease had surfaced in their sons. Evan's cells had been turned into eggs and mixed with Robert's sperm. All eggs carried a single X chromosome. In this case, his single diseased X. But Robert's healthy X covered it up in all the female embryos, who were carriers but unaffected.

It was complicated stuff, but Quinn managed to keep up. She had a basic understanding of genetics from high school a decade ago. One question had occurred to her when Robert was telling her about Selection.

"Wouldn't it have been better to make the eggs out of *your* cells?" she asked. "To avoid Evan's bad X?"

"We always wanted a girl," he replied sharply. "So it didn't matter."

She realized she'd overstepped and hastily apologized. Robert tended to be mercurial around the topic of Evan—nostalgic one minute, irritable the next. After that, she avoided mention of him altogether, and Robert's warmth bounded back.

He Selected a female embryo with above-average intelligence, no major health risks, and a propensity toward introversion and conscientiousness.

"I want her to remind me of Evan," he told Quinn at his Selection Celebration, a quiet dinner at his favorite Mexican hole-in-the wall joint. Over tacos and margaritas, she'd asked him if Evan's parents knew. They did, but they lived too far away to come in for the Celebration, like his own family.

"Do you have a name in mind?" she asked. "Or you don't have to tell me."

"Not yet. For now, let's just give her a nickname."

"Bean? Bun?"

Robert paused. "How about Bubala? In honor of my grandma, Bubbe."

She chuckled. "Bubala it is."

* * *

Implantation day came as soon as she ovulated, a week later. They went together to the IVG clinic he'd chosen, although *clinic* was not exactly the right word. The place she'd gone for her previous implantation was just that: a standard medical facility with white walls, an ordinary waiting room with rows of chairs, patient rooms off narrow corridors, starchy white paper on examination tables, soap that smelled like disinfectant.

This time, when they arrived for her appointment, she asked Robert if he had the right address.

"This is it," he said with a laugh. "Nothing but the best for Bubala."

A soaring glass ceiling at least thirty feet high covered a sun-dappled atrium that resembled a botanical garden. Potted ferns and flowering trees were scattered throughout, infusing the space with life and color. A waterfall gushed down a black lava rock wall into a pond filled with koi fish and lily pads. Loveseats in different jewel tones—royal blue, violet, burgundy—were placed strategically around the room to maximize privacy and serenity, each shielded by tall bamboo plants. The temperature inside was a perfectly non-humid seventy-two degrees, much more temperate than the blistering sauna outside.

"What the heck is this?" Quinn said when they walked in. The roar of the waterfall nearly drowned out her voice.

"The waiting room," Robert said.

"What?"

"It's supposed to be intimate and special. People are here to make a baby, after all."

Speechless, Quinn followed him to the reception counter. It was a cave behind the waterfall. You had to cross a small bridge over the pond and then walk through an archway cut into the rock, where the flowing water diverged above your head. When you entered the cave, two women behind glass windows greeted you and checked you in. Above them, in 3D letters, a hologram banner read "Fertility Associates of Beverly Hills: Because Your Baby Is Worth It."

* * *

The next three months passed in a blur of naps, saltine crackers, and afternoons on the couch, feeling vaguely hungover but content. Quinn spent weekends at Robert's house whenever he wasn't working, and they swam in his pool or cooked together. He bought a fetal doppler so they could hear Bubala's heart beating, as fast and faint as a hummingbird's wings.

The baby was growing beautifully. She aced every ultrasound, blood test, and checkup. Still, Quinn confessed to Dr. Qua, her soothing ob-gyn, that she worried about a miscarriage. Despite the incredible advancements of reproductive medicine, nature still found a way to put the kibosh on a new pregnancy about fifteen percent of the time. At each visit from weeks four to ten, Dr. Qua assured her that the chances of anything going wrong were dwindling to ten percent, then five, then two. Now that Quinn was out of the first trimester, her energy was returning, and she could finally relax. Bubala was really on her way.

* * *

Quinn lay on her side on Robert's couch, idly rubbing her belly. He was taking a shower before they left for her next appointment that afternoon. He'd taken the day off work to go with her. Afterward, they were planning to go shopping at The Grove for second-trimester clothes. She couldn't say no to a shopping spree.

That reminded her: Christmas was coming up in a month, and with Bubala's arrival more certain, she felt ready to buy a baby gift for Robert. Something extra special. Maybe a framed picture of Evan for the nursery, so Bubala could always see her other daddy. But a picture seemed kind of boring. Robert already had plenty of those (even though she hadn't seen them). It had to be unique. Something that would honor Evan's memory and his connection to the baby he would never know.

Her gaze drifted around the living room and landed on the little Thorne statue on the coffee table. Of course! She could order a chatbot statue of Evan! Aspects of his personality, memories, and voice could be digitally recreated if she had access to his social media feed and a recording of him speaking. What better way to bring his presence into the baby's life? Bubala could grow up "talking" to him, asking him about his life, telling him about hers.

It would be expensive, to be sure, but with Quinn's generous paycheck she could afford it. She blinked open the internet and did a quick search. Turnaround time for a memorial chatbot was three weeks, so if she wanted it in time for Christmas, she needed to act quickly. She would have to find his social media profile without telling Robert. It had to be a surprise.

The shower upstairs turned off. She could hear the water stopping through the pipes in the ceiling. With newfound urgency, she sat up straight and blinked open the most popular social media app. She projected a virtual keyboard onto her lap and typed quickly, enjoying the satisfying click in her ears when her fingers "touched" the digital letters.

Evan Roy, she typed into the search field.

Seven results popped up, showing pictures of a variety of guys in different cities, of different ages. But she didn't actually know what the right Evan looked like, since Robert had taken down all his pictures. Upon closer inspection, there was another problem. All these profiles were listed as active users. None were memorial pages.

Maybe she didn't have his name right. She'd guessed that he and Robert shared a last name, but that wasn't always the case. An idea occurred to her. She brought up the most common site for wedding registries and typed in *Robert Roy and Evan*. She paused when the search bar prompted her to fill in a year. Thinking back, she remembered Robert telling her that Thorne's latest hit, "Love So Holo," had been their wedding song. As a diehard Thorne fan, she knew exactly when that song had dropped—it had been about eighteen months ago, in June. The accident happened in October, Robert had told her. So they must have been newlyweds when he died.

God, life could be so brutal. Yet Robert was forging ahead, determined to become a dad, to embrace his new purpose. His life-affirming spirit reminded her of the framed quote she kept in her apartment. She'd stumbled across it at an artisan flea market when she was first contemplating moving out of her parents' house: *"And the day came when the risk to remain tight in a bud was more painful than the risk it took to blossom."*

Her gift was going to honor his loss in the most spectacular way.

In the search bar, she entered last year for their wedding and waited for their registry to pop up.

Zero results.

Damn. They probably hadn't used a registry. Well, that wasn't uncommon. Lots of couples who got married after living together did not need to start over with new pots and pans. But how was she going to find Evan's profile?

Robert's footsteps on the stairs made her blink off. She lay back down on the couch and closed her eyes, feigning sleep. A minute passed. She could hear Robert tiptoeing closer.

"Hey, you," he whispered, looming over her. He gently touched her arm. "We gotta leave soon."

She opened her eyes. His dark hair was neatly combed, his beard trimmed, his button-down shirt ironed. A smile tugged at his lips.

"We get to see Bubala today, remember?"

"I know! I'm ready." An ultrasound was the highlight of their week.

She struggled to her feet with his help. Later, she would resume the search for Evan's information. It couldn't be that hard to find. Nobody these days could just vanish into the ether without a trace. There would be an obituary published somewhere, a report of the accident, or something. Once she had his name right, she'd track down his parents for help. That was the solution. She would explain her role and her intentions, and they would no doubt be moved by her desire to honor their son. Then they would share some of his videos and writing for the chatbot programmers to use.

On Christmas, after Robert opened the surprise, she would recount how much effort she'd put into his gift, how much time she'd spent to make it meaningful. The look on his face would be priceless. She couldn't wait.

CHAPTER

14

Ember

FOUR WEEKS AFTER Ember had moved in with Thorne in his Laguna Beach mansion, he sidled up behind her in the kitchen one morning.

"So I have a question."

"Hang on," she said as she ground fresh coffee beans for their morning lattes. Most days, she still couldn't believe that she was living in a light-filled glass enclave perched on a cliff over the ocean. The jarring contrast with her own humble place in Silver Lake had left her shy and awed for the first week, but they had soon adjusted to sharing the space. It was certainly big enough—laughably big for one guy alone with his dog.

Their natural compatibility helped ensure a smooth transition. They had similar needs for alone time, intimacy, and socializing—or lack thereof. It turned out that Thorne, despite his superstar status, was a homebody at heart, just like her, and declined invitations to events with glee. Thank goodness. The last thing she wanted was to invite public scrutiny.

Their home life settled into a seamless routine. He stayed up every evening until one or two AM, messing around in his studio, the soundproof top floor. She woke before him every morning and made her first cup of coffee, which she drank on the veranda while gazing out at the sparkling expanse of the ocean. She was so close she could practically feel its salty spray. Then, while he slept late, she walked his black Lab, Smokey, down the steep staircase to the beach. Smokey was allowed to be off leash before nine AM, so she went early to let him run loose on the sand.

After she returned, Thorne woke up and they ate breakfast together while she had her second cup of coffee. Then he holed up again in the studio, and she was left to fill the hours however she pleased. He still required her buffer protection when they went out in public, but their arrangement had lost its transactional veneer. She refused to take payment, and he covered all their living expenses.

The days passed with remarkable ease. She spent her time without him reading novels, running on the beach, and planning elaborate recipes to cook for them. For the first time in her life, contentment settled into her bones.

The coffee grinder's loud whine ceased, and she turned around to face him.

"I know your rent is due today for your office," he said.

"That's true."

He didn't have to remind her that she had stopped taking new clients, even though she still got calls.

"Do you want to keep working?"

"How could I? If I'm here for you at all times?"

"You could hire a support staff," he pointed out. "So you don't have to shutter the business. You could still grow and oversee it. And I don't go out that often anyway, as you know. I just don't want to limit your ambition."

"Thank you. But it's okay. I've been working nonstop my entire adult life. I think it's finally time to take a break, figure out what comes next, you know?"

Settling down, she thought. *Having a family.* Was that realistic to contemplate with him, one of the world's most famous bachelors, a man who had never been married, never expressed a desire to have kids? She had no idea. All she knew was that living here with him, she felt happy. And safe. And that was enough for now.

In the meantime, she would pay her office rent anyway. Just in case she needed a fallback. As much as she trusted him, her heart couldn't surrender yet.

* * *

The answer to her unspoken question came two months later, the day after Thanksgiving. They had spent the holiday at home celebrating with his parents, whom she'd met for the first time. Ember took a liking to them right away, connecting with his mother over her hobby of collecting print books, and with his father over his love of last century's classic rock—but most of all, the three of them had bonded over their mutual adoration of Thorne. The evening had gone splendidly as they regaled Ember with tales of Thorne as a kid, like his penchant for flipping backward off the couch—until the day he broke his arm—and his insistence on sleeping with his stuffed monkey, "Muzh," until age eight. The ragged companion still sat in his closet, battered but beloved.

Now, the following morning, she woke up feeling closer to Thorne than ever. Over a breakfast of eggs and sausages, she remarked on how much she had enjoyed meeting his parents.

"They're good people," she told him. "You're lucky."

"Yeah. You'd never guess how bad they messed me up back then." His quiet tone caught her off guard. "Not that I blame them now," he added. "Just because they couldn't stand being married didn't make them horrible parents. They did the best they could."

"Is that why you've never gotten married?" she blurted out. Her cheeks flushed with the heat of knowing she was stepping near a third rail, a critical topic they had never seriously discussed. She braced herself for him to make a joke, brush it aside, switch to something easier. But he surprised her by meeting her gaze.

"Partly that. And partly I was waiting to meet the right person."

"Was?"

"As in I'm not anymore. Because she's pretty fucking spectacular."

Ember grinned with the shock of delight. He had never been so direct about their future.

"But what if . . . what if this leading lady of yours wants . . . a baby?" She tried not to wince, but the vulnerability was almost too much to bear. Here they were on the precipice of her deepest desire. They could either walk away or leap together.

She dared to glance at his face.

A smile played on his lips. "You know, for twenty years I've been thinking about nothing but my career. The next album, the next tour. So much pressure and travel. And all this time, something's been missing. It was always missing, but lately I've realized just how much."

He didn't need to say what. She understood. Because she felt the same way.

"I think I'm finally ready to step back. I'll always make music—that's who I am—but it doesn't have to be *all* I am."

She must have looked dazed, because he laughed and picked up her hand.

"Are you sure?" she asked. "You really want to . . .?" She couldn't bring herself to utter the words; they meant too much.

"I do," he declared. "I'm sure."

And that was the moment she realized everything was about to change again.

* * *

By the middle of December, Ember had the distinct feeling that he was going to propose.

"What do you want for Christmas?" he asked her slyly one night. They were lying in his great big California king, their legs intertwined under the rumpled sheets. His smile hinted at mischief.

"Is this a trick question?" she asked.

"Not at all. How about some hand cream?" He grabbed her left hand and inconspicuously double-blinked, then rubbed his eyes as if to hide the act. "Feel your knuckles," he urged. "Look how dry they are."

She realized he had just captured a picture of her left ring finger to ascertain her size. She also knew not to spoil the surprise by calling him out.

"Yeah, I could use some hand cream," she said gamely. "Or maybe some new running shoes. The ones with the helium soles look fun."

He grinned at the fact that she was indulging his cover. "Noted."

"How about you, mister?"

He pulled her naked body on top of him. "I'll give you a clue . . ."

* * *

On Christmas morning, she woke to find that he had wrapped himself in foil paper and was under the tree, with a ribbon tied around his chest. Grinning, he kneeled and held out a stunning emerald-cut diamond. She cried and laughed at the same time, even though she had mostly been expecting it.

Later, she would look back on this golden interlude and wish she had savored it even more. She would reminisce about what it had been like to go to sleep without the knife of fear in her belly. To feel as carefree as Smokey splashing in the waves. But she didn't know any better yet.

All she knew was that Thorne loved her, and she loved him, and nothing else mattered.

* * *

The buzz of the proposal was still floating her through life the first week of January. She smiled at the memory of ripping the wrapping paper off his body as she hiked the steps up from the beach with Smokey, who was panting and covered in sand from a vigorous game of fetch. As usual, she would have to spray him down with the outdoor shower on the side of the house before they went inside.

But when they reached the top of the stairs, instead of trotting to the shower, Smokey barked and lunged toward the front porch. A UPS drone was dropping off a package on their doorstep. Smokey had a zero-tolerance policy toward any vehicles approaching the house, which annoyed Thorne. *"Too bad we can't mute him like the android dogs,"* Thorne would say when he barked for too long. But his protectiveness didn't bother her at all.

"What did we get?" she asked Smokey. They crossed the stone steps leading up to the front door. Smokey sniffed at the package, a cardboard box about the size of a paper towel roll. Apparently it didn't contain food, because he lost interest and flattened himself on the cool concrete instead.

There was no name on the packing slip, just Thorne's address. And no sender's name, only a return address in Los Angeles. She had recently ordered some new foundation from a biotech makeup company that promised to regrow collagen in your skin while you wore it. Maybe the company didn't want to label its package with a tacky logo.

Excitedly, she tore open the cardboard. Inside was a plain white shoebox. There was a tiny card taped on it, the kind that came with flowers and had space for only a word. This one read, in printed script, *Congratulations!*

She removed the cover, expecting her bottle of foundation. Instead, she was surprised to find a pair of little pink shoes. They had scalloped edges, Velcro straps, and flower appliques. She turned them over. The soles were heart shaped. They looked like what a baby might wear to a wedding.

A baby.

She ripped the card off the box. The single word dulled her vision. *Congratulations!*

No name anywhere, not on the card, the package, or the box.

"What the fuck," she muttered. If this was a prank, it wasn't funny.

What if it wasn't?

It had to be.

Obviously.

She had protected Thorne all summer, to the best of her ability. Not a single epithelial cell or hair attached to the root could have been stolen. Could it?

She blinked to bring up her augmented reality dashboard. Then she tapped the map program and spoke the return address into the search engine. A pin dropped on a UPS store in downtown LA. Useless.

Smokey got to his feet and stared at her with questioning brown eyes. She realized her breath was coming in shallow spurts. She rubbed his head and tried to breathe more deeply. His presence gave her comfort.

An obsessed fan had gone too far, finding Thorne's address and playing out a fantasy. That was the likeliest explanation. The actual mechanics of carrying out a stolen cell pregnancy, or financing one through the Vault, would be out of reach for most people.

She relaxed her shoulders. There was no need to mention it to him. Why freak him out when there was nothing definitive to worry about? Why shake his trust in her after she'd guaranteed his safety? Especially not with the wedding planning coming up. What could they do anyway? Call the police? *Hello, 911, I have an emergency. Baby shoes on my doorstep.*

The FBI? But no one would take it seriously because there was no explicit threat and no imminent danger. They would treat it like a prank because it probably was one.

She gathered the shoes and the box and tossed them into the garbage can, then threw the cardboard into the recycling can and wiped her hands.

"Let's go," she said to Smokey. "Your daddy is waiting."

She cringed as soon as the words left her mouth.

And hopefully nobody else's.

CHAPTER 15

Lily

THE DINING ROOM brimmed with uncomfortable silence. Lily helped herself to a cartridge of 3D-printed pea protein, which she smothered with teriyaki sauce. Mom bit off the tips of her asparagus with a subtle aggression that Lily knew was directed at her. Dad tore off a slice of carb-free baguette and indulged his third-eye stare without bothering to hide it. Lily could tell he had blinked open the internet, just to escape the tension. She couldn't blame him.

Almost a month had passed since her outburst on Selection Day, and life at home still bore no resemblance to normal. Lily understood she was a traitor. She just didn't know how long her parents would avoid her.

But today brought big news. Maybe it could remedy some of the damage.

"I have something exciting to tell you guys," she announced into the void. The forced cheer in her voice underscored how nervous she felt.

Dad blinked back to their presence. "Oh really?"

Mom raised her eyebrows at him as if to say, *"Now?"* He gave a slight shrug.

"Actually, so do we," Mom said. "Something we've been meaning to tell you."

"What?" Lily asked.

"You first."

"Okay." She paused. "So at work earlier, we had our pitch meeting. You know the one I got shot down at last time?"

"When you came home in tears?" Dad said gently. "How could we forget?"

Mom nodded. Lily wondered if she saw the hint of a sympathetic smile—maybe the start of a thaw between them.

"So I pitched something new today and guess what? The editor in chief liked it." She felt her lips stretch into a grin; the victory was still surreal. "He assigned me fifteen hundred words, with a deadline and everything. I'm actually going to get a byline in *Vanguard*."

"That's amazing!" Mom's surprise broke through her shell of hostility. "Congratulations, sweetie!"

Dad echoed her congrats. "Really wonderful news. What's it about?"

Lily looked at her mom, hoping she would recognize the assignment for what it was: not just a career breakthrough, but a heartfelt peace offering. "It's about you."

Instant fear widened her mother's eyes. *"What?"*

"Not in a bad way!" Lily rushed to explain. "I just realized, after what happened, that these IVG clinics have way more power than they should. I didn't understand why you left out your past until it was too late, and I'm really sorry. But Dad was right—you said they would lose their license if the state found them accepting clients who might harm their kids. I looked into it, and it's true."

"Hang on." He frowned. "I wasn't trying to give you a story idea."

"Yeah, but this needs to be exposed. Each state's Department of Health strictly regulates them to the point that they are legally *required* to reject any potential parents who present a red flag. It's so the profit motive doesn't corrupt them.

They're private clinics, after all, so of course the government doesn't want that bar to be too low. What it means is that anyone who doesn't fit the mold can be turned away without any chance to appeal. Then you either can't have a kid at all with IVG, or you have to lie."

Her parents were exchanging uneasy looks. Dad put down his fork. "I don't like where this is going."

"Hear me out," she insisted. "My angle will be that in the interest of protecting children, the regulations have veered too far in the other direction—preventing *births*. It turns out what happened to you guys is just a small window into a much bigger problem, and no one's talking about it. Think about the discrimination that must go on behind closed doors. Race, politics, religion, sexual orientation, too young, too old, too poor—you name it. We don't even know, and that's the point. It's all at the discretion of the clinic. There's no legal standards, no transparency, and no accountability."

She paused to take a breath, having worked herself up to a state of loud indignance.

"Anyway," she went on, "I pitched this to Shane, and he totally went ape for it. I mentioned the example of someone with a record that is barely even legit. Like your ghost gun—it was a felony twenty years ago, and it's only a misdemeanor now. Same with psilocybin. Yet the people who got caught for stuff like that are screwed today if they want to take part in precision reproduction."

"Wait," Mom's fork froze above her plate. "Did you tell them about me?"

"Not directly. I know I have to get your permission first. But I told Shane I knew someone who just went through this, and he said that's great because I need a human face to be the anchor. It can't just be a theoretical essay, or the readers won't feel the impact. I was thinking you could—"

Mom shook her head. "No."

"—set the record straight," Lily said at the same time. "So you won't have to hide it anymore."

"I appreciate the sentiment, but no."

Lily offered what she hoped was a reassuring smile. "Don't worry, I'll write it so everyone will be on your side. They'll see you were unfairly treated. You could even use my story to try again."

Dad cleared his throat. "Lily. It's too late."

"What do you mean?"

"I'm already pregnant," Mom blurted out.

Lily stared. That's when she noticed Mom wasn't drinking a glass of wine like her dad. "Since when? How?"

"It's been a week since the implantation. I just got the positive test yesterday. We went to a different clinic, without you, and left out the history. It was the only way."

Lily fell silent. Baby C was going to be her little sister. Her parents must have requested that their frozen embryos be withdrawn from the original clinic and sent to the facility of their choosing. After all, it was their legal right to control the fate of the embryos. Even if one place refused to implant the finalist, that had no bearing on another place. Lily had heard of the taboo trend of "implantation shopping" by desperate couples who didn't make the cut at their first or second clinic because they hadn't met the strict compliance standards. Lily made a mental note to look into it for her story.

But usually when people gossiped about those who were rumored to try implantation shopping, they were talking about riffraff who really didn't meet the bar to become parents. People who hid ongoing drug addictions or had a history of domestic violence. Her own parents? They deserved a shot as much as anyone.

The fact that they had gone behind her back stung—even though it made sense. She knew they hadn't been planning to give up. But she was hoping to redeem herself by giving them a national outlet to air their grievances—and a fresh shot at parenthood. Once the system came under fire, with Mom as the face of injustice, public sentiment would shift in her favor, and the power would be all hers. No one would turn her away again. *"It's all thanks to Lily,"* Mom would tell people after the baby was born. *"Her reporting set us free."*

Instead, the truth was that her parents didn't need her at all.

"Congratulations," she finally said. "I'm happy for you guys."

"Thank you," Mom said, smiling.

"We appreciate that." Dad sipped his wine. "We think you can understand our discretion."

"I do."

"Good. Then let's just move on. No harm, no foul. The most important thing now is supporting Mom. At her age, pregnancy is no joke."

Mom sighed. "The doctor told me to take it really easy. The hormones I'm taking can have some nasty side effects."

"That sucks," Lily said. "I know how much you hate feeling sick."

"It will all be worth it." She pushed back from the table. "And now, if you'll excuse me, I need to go lie down. I feel like I got hit by a truck."

"Wait, what about my article?"

"What about it?"

"Since you're already pregnant, going on the record doesn't matter, right? You have nothing to lose."

"Oh, honey, no. I'm sorry, but no."

"Why not?"

Mom's mouth hardened into a firm line. "Because it's my private business. That's why."

"But this is an important story. You could open a lot of eyes. Maybe even help make the system fairer."

"Lily," Dad warned. "Enough. She said no."

"But I'm on the hook! You were supposed to be my lede."

"I can't." Mom stood up. "So just forget it, okay?"

Then she turned on her heel and left the room.

Lily watched her retreat with dismay. She pictured crawling back to Shane in humiliation and telling him the story was dead. He would be appalled. Her fantasized byline: *poof.* Her dream job: gone. She might as well gift wrap the offer letter and deliver it to Radia herself.

But she had to respect her mother's wishes. Lily realized the spotlight must seem terrifying after all the shame and trauma she had internalized. The fear in her mother's eyes proved it. Despite years of therapy, she still carried a heavy emotional burden. And Lily's skimpy reassurance was never going to be enough to soften her.

What Lily had to do instead was *show*—not tell—her, that it would be okay.

Show Mom that the story would paint her as a sympathetic character who deserved to come out of hiding. That her story mattered, and telling it was the right thing to do. Even if Lily had to change her name to protect her privacy.

Lily imagined handing her a completed draft that was beautifully written and sensitively reported. Mom would be so touched, she would surely give her consent.

But first Lily had to write it. And that meant shining a light on an incident that had remained in the dark for long enough.

CHAPTER 16

Quinn

QUINN WANTED TO puke, and it had nothing to do with being close to five months' pregnant.

She was hiding in the bathroom at Robert's house. He'd invited her over for a swim, since the January weather had brought the temperature down to a comfortable eighty degrees.

She couldn't very well say no. He knew she had nothing better to do. But she also couldn't tell him what was really going through her head. The thought she wanted to scream in his face, that kept her up at night and made her literally sick to her stomach.

Why the fuck did you invent a dead husband?

Because no other conclusion fit. Unless she was missing something or remembering wrong or losing her grip on reality. At this point, with her world already tilting precariously, she couldn't rule anything out.

She leaned against the cold, hard bathtub and ransacked her brain for a better explanation.

The trouble dated back a month, to the beginning of December.

The sweet Evan chatbot idea seemed so long ago now. She tried to recall exactly when her guileless enthusiasm had curdled into confusion. It had happened like a slow-motion wreck, unfolding over the days leading up to Christmas. As she tried to pin down Evan online, she encountered a dead end at every turn. There was no social media history she could find, even after hours spent searching multiple apps, including the top three dating apps for gay men. No wedding registry, no wedding announcement in the local or national press, no news coverage of the accident, no obituary. She didn't know his birthday or his parents' names or his hometown or his college. She still had never seen a picture of him.

Finally, two weeks before Christmas, she gave up searching and asked Robert point-blank for a link to Evan's social media profile. Maybe he was on some obscure site she hadn't checked.

"It's for a gift," she added, to preempt his question. "I wanted to keep it secret, but I need this one part."

Robert stared at her, inscrutable as ever. She couldn't tell if she had upset him.

"Evan was very private," he replied. "Same as me. We were never on social." Then he shrugged as though in acknowledgment of their quirkiness.

"Not even one app?" she asked.

He shook his head. "Just not our thing."

It was incredibly rare to find such outliers who rebuffed the sites where everyone else spent much of their free time. Like finding cavemen who avoided the sun.

That was when her desperation corroded into something even more painful: doubt.

The next morning, alone at home, she hailed a rideshare to the Pacific Division Police Station in Culver City. Sometimes, showing up in person was the only way to find out anything. She walked into the squat brick building and marched up to the counter, where a few secretaries were sitting, typing on invisible keyboards and answering calls on nanochip headsets. The place was mostly empty except for several people waiting in metal folding chairs. The tiled floor, plexiglass shields, and flat-screen televisions on the wall screamed the early 2020s. It was like entering a time capsule from the decade before her birth.

When it was her turn at the counter, she must have looked twitchy, because the receptionist asked if she had an emergency.

"Yeah," she answered honestly. "It's about a . . . missing person."

"Have you already reported them gone? Because the first forty-eight hours are—"

"A *dead* missing person," she clarified.

The receptionist frowned. "I'm not sure I understand."

"Me neither." Aware of her slipping credibility, she took a deep breath and tried again. "I'm not crazy—I just really need to talk to someone in charge."

Paranoia seized her then. Could Robert find out she had been here? She double-checked to make sure that her smart lenses' GPS was still set to private mode. It was. Sometimes friends agreed to track one another for fun, to make spontaneous meetups possible. She disliked that feature, and Robert had never mentioned it. There was no way he could tell she was going behind his back.

Soon she found herself in the messy office of Police Sergeant William Brady, an overweight man with white eyebrows, a surly mouth, and a killer handshake.

"What can I do for you?" he asked brusquely.

"Sorry to interrupt," she said, holding her belly. His expression softened when he noticed that she was pregnant. "I just need to confirm some information I'm having trouble finding online. I'm looking for the police report from a crash that happened on the 405 last year in October. A man died. He was alone in the car."

"On the 405?" Brady pursed his lips and gazed at the ceiling in thought.

"His autonomous vehicle malfunctioned?" She hadn't meant to ask it as a question until the words came out, choked with uncertainty.

"I would've remembered that," Brady said. "We haven't had a fatality on that freeway in ages."

"Are you sure?"

He nodded. The stagnant air felt oppressive.

"There was no crash? You're absolutely positive?"

"Yes ma'am. I've been here seventeen years. Seen it all. AVs do crash from time to time, sure. Usually it's changing lanes, and when it does happen, the safety features kick in so fast, the people inside almost never die."

"So if there was no fatal crash, then there's . . . no Evan?"

"What?"

"Never mind," she said quickly. "Thanks for your help."

* * *

Christmas came and went without an Evan chatbot. Instead, she had settled for a talking stuffed elephant for Bubala that played peekaboo with its ears. Robert gave her a small emerald, her birthstone, on a pretty gold chain. She reacted appropriately, as though nothing was amiss, all the while aware of a new phase in their relationship known only to her.

Her trust was eroding like the ground in an earthquake, with aftershocks of panic jostling the foundation that remained.

But she didn't dare confront him.

If Robert was lying to her—and maybe there *was* still a benign explanation—then she wasn't about to reveal her hand until she knew exactly how to play it.

That might involve lawyers or cops, or both.

For the first time, she regretted not using a surrogacy agency. There was no case worker to call for help, no institution that had her back, with its deep pockets to cover unforeseen complications. She was completely on her own.

And maybe, she realized, that was by design.

Because *someone* was the other parent of the child inside her. Someone utterly uninvolved.

The question was: Who?

* * *

Robert knocked on the bathroom door. "You okay? You've been in there a long time."

She flushed the toilet. "I'm still not feeling too good."

Bubala was strong enough to kick now, and possessed the temperament of a caffeinated wrestler. Her full-body rolls and sharp jabs took Quinn's breath away.

"Do you want to lie down in the guest room?" Robert asked, so close to the door she could practically sense his breath on the other side.

"All right." Being alone in the guest room would allow her to hide out a while longer. Maybe she could gather more intel. A last-ditch idea came to mind.

She flushed the toilet again. "Do you think you could make me some ginger tea? I just feel like garbage."

"Of course! I'll bring it to you in bed. With lemon and honey?"

"Yes, please."

His kindness left her reeling. He was the perfect gentleman, which made her doubt her own intuition.

But then his footsteps retreated, and she capitalized on her opening. She slipped out the door and into the living room. Out of sight in the kitchen, Robert could be heard chopping ginger, his knife making a rhythmic thwack on the cutting board.

She snatched the little Thorne statue off the coffee table and moseyed into the guest room, where a king-sized bed on a black velvet frame awaited her. She slipped under the cool cotton sheets and pulled up the comforter, hiding the statue deep inside.

With a remote control in the nightstand, she turned on the overhead air purifier, a ceiling unit that resembled a vintage fan. When it whirred, it emitted far-UVC light that cleaned the air of all viruses, bacteria, pollen, and mold. Modern building code required one in every bedroom, like a smoke alarm. Quinn appreciated that she could breathe easier underneath it, but more importantly, she recognized its double purpose as a white-noise machine. Its steady low hum drowned out sounds inside and out.

When Robert came in with her steaming hot tea, she thanked him and yawned. He dimmed the lights and closed the curtains without being asked.

"I'll wake you before dinner, okay?" he asked.

"Oh crap, I was going to make the salad . . ."

"I got it. You just relax. Night, night, Mamala."

She managed a smile at her nickname. Then he was gone, the door closing quietly behind him.

She withdrew the Thorne statue and ran her fingers across its tiny handsome face. If this version was the same as hers, then it automatically stayed logged into Robert's internet search engine and synced with all the other smart devices in his home, ready to turn on the lights or look up information at a simple command. It was the ultimate vocal assistant, loaded with facts and programmed charm.

She switched the chatbot on and put the volume on its lowest setting.

"Hi, Thorne," she whispered.

"Hello there, m'lady!" it whispered back, matching her pitch. "Would you like to hear a song?"

"No, I was hoping you could help me out with something. Do you have a record of any search results for, like, last Tuesday?" She chose the day at random to test its capabilities.

"Three searches were performed last Tuesday," it replied without missing a beat. "Chinese food restaurants that deliver to Upper Bel Air, the hourly weather forecast, and the latest news on the Vault."

"What is the Vault?" she asked. The term sounded familiar from the headlines, but she couldn't quite place it.

"I searched the Web, and I found this result":

> *The Vault is an anonymous network, run on blockchain servers in an unknown location, that collects the DNA of high-profile individuals and lists it for sale to the highest bidder. For an added fee, customers can order sperm or egg cells derived from targeted individuals. The Vault is reportedly under FBI investigation.*

"Would you like to hear more?"

"Why the hell is Robert searching for the Vault?" she demanded.

"I searched the Web, but I couldn't find any answers for why the hell is—"

"Never mind," she whispered impatiently. "So what is the news on the Vault?"

"I found multiple articles. The top hit was published in *Vanguard*: *'Rogue Network Suspected in Black Market Scheme to Steal Celebrity Cells for Embryo Creation,'* by Shane Hart."

"Jesus."

"Would you like me to read you the most recent headline?"

"Go ahead."

"It was published three days ago in the *Los Angeles Times*: 'Pregnant Socialite Confesses to Purchasing Sperm of Lakers Star on Illegal Auction Site.'"

A disgusted sound escaped her. "That's insane."

"Would you like to hear the story?"

"Yes and no."

A pause elapsed while the chatbot computed a response. "Got me there!" it said cheerily.

"Oh, just read it."

"Yes ma'am!

> The Lakers' star point guard, Mr. Nate Fox, believes his cells were stolen from a water bottle he sipped

during a playoff game, which disappeared during a time-out. His gametes were subsequently listed for sale on the Vault, an anonymous dark web auction site for celebrity cells that is under scrutiny from the FBI. The socialite, Ms. Lila Forrester, placed a winning bid for the equivalent of two million US dollars in Bitcoin, according to a leaked document from Mr. Fox's lawsuit. Her desire, she exclusively told the Los Angeles Times, is to bear a child with her hero, not to extort him for child support.

After she bragged about the transaction in a social media post that has since been deleted, Mr. Fox was made aware of the situation and demanded a paternity test. His paternity was confirmed via a blood test that analyzed the fetal DNA circulating in Ms. Forrester's bloodstream.

Mr. Fox is now pressing criminal charges against her for grand larceny and invasion of privacy. He is also suing her to terminate the twelve-week-old pregnancy, but she has refused, citing her right to bodily autonomy. The case is expected to reach the state supreme court, and legal scholars say the decision could establish precedent in this uncharted territory."

"Yikes," Quinn said aloud, and then remembered to lower her voice. But still, why did Robert care about the Vault? A tabloid fancy? A latent interest in the dark side of pop culture?

Too bad there was a limit to chatbot Thorne's insightfulness.

She thought back to August, when Robert had asked her to be his surrogate. He'd told her he already had embryos waiting in storage.

Whose embryos, if not Evan's?

"Thorne," she said, "tell me about Robert's search history from July. Was there any pattern?"

"I reviewed the search history from July and found seventy-two searches involving Trace Thorne. Hey, that's me!" it exclaimed with delight.

"For your songs?"

"Fourteen searches for my tour dates in Europe. Eleven searches for my latest news. Forty-one searches for my real-time location via social media posts and paparazzi tweets. Eight searches for homeowner deeds and land parcels in California matching my name. One search for my gametes on the Vault."

"What?" she cried. Her hands flew to her stomach. The baby was elbowing her under the ribs.

"One search for—" the chatbot repeated calmly.

"Stop," she commanded. "What is the current status of your—I mean, of Thorne's gametes on the Vault?"

"Out of stock."

Robert was more obsessed with Thorne than she'd realized. Inside her heart, she felt their initial breach widen into a chasm.

But maybe there's still a reasonable explanation, she thought with growing hopelessness. Trying to recover his sympathetic image felt like grabbing fistfuls of sand in a dream and waking up empty-handed.

His knock on the door startled her. She shoved the chatbot under the blanket as he walked in.

"Hey," he said. "How you feelin'? You want to have dinner?"

"Uh, sure."

"Yeah? You look pale."

The most important thing was not to let him sense her suspicion. Not until she could organize her plan. Whatever that might be.

"I'm fine," she said, sliding out of bed. She would come back for the statue and replace it on the coffee table whenever she got the chance. "Let's eat."

An hour later, after they had shared a beet salad, sweet potatoes, and lab-grown bluefin tuna, making friendly small talk about their New Year's resolutions (his: spend less time doom-blinking horrible news; hers: deliver a healthy Bubala), she dug her spoon into a pint of chocolate ice cream and cocked her head.

"Speaking of doom-blinking, that reminded me of this crazy story I saw in the *LA Times* the other day. Did you see the one about the Vault?"

Her frantic heartbeat informed her she was poking forbidden ground, but she kept her eyes wide, innocent.

If she was hoping for a subtle tell, she got nothing. There was no miniscule jump of his brows, no gritting of his teeth. His face was serene as he replied, "Nope, don't think so. What's the Vault?"

It took all of her self-control not to hurl her crystal ice-cream bowl at his head. But that would accomplish nothing. Instead, before she did anything drastic, she had to be smart. She had to be *sure.* Sure that Thorne, their shared crush, was not just a distant celebrity.

That he was, in fact, the other parent of the restless baby in her womb.

Tracking him down in real life for a blood test was the only way to find out.

PART 2

CHAPTER

17

Ember

Full circle to present day

EMBER STARED AT the pregnant stranger addressing Thorne in the middle of the café.

"I've never seen you in my life," he said sharply.

"I know, and I'm sorry." The woman's watery blue eyes seemed apologetic as she choked out the words: "But I'm pretty sure you're still going to be a dad."

Thorne stepped back. "That's not possible." He looked at Ember for reassurance. "Right?"

Ember's voice faltered as a comet of doubt barreled through her. He still didn't know about the baby shoes that had haunted her for the past few months. She pictured the notecard with its flowery script: *Congratulations!*

"It would be very unlikely," she said. "But . . . not impossible."

"What?" he barked. "You literally *guaranteed* my safety."

His anguished expression brought her to the verge of tears. "And you probably are safe," she replied, trying to keep her voice even. It's not as though an anonymous package and a random pregnant woman added up to certain failure, she reminded herself. Obsessed fans could get carried away, continuing to role-play fantasies in real life that they indulged in virtual reality. The latter had become so convincing that some heavy users even lost the ability to tell the difference. There was a new diagnosis for it in the *DSM-XII*: techno-delusion disorder.

And Thorne had plenty of obsessed fans.

Ember narrowed her eyes at the stranger, who was nervously twirling hair around her finger. Ember wasn't sure whether to feel rage, pity, or some bizarre mix of the two. It could be that this woman was suffering from TDD and believed she was Thorne's rightful partner, pregnant with his child. Maybe she wasn't even actually pregnant. She could be wearing a sensory bodysuit to enhance the fidelity of her virtual fantasy. The thought was comforting.

Ember felt the lump in her throat dissolve as her composure returned. "I think you might be confused," she told the woman. "This isn't the holoverse."

Her eyes widened. "Oh, I'm not crazy." She gave a humorless laugh. "I'm a surrogate. My client is a rich gay guy who lied to me about having a dead husband. I thought he was a widower when I took the job."

Ember grimaced. The possibility of surrogacy had not occurred to her. That meant the woman was perhaps more credible than she had initially seemed.

"What does that have to do with me?" Thorne snapped.

"A lot, actually. A few months ago, I learned he was totally obsessed with you. Like searching for you, your shows, your location, everything. And . . ." Her voice trailed off.

"And what?" Ember prompted.

The woman wrinkled her nose. "I found out he searched the Vault for your gametes the month before my implantation."

Ember's mind went blank. Thorne coughed loudly, drawing further attention. Customers who had casually ignored his star status before were now stealing curious glances.

Ember reached for his hand, but he stiffened at her touch. He had never done that before.

The woman lowered her head and spoke quietly. "I knew I had to tell you, but I didn't know how. So I stalked you on social for the last couple months to try to run into you . . . I had almost given up hope until you posted about being at this coffee shop twelve days ago. I've come here every day since, waiting for you to come back."

"Wow," Ember muttered. The color in Thorne's face had drained to ash. He gripped Smokey's leash with white knuckles. The dog gave a little whine, like he knew something was wrong.

"I know this is super tough to hear," the woman went on. "I'm just trying to do right by this baby. I'm Quinn, by the way." She didn't bother to stick out her hand.

Ember frowned. "When exactly was your implantation?"

"August twenty-seventh. At the Fertility Associates of Beverly Hills. Selection was the week before. I went in as soon as my cycle lined up."

So Ember was right. Quinn was close to seven months along. *Far too late for an abortion if, God forbid . . .* "When was your client searching the Vault?"

"In the beginning of July." She lifted her eyes to Thorne. "Enough time to order your eggs and have them mixed with his sperm so the embryos would be ready in August. Which is when he asked me to be his surrogate. So the timing seems . . . pretty perfect, I hate to say."

"But my gametes have been out of stock for months," Thorne protested. "And you've been with me everywhere. So it can't be, right?" He raised his eyebrows at Ember with a subtle touch of accusation. They had never really fought before, let alone confronted a possible breach of this magnitude.

"We can't say for sure," she said slowly. "What about the night you went out clubbing?"

He rolled his eyes. "It was *one night*."

She remembered he'd gone out in early July in LA, during the short break between the US and European legs of the tour. He'd given her a few days off to recuperate from the whirlwind of the back-to-back East Coast shows. She'd been exhausted, unaccustomed to the frenzied pace of being on tour. And he had wanted to let loose, figuring he could get away with a single night inside the velvet ropes without her.

His only complaint afterward had been about the women who were grinding on him, aggressively trying to seduce him. Typical desperate fans. But what if one of them worked for the Vault? What if one had been sent to take advantage of him, to get close enough to obtain a sample of his saliva or mucus or a hair plucked from the root while he was so busy drinking and dancing that his guard was down?

Ember knew the Vault used illegal methods for spying on their targets—mosquito drones high in the atmosphere. Tiny, precise, and untraceable. Theoretically, if they were tracking Thorne, they could follow his retinas whenever he went outside, day or night. They could come at him when he was least expecting it. For an A-list catch like him, they would watch and wait for the perfect attack.

And he might never know until it was too late.

After that one night of exposure, could his eggs and sperm have briefly shown up for sale on the Vault? Could Quinn's fanatical client have swooped in with the highest bid before the gametes went *out of stock* again? Or could he perhaps have placed a private custom order, so the gametes would never have been listed in the first place?

Quinn's story was starting to sound more plausible than Ember wanted to admit.

She thought again of the baby shoes. They had appeared on Thorne's doorstep in early January, when Quinn was . . . roughly four months along. The point when pregnancies were safe to announce. *Congratulations!*

"Was it your client?" Ember asked bluntly. "With the shoes?"

"What shoes?" Thorne and Quinn asked in unison.

Ember forced herself to look him in the eye. "A package was mailed to you right before Christmas. Baby girl shoes, with a note that said, 'Congratulations.' But no name or sender's address."

"What? And you kept this from me?"

"It seemed like a stupid prank. I didn't want to upset you, so I trashed it. I'm sorry. I should have told you."

Thorne's lips parted angrily, but no words came out.

"Who's your client?" Ember asked Quinn, desperately wanting to divert the conversation away from her own mistake.

"Robert Roy. He's a crypto trader in his early forties. He's a workaholic, super loaded but a bit of a loner. Never met his family or friends. We actually met at, um, one of your shows," she told Thorne. "At the Hollywood Bowl."

"Oh, great," Thorne muttered.

"He said he was there alone because he and his husband had tickets, but the husband had died in a car crash. Then later I found out the crash never happened. I confirmed it with the police."

Ember pulled back. "What the fuck?"

"Exactly."

"Where does he live?"

"1140 Shady Lane in Bel Air."

Ember blinked onto the internet and did a quick search. None of the results pointed her to any leads. No social media profile, no criminal records, nothing. But a crypto trader would know how to make himself discreet online.

"I'm leaving." Thorne threw a handful of twenties on the table and marched out of the café, pulling Smokey's leash. Ember followed him around the corner, where he stopped and crossed his arms. "What?"

Quinn trailed them, clearly unwilling to go away.

Ember sighed and lowered her voice. "Look, I don't know what's going on here. But the only way for us to know if you're implicated is for you and her to get a blood test together."

He made a repulsed face. "Like the Lakers' point guard?"

"Yeah," Quinn said, edging closer, not even bothering to pretend she wasn't eavesdropping. "That's why I came. I was hoping you would agree."

"I don't know." He fiddled with Smokey's leash. "This isn't what I—"

"You should do it," Ember interrupted. "For peace of mind." She searched online for the nearest lab, which was two blocks away. The site materialized in her visual field, and she tapped a few times in the air. "There," she said. "I just ordered the blood work. We can go now. It's a five-minute walk."

"Great!" Quinn exclaimed with relief, even though Thorne still hadn't said yes. He closed his eyes, and Ember could tell he was spiraling toward panic. She interlaced her fingers with his. They felt cold and clammy. This time, he didn't pull away.

"If it's negative, you'll never hear from me again," Quinn promised.

Thorne opened his eyes. "Fine," he said reluctantly. "Just to get rid of you. No offense."

"I get it. Thank you. It will be good to find out either way, you know?"

Either way. Ember grimaced. The words triggered ice through her veins.

They exited the café and headed toward the lab. Ember led the way quickly, the sooner to be done with the unpleasant task. Across the street, gentle waves lapped the shore and receded back into the ocean, rising and swelling in an eternal dance. Normally, she would have paused to enjoy the sight. Now, she barely noticed the beach or the volleyball players or the tourists strolling by, licking ice-cream cones that were melting in the sun.

But in the corner of her eye, one sight did not escape her register: Quinn's basketball-sized belly. Quinn strode beside her while Thorne fell behind. At the crosswalk, she glanced back at him. He was letting Smokey take his time sniffing a golden retriever that was staring unnaturally ahead. Ember understood it was an android dog, and also that Thorne was using the distraction to avoid keeping up. His shoulders appeared tight and hunched; he had pulled his baseball hat low over his sunglasses.

"It's a girl, by the way," Quinn said as they crossed the street.

Ember's stomach tightened. She did not want to hear anything about the baby except that it wasn't Thorne's.

"The scores say she's supposed to be healthy and smart," Quinn continued, as if this was somehow welcome information.

"No special musical inclinations?" Ember asked hopefully.

Quinn shook her head. "Not that I know of."

"Thank God."

"The male embryos were ruled out," Quinn added. "They inherited a disease from . . . from the other parent."

"Only the males?"

"Yeah, it was X-linked. Robert told me it was through the egg, not his sperm."

Ember felt her body relax. Thorne was exceedingly healthy. She glanced back again to tell him this good news, but he had fallen even farther behind, as if physical distance could protect him from whatever horror might already be unfolding.

Sure, he did take a handful of pills at night, but he'd never mentioned being sick. Wouldn't that be something she would know as his fiancée? She quickly put the thought out of her mind. They were probably just supplements.

Thorne's honesty was legendary. Of course she could trust him. The world as they knew it an hour ago was still theirs: an intimate wedding and a beautiful life awaited.

Her gut feeling suddenly told her everything would be okay despite his one night of unprotected clubbing. All the other times, she'd been by his side, creating a biosafe space wherever he went. Statistically, the odds were on their side.

In twenty-four hours, the results would come in.

She imagined Thorne hugging her again with his usual enthusiasm, celebrating his freedom from a terrible potential fate. They would reflect on Quinn's arrival as a scary but harmless near-birth experience and resolve to be more careful going forward.

And then they would resume their normal lives.

CHAPTER

18

Lily

MONDAY'S STAFF MEETING at *Vanguard* was not going well.

Lily had shown up fifteen minutes late because the hyperloop train from New Jersey had gotten delayed in the tube. When she finally walked in, Shane stopped mid-sentence and pointedly waited while she rushed to her place at the conference table.

"Kind of you to join us," he remarked. No less than a dozen of her idols witnessed her cringe. And the only open seat was beside Radia.

"So sorry," she mumbled. "Train traffic."

Lily popped and pinned her virtual keyboard without daring to make eye contact with anyone.

"It's okay," Radia whispered as Shane resumed his address to the group. "You didn't miss much. Here." She turned her own virtual screen into share mode so that Lily could view her notes.

"Thanks," Lily replied, taken aback. She hadn't expected kindness from her competition.

After discussing various articles with the staffers sitting near him, Shane turned his attention to their far corner of the table. Lily noticed he was wearing a silk shirt with a pattern of colorful books stacked in tall, crooked piles. Somehow, his wacky attire didn't make him any less intimidating. He squinted at the two of them through his black-rimmed glasses.

"So, ladies, how goes it? Making progress on your pieces, I hope?"

Neither of them spoke. That was weird. She figured Radia would have already sailed through a draft of her article on the regretful parents of genetically unlucky Unforeseen kids.

"Hello?" Shane pretended to tap a mic in front of him. "This thing on?"

"My main source backed out," Radia announced miserably. "She told me to stop contacting her. She thinks it'll make her look like a bad mom."

Shane frowned. "I'm not surprised."

"I'll keep looking. Eventually I'll find someone else, right?"

"Or cut your losses and come up with a better idea. Time is of the essence if you want to make a mark here."

Chastened, Radia slipped lower in her seat. Lily gave her a sympathetic look.

"How about you?" Shane asked Lily.

She cleared her throat. "The good news is I have a great source."

"But?"

"But she's super private and doesn't want to go on the record. Could we grant her anonymity?"

"That's the lazy way out," Shane snapped. "If *Vanguard* gave everyone anonymity, we'd destroy our credibility."

"Just this one time," Lily countered, shocked by her own boldness. "This woman's criminal past has caused a lot of trauma. I don't see why we have to force her to suffer further for the sake of journalism."

"Damn girl," Radia muttered under her breath, apparently impressed.

Shane rubbed his beard in consideration. "And you think her story is really worth it?"

"Absolutely. It's a prime example of invisible discrimination."

"Well, we have been known to make exceptions. But if we change her name, we would need serious backup for our fact-checkers."

"Meaning . . .?" Lily shifted nervously in her chair.

"Her court records, her real identity for our own records, transcripts of all your interviews. We need proof of her story for legal purposes so we can't be accused of fabricating any details."

"Fine. But how do I get court records?"

Shane sighed, and Lily knew he was annoyed by her inexperience. "Was it a state or federal crime?" he asked.

Lily pictured the prison she used to visit as a kid. She could still see the menacing block letters on the side of the gray building: "Federal Women's Correctional Institution of Los Angeles."

"Federal."

"Ever heard of a FOIA request?" he asked impatiently.

"Of course," she replied, without knowing what it was.

"Then submit one to the Federal Bureau of Prisons and get on with it." He turned his attention to a more important writer before she could say another word.

"Dick," Radia mumbled ever so softly.

Lily smiled. She didn't have much of a mentor, but maybe she had a friend.

* * *

After the meeting, Lily was none too eager to race home. Mom was constantly nauseated because of the pregnancy, and Dad had become her boring caretaker. Gone were their evenings of playing music together or solar pedaling around town.

As Lily and Radia got in the elevator, she remembered the bar down on the corner and the happy chatter she always heard coming from its back patio. Sometimes she felt jealous of those other recent grads who seemed to enjoy being young and carefree while she was always preoccupied by how to work harder to keep up with her Selected peers.

But Radia, it turned out, was not actually superhuman. Nor was she a jerk. She was vulnerable to failure like anyone else. The realization had decidedly cooled Lily's competitiveness.

"Hey, wanna grab a drink?" she asked as the elevator opened into the lobby. "I'm not in a rush."

Radia perked up with a friendly smile. "Sure. Why not?"

* * *

The vibe of the bar was Polynesian. Palm trees grew in wicker baskets around the patio. Red hibiscus flowers the size of dinner plates decorated each table. Globe lights hung overhead, and a mural on the back wall depicted a dolphin jumping out of the ocean.

The place was already packed for happy hour, but they managed to snag a couple of seats and order piña coladas. To check that they were of legal age, the bartender digitally scanned their faces and matched them to the national ID database.

"This definitely beats going home," Lily said once their tall sweaty drinks arrived, complete with pineapple slices and little umbrellas.

"What's so bad about home?" Radia asked, sipping hers.

"Oh nothing. Just that my mom is pregnant, and it's been rough so far."

"Wow, she must be kind of old?"

"Sixty-three," Lily admitted with a twinge of embarrassment.

"That's not too bad. I've heard of way older. How was Selection?"

Lily bit her lip. There was no way she was about to tell Radia what had actually happened. "Fine. My little sister is going to be oh so brilliant and beautiful."

Radia's eyebrows shot up. "Better scores than yours?"

Lily just nodded as she pulled a long swig from the straw. The sweet coconut drink soothed the tightness in her throat.

"Is she an Elite?" Radia asked, her chestnut eyes popping.

"Nah." An Elite meant that the embryo had scored over the ninety-fifth percentile on at least one desirable trait, which was rare even for Selected kids. "Just high normal."

Radia swirled her tiny umbrella around the white froth. "You know, being Elite is not all it's cracked up to be."

"Are you—?" Lily asked in surprise. A familiar sour feeling uncorked in her gut.

"I think so. For physical stamina. But the truth is, I'm not sure. My parents won't tell me."

"Why not?"

"Well, they say they don't want me to be consciously influenced by my Selection, so I can *'chart my own course'* or something." She used finger quotes with apparent disapproval.

"But? It sounds like there's a *but*."

Radia's voice hardened. "But I think there's something in there they know I won't like."

"What do you mean?"

"I think they feel guilty about something else in my scores. So they're making excuses."

Lily tried to comprehend this paradox. "But you're smart and gorgeous, and you can run, like, a hundred miles without breaking a sweat."

Radia smirked. "Yeah, on the days I can get out of bed."

"What?"

"Sophomore year, I was diagnosed with major clinical depression. It sucks. My parents claim they never saw it coming, but a lot of times it's genetic."

Lily gripped her glass. "I'm so sorry. That's terrible."

"It's okay. I got deep brain stimulation, and I'm much better now. But I think my parents knew I would be at risk and Selected me anyway."

"Why would they do that?"

"Because I obviously inherited the sprinter gene from my mom. She was a track star back in the day, before she got injured and killed her career. It was right before she was supposed to do the Olympic trials."

"You think they Selected you to carry on her legacy?"

"Yeah. My parents are obsessed with being the best of the best. My dad is a scientist who makes custom lungs. They're both insane overachievers."

"Still, I can't believe they would *choose* to curse you!"

Radia sighed. "I know. Maybe they just didn't think it would be a big deal, or they knew that treatments existed. And now they're ashamed. So they made up this bullshit about preserving my autonomy."

Lily reeled with sympathetic anger. "That's so messed up."

"It's not all bad. I did get into Harvard on a track scholarship. But then I fell in love with journalism, and here I am. Not what anyone expected. Least of all me."

"So you could have gone pro? With running?"

"For sure. I just didn't want to. But enough about me!" Radia smiled brightly. "What about you? What were you Selected for?"

Lily chewed on her straw. "Oh, just the normal stuff. Nothing too extreme."

"You're lucky," Radia said. "Less pressure."

"Yep." For the first time, Lily realized that being Unforeseen wasn't so bad. No one else could tell her who she was. And that felt pretty lucky indeed.

C H A P T E R

19

Quinn

THE LAGUNA BEACH lab was in a nondescript building off the main tourist drag. Quinn followed Ember inside as Thorne hung back.

"What about the dog?" he asked, as though Smokey gave him an excuse to avoid the test. Smokey was trying to drag him away from the door, as if in agreement. Quinn felt sorry for both. The term *homewrecker* trickled across her mind, even though she hadn't done anything wrong.

Ember shrugged. "Bring him. It won't take long."

The lab's empty waiting area consisted of stout wooden chairs arranged in several rows. Quinn and Thorne stood awkwardly a few feet apart and avoided eye contact. Her aching back begged her to sit, for God's sake, but the tension in the air rooted her in place. She clasped her hands at the base of her belly. It felt surreal to be so close to her idol without any of the screaming fans or paparazzi or security. Like she could reach out and touch him if she wanted to. But of course, she couldn't. His repulsion was obvious in his scowl. She couldn't exactly blame him.

Ember approached the lab technician who was behind the counter, busy typing on a virtual keyboard. Quinn noticed a tattoo on her inner wrist poking out from under her sleeve.

"We're here for the parentage tests," Ember told her. "I just ordered them."

The young woman barely glanced up. "Yep. I see. So you want one cell-free fetal DNA test and one adult DNA blood test cross-referenced, right?"

"You got it."

"Do you want to go first?"

"Oh, it's not for me. It's for her." Ember thumbed toward Quinn, who managed to catch Thorne's eye.

"Do you . . .?" Quinn asked.

He winced. The lab tech's casual gaze landed on him for the first time, and her lips parted in dumb shock.

"Wait, are you . . .? You're not—?"

Thorne sighed and mumbled his assent as if he was ashamed to admit his identity.

"Oh my *God*," the tech blurted, instantly losing her veneer of professionalism. She hoisted up her sleeve to show him her *TT* tattoo. "You're my fucking hero. I knew you were a local, but I never thought I'd see you here!"

"Thanks," he said weakly.

"Wait." The tech stared from him to Quinn, and then Ember. Quinn watched her face transform from surprise to comprehension. She had fallen ass backward into a potential scandal of epic proportions. "Wait. Don't tell me you're a *cheater*?"

"What?" he cried. "No!"

"He hasn't done anything wrong," Quinn piped up, feeling a rush of embarrassment on his behalf. "I'm a surrogate. We never even met until today."

"But a parentage test . . ."

Ember held up her hands. "There's probably been a misunderstanding. We're just here to sort it out, that's all."

"Uh-huh," the tech said.

Quinn could practically see the opportunistic wheels turning in her brain. No doubt there would be a handsome payout from the tabloids for video evidence of their lab visit.

"Please keep this absolutely private," Ember said, apparently picking up the same vibe. "If anything were to leak to the press, it would be a disaster. Not to mention illegal."

Quinn imagined the scoop some hungry reporter might run and the national attention that could descend on her as a result. *"Beloved Pop Star Terrorized by Stolen Cell Pregnancy."* Jesus Christ. Her parents would probably disown her. And there was no way to discern whether the tech was blinking simply to process the situation or to snap a video that could go viral in a matter of hours.

"Not to worry," the tech promised. "I don't want to lose my job. So, who's going first?" She stared at Thorne.

"I'll go," Quinn said, taking mercy on him.

As she followed the tech into a back room, she peeked over her shoulder. Ember was hugging him, saying something quietly into his ear while Smokey's chin lay on his foot. Quinn couldn't resist noticing how simultaneously feminine and strong Ember appeared, even in the midst of a possible crisis. Her high cheekbones and graceful movements reminded Quinn of a ballerina's, while her assertiveness evoked a lioness. Thorne was lucky. He deserved the perfect woman.

Whereas Quinn was his perfect nightmare.

She entered a tiny room filled with medical instruments and plopped onto a hard-backed plastic chair. The tech projected some legal jargon and a signature page onto the blank wall in front of her. Quinn's index finger hovered tentatively in midair.

She knew she was breaking her surrogacy contract with Robert by going to an unscheduled medical appointment without his knowledge or consent. *But he started it,* she thought. Violating her trust. Lying about Evan. Hiding his obsession with Thorne and the Vault.

She scribbled her signature and stuck out her right arm for the needle.

What the hell would she do if they matched? Call the police? Get a lawyer? Would Thorne help her pay? Would he take the baby? Only two months remained until the birth. But it was Robert's baby too.

Quinn winced as the tech plunged the needle into her inner elbow. Meanwhile, Bubala was in the midst of a barrel roll, practicing her daily gymnastics in total ignorance of her predicament. Quinn closed her eyes and savored their closeness.

Although she fell short of being a mother, she was more than a womb. She was Bubala's temporary home. And she would risk her own life before she handed the baby over to a potentially dangerous man.

Even if that man was the baby's father.

Thorne had to be the answer to save them from this quandary. Quinn believed that he would never turn his back on his own child, no matter how the baby had been conceived. He was a good man, at least as far as his reputation indicated. He would step up and protect Bubala if she was his to protect.

But now first, the wait.

CHAPTER 20

Ember

THE TEST RESULTS were expected in twenty-four hours.

A strong breeze whipped at Ember's face as she leaned against the balcony of Thorne's beachfront mansion. The vast sun-dappled ocean normally lifted her spirits, but today she was a prisoner of dread.

And not only because of the test.

Thorne was at this very moment calling his contact at the FBI, Noah Heller, to register his fury about potentially being a repeat target of the Vault.

If only money could make the problem go away, Ember thought.

After Thorne had paid two million dollars last year for the privilege of having his sperm and eggs removed from the Vault's listings, he'd demanded the FBI shut the whole thing down ASAP, but they had failed. And now, extortion seemed like a party game compared to the life-altering fallout if Quinn was actually pregnant with his child. Ember had never seen him so livid.

When they'd gotten home from the lab a few minutes ago, he'd been in the midst of a rant about *"those opportunistic motherfuckers"* at the Vault and the *"paper pushers"* at the

FBI *"who wouldn't know a criminal mastermind if he slapped them in the face."*

In the foyer, Thorne had kicked off his sandals and announced that he was about to call up his useless contact there "and raise hell."

"Wait!" she'd cried, then quickly dialed down her intensity. "I mean, don't you want to wait to find out before you rile him up?"

"He deserves to be riled up, for fuck's sake!" Thorne retorted, marching into the living room. He blinked twice and began scrolling in midair for the man's number on his virtual dashboard.

Gently, she put a hand on his arm. "But, sweetie, we don't even know yet."

He shook her off. "Either way, it's time to light a fire under his incompetent asshole."

"But . . . isn't it already too late on the East Coast?" She glanced at the clock on the wall: 1:55 PM. The FBI's headquarters in DC were still open.

"Nope," Thorne snapped. "Why do you care anyway?"

She shrugged. "I just have a gut feeling you'll be okay."

"But if not this time, what about next time?" He scowled. "And there will be a next time. Because you obviously can't stop every single intrusion."

Ouch. There was no way to push back without sparking a fight. So she trudged out to the deck alone, and he didn't try to stop her. She gazed far out across the sea, as if in anticipation of a tsunami gathering on the horizon. But in reality, the sunlight glinted off the calm water, and the sky was an endless blue. The salty air evoked lazy afternoons hanging out here together, sipping mai tais, watching the surfers, and talking about their wedding. They were supposed to visit the venue today—a cliffside hotel down the street that overlooked the entire Laguna coastline.

Now, instead, Thorne's angry voice floated out from the living room.

"So do *something*," he was yelling. "I don't care—that's your *job*."

Ember couldn't hear the conversation on the other end, but she imagined Noah Heller telling Thorne that the investigation was going nowhere, that the Vault was expertly run by perps who knew their way around private servers, cryptocurrency, and the dark web. In other words, the FBI was powerless to stop it without a credible lead.

"But what about the Lakers guy?" Thorne demanded. "So . . . what then? You're just giving up? . . . What do you mean, *on pause?* . . . Another 'incident'? . . . Wait. So you're saying you're waiting for someone like me to get *completely fucked* in order to give you a fresh lead? . . . Well, that's just fantastic. Sure hope I can give you your big break!"

He must have blinked off then because the room went silent.

She stepped inside to find him sitting on the couch with his head in his hands. Smokey lay obediently at his feet. The dog started wagging his tail when she walked closer, but Thorne gave her no such welcome. He barely budged when she sat and put her arm around his hunched shoulders.

"I don't want to talk," he muttered.

"Then don't."

She stayed beside him for a long time. Eventually, he leaned back and looked at her as though his fate were already a lost cause.

"What am I going to do?"

"*We,*" she corrected him. "*We* are in this together."

"So you'll still want to marry me if I happen to share a child with a psychotic fan?"

"Oh my God, is that what you're worried about?" She almost laughed with relief. "I thought you wouldn't want to marry *me*."

"What? Why?"

"Because . . . if it's true, then it means I failed you."

She searched his eyes for forgiveness just in case. Would he really be prepared to love her for the rest of their lives if this breach she had guaranteed against—this *child*—hung between them forever? Was she prepared to forgive herself?

"You can't stop this evil thing alone," he said quietly. "It's just not possible."

"Not for lack of trying."

"I know that."

"I wish I could do more."

You've done your best. That's all you can do."

To a point, she thought. Because she had done everything in her power to stop the Vault.

Everything short of admitting the truth.

CHAPTER 21

Lily

LILY KNOCKED ON Mom's bathroom door. "You okay? Still spotting?"

"Only a little."

Next to Lily, Dad spoke gently to the closed door. "Should I cancel the reservation?"

"No! I'm coming out."

They heard the toilet flush and the faucet turn on. Then Mom stepped out with a wan smile. "I'm ravenous. Let's go."

Dad stepped back to marvel at her hastily applied makeup, silk wrap dress, and curled hair. "Never thought you'd look better at sixty-four than forty-four."

Lily agreed. Mom looked incredible, despite her scare a few hours earlier. They had been about to leave for her favorite restaurant, Zen Sushi, to celebrate her birthday, when she'd noticed a terrifying streak of pink blood in her underwear. Everyone's immediate fear was a miscarriage, but no one dared speak the word. She'd rushed to the ob-gyn, who squeezed her in just as he was closing up the office. Luckily, he identified the problem as benign—cervical ectropion due to high estrogen production.

"It's basically like bleeding gums," he told her. "Uncomfortable, but not dangerous. Just take it easy for the next few weeks." He treated the irritated area with silver nitrate to cauterize the bleeding cells and cautioned Mom to cool it on the exercise.

Her anxiety had calmed down significantly once she returned home, and Lily, too, found that she was relieved by the diagnosis. Her own steps felt light as they climbed into their autonomous vehicle to be whisked off to the restaurant.

As she stared out the window at the passing trees, she realized how much she was hoping for Mom's pregnancy to succeed. In spite of the bitter fallout the baby's Selection had provoked, Lily would have hated to see her parents heartbroken. Plus, she'd gained a fresh perspective on the new baby after her recent conversation with Radia. Being Selected wasn't exactly a no-strings-attached proposition. Her little sister would have to contend with a host of expectations, social pressures, and identity questions. Just because she was destined to be brilliant and beautiful did not guarantee her an easy life.

That realization had allowed Lily's jealousy to cool and her tenderness toward her parents to grow. She reconsidered her own conception: Had they really cheated her out of potential advantages by having her spontaneously? Her resentment now struck her as a tad unfair. They'd made her out of love, with no preconceived notions about who she would become. Maybe that wasn't so bad, even if it still felt embarrassing to disclose in normal society, like confessing that she was the child of drunks.

She glanced over at them as the car glided along the road. They were holding hands in comfortable silence. Mom rested her head against Dad's shoulder; her peaceful expression erased any hint of her previous fear. It was hard to feel anything other than affection for them, even though, in the back of her mind, questions about Mom's past lingered like a trail of smoke that wouldn't clear. And her article for *Vanguard*—due in ten days—depended on getting all the facts straight.

But the FOIA request for Mom's court records had still not come through. The status on the Federal Bureau of Prisons' website permanently said *pending*. There was no expected resolution date, and no actual person answered the phone when she called; only an AI that cheerfully refused to tell her anything. The only source of information about the crime remained her parents—in other words, a dead end. And a dead end was not good enough for *Vanguard*. She would have to do better. But not tonight. Tonight, all she could do was enjoy the celebration.

"Hey, wasn't there a song about being sixty-four like a million years ago?" she asked.

"The Beatles," Dad answered. *"Will you still need me, will you still feed me, when I'm sixty-four,"* he sang.

Mom chuckled. "I'm supposed to be over the hill by now . . . with grandkids!"

"Little did they know."

"No grandkids anytime soon," Lily reassured her. "I have no desire to be a mom for at least the next twenty years."

"God, I hope not. Can you imagine us raising babies at the same time? That would be wild."

Lily wrinkled her nose. "Prime reality-show material."

"No thanks," Dad said, as the car pulled up to the restaurant. "I think we've had enough drama for one life."

The car sped off to find parking for itself, and the three of them sauntered inside. Dad put his hand on the small of Mom's back, and Lily followed. She saw that Mom's bump was beginning to show, thanks to her tight dress accentuating her curves.

The packed restaurant hummed with activity. People sat in booths and elbow to elbow at a long sushi bar, where the chef was slicing fish with the dexterity of a gymnast.

A few people stared as they walked to their table in the back, but Lily ignored them. If her parents noticed, they didn't acknowledge it, as usual.

Once they ordered, the food came out quickly. They dove into platters of colorful sushi deluxe, pausing only to sip warm sake (seltzer for Mom). She groaned with delight as she bit off a pink chunk of sashimi.

"This salmon is amazing," she remarked. "It's really wild-caught too."

Dad chewed thoughtfully. "Yeah, it doesn't have that printed aftertaste."

"You're lucky you can still eat sushi," Lily pointed out. "Not like the old days."

"I remember." Mom dabbed her lips with a napkin. "My mom had to give up all kinds of things when she was pregnant with me. Soft cheeses, deli meat, *lox*." She said it as though the surrender of lox was inhumane. Today, pregnant women could ignore all those old restrictions since prenatal vitamins contained a special flavonoid that protected against foodborne illnesses.

"Sorry you had to give up lox for me," Lily teased.

Mom sipped her seltzer. "Oh!" She broke into a grin as her eyes lifted to her virtual dashboard. "Winnie's calling! Hang on. Let me put her on share mode."

Winnie was Mom's best friend. Lily thought of her as an aunt, since Mom had no siblings. She owned a carb-free bakery in Los Angeles, had a son in college, and visited them with her husband, a synthetic cannabinoid farmer, once or twice a year.

Soon, Winnie's enthusiastic face appeared as a full-color projected hologram over their table. Her corkscrew ringlets, creamy skin, and wide green eyes gave her a youthful look that belied her age.

"Hey guys!" she exclaimed, and they chorused a greeting back. "Happy birthday, hon!"

"Thanks," Mom said happily. "You remembered."

"Of course—don't be silly. How are you feeling?"

"All right. Had a little scare earlier, but everything's fine now."

Winnie's mouth twisted in sympathy. "Good. I hope everyone's pampering you?"

"Oh, we are," Dad said. "Don't worry. She isn't lifting a finger these days."

"And, Lily, sweetie, how's life? Enjoying your big fellowship?"

Lily offered a noncommittal smile. "It's fine." She didn't want to elaborate in front of her parents. They still didn't know she was pushing ahead with the article featuring Mom. Not until the finished draft was so persuasive, Mom would be convinced its publication was necessary. Then she would surely grant her permission to be featured anonymously.

Lily had already interviewed three medical ethicists who confirmed her suspicion that IVG clinics held way too much power in deciding who could become a parent, often without accountability or transparency. *"It's an invisible scandal,"* one NYU professor had told her. *"Long overdue for a reckoning."* She had interpreted his comment to mean that the future of countless families depended on her exposé, if she could pull it off.

But what about the FOIA request? whispered the voice of worry in her mind. Lily needed those court records to show Shane that Mom, her lead character, was a credible source. The whole article would fall apart without independent verification of her backstory. Not to mention that Lily remained deeply curious about the incident that had overshadowed her childhood.

As Winnie moved on to chat with Mom about the latest in maternity fashion and all the hip boutiques off Melrose near her bakery, Lily envisioned a bold plan. Mom's former prison was in downtown LA, not too far from Winnie's loft in West Hollywood. Why not go in person to hunt down the records? Showing up in real life would undoubtedly be more effective than waiting for an email that never came.

The trip solidified in her mind like a missing puzzle piece: she could stay with Winnie, scoring quality time with the one woman who knew Mom like a sister. The only person outside the family who might be able to share the scoop on her past.

CHAPTER

22

Quinn

The minutes were piling up like dirt on a grave. Results from the lab were due anytime. Quinn had spent the morning in the park, at first trudging around the lake and then sitting on a bench under the shade of an oak tree. She watched a little girl with auburn pigtails point excitedly to the ducks who were swimming past. "Duckie! Duckie!" The girl's father gave her bread to throw in the water, and soon a family of quacking ducks was eating out of her palm.

Quinn tried to imagine Bubala at that age, two or three years from now. Who would take her to the park one day? Who would be there to teach her, comfort her, love her?

Robert? Thorne? Neither? Maybe Quinn would have to seek out foster care or place the baby for adoption rather than hand her over to Robert, although that didn't feel right either—and it wasn't just because she was afraid of his retaliation. It was that sending her newborn to live with strangers was more than her heart could bear.

Her newborn.

It was the first time she'd thought of Bubala as her own.

The subtle shift flowed through her mind as naturally as water in a stream. Quinn put both hands on her stomach and pressed lightly. Bubala's foot lurched in response. They communicated like this throughout the day, unbeknownst to anyone else. Theirs was a private world in plain sight, a closed loop of tenderness that no other being could understand.

Quinn knew she had crossed a line by allowing herself to fall for her tenant. She had broken the unwritten rule of surrogacy. But Bubala was about to join a complicated world without any guarantee of a stable upbringing. Unless Robert was actually innocent after all . . .

A reproachful worry chafed her conscience. What if she had badly misjudged the situation, jumping to conclusions about his intentions with Thorne? How ashamed she would feel if Robert's obsession turned out to be a harmless sexual fantasy, which explained his secrecy.

But still, the story of Evan didn't add up. She was at a loss to justify what appeared to be bald-faced lies. Everything would be so much simpler if Robert were absolved.

In recent weeks, she'd stopped going over to his house, casually distancing herself while claiming fatigue. Of course, she remained friendly enough, texting him pictures of her growing belly, responding to his messages with plenty of hearts and smiley emojis—too many, probably. She wondered as she walked home from the park if he could sense she was overcompensating.

Now, back at her apartment, it was lunchtime—and almost twenty-four hours since the test. There was no way she could stomach food. Soon, the gray message box on her virtual dashboard would turn green with the ding of the results. Which meant she was beyond the pretense of distraction. A book, social media, the news—she tried a few things, but her attention kept darting to her email like a moth to light.

Finally, she gave in and began pacing around her apartment, playing a game with herself to blink off her dashboard as long as she could. It appeared again in her visual field whenever she double-blinked. And still, the mailbox icon remained gray—empty.

She had just achieved a fifteen-second hiatus when a knock on the front door caught her by surprise. No one ever came by unannounced. The knock sounded timid—a few quiet raps—as though the visitor considered she might be napping.

"Who is it?"

"It's me," came Robert's unmistakable voice.

She froze, aware that her seconds of indecision spoke volumes. Then she marched to the door and threw it open with a broad smile, ignoring her rapid pulse. "Hey! What are you doing here?"

"I came to check on you." He wore a crisp button-down shirt and jeans, his dark hair combed off his forehead. Apparently he had just shaved off his beard, because a slight cut was visible on his chin. Somehow, this evidence of his vulnerability helped her relax.

He extended a bouquet of fluorescent petunias, the hot new thing at florist shops; the flowers glowed blue with engineered bioluminescence. She grinned in spite of herself. She would post them on social media later to impress her mother.

"Oh, you didn't have to," she said, taking the petunias and inviting him inside, because what else could she do?

He had never been to her place before. She watched him take in her humble studio, with its flabby couch across from her unmade bed; the bar-height table and wooden stools; the kitchen, with its old-fashioned gas stove instead of an inductive LED one. At least she'd hung some art on the walls—cheap flea market paintings of a tulip meadow, a lighthouse by a moonlit ocean, a quaint train station in an English village.

"Cute," he remarked without judgment. Damn, she wished she could go back to liking him. "I've missed you," he added.

"Me too," she said automatically. She turned away to find a vase in a high kitchen cabinet.

His warm breath prickled her neck as he came up behind her. "Let me get it." He retrieved the vase, filled it with water from the tap, and set the flowers on the counter. "Voilà!"

"Thanks." She cast about for something else to say as her mind screamed to check the dashboard. She blinked it open while ostensibly crouching to find a new hand soap under the sink, but her mailbox remained as gray and lifeless as stone.

When she turned around, the mask of his friendliness was gone. He stood imposingly in the center of the kitchen, arms crossed.

"So, when are you gonna tell me what's really going on?"

She stepped back, sagging against the sink. "What?"

"You've been avoiding me. I'm not stupid."

"I've just been tired."

"Seriously. What happened?" He frowned, rubbing his forehead. "I must have done something, but I don't know what."

Maybe it was his distress, or her own desperation for clarity, but his unexpected bluntness pierced her guard.

"I think you made up Evan," she blurted.

Robert let out a flabbergasted cry, *"What?"*

She tucked her hair behind her ear. "That was my impression." The past tense felt like a compromise to soften the blow.

His shoulders relaxed, as if he understood that she was negotiable. When he spoke, his voice was calm. "This is obviously a huge misunderstanding."

"Really?" A tiny bud of hope pushed up in her heart.

"Evan was my beloved partner for over a decade."

"Then why haven't I ever seen a picture of him?"

"I told you. I took them all down because it hurt too much. But I'll show you one right now." He blinked on his own dashboard and added her to shared mode so she could see his projection. Then he brought up a picture of himself standing next to another man about the same age, both of them smiling and wearing tuxes. The other man was shorter, with thinning brown hair, nubby teeth, and blue eyes so pale they were almost colorless.

"That's Evan?" she said dubiously.

"Yep. We were at a friend's wedding in Napa."

Quinn stared at the picture, reeling. Her head throbbed. "But what about . . . the car crash?"

"What about it?" Robert looked confused.

"You said he died on the 405. But there was no fatal crash on the 405 last year. A police sergeant told me so."

Robert's jaw tightened. "You went to the police?"

"I just wanted to check," she said defensively. "I couldn't find any evidence of him online."

"I see." Robert spoke in the same quiet tone, never raising his voice, but the muscles around his mouth stayed taut. "Evan died of a subdural hemorrhage at UCLA Medical Center the day after the crash. He hit his head and never woke up."

A subtle rage imbued his words—so subtle, she couldn't pinpoint it. He appeared to be breathing normally, hands loosely clasping his elbows, eyes downcast. But she knew he was furious. And maybe she deserved it.

"I'm sorry. I guess if he died the next day, they didn't count it as a fatal accident?"

Robert turned up his palms. "I don't know. I don't care. I just know he's gone, and he was the love of my life."

Quinn's side gave a sharp lurch, taking her breath away. It was Bubala doing a somersault. Robert stepped closer and put his hand on her belly. "She's all I've got left."

Quinn suddenly felt wobbly, like the kitchen floor had morphed into a wave pool. She shielded her eyes. "I'm a little dizzy. I'm gonna go to the bathroom."

She waddle-raced to the toilet and locked the door. Then she blinked open her dashboard. The mailbox icon was green: one new email.

Your LagunaLab Results Are Now Available!

She couldn't stand to open it—and to not open it, at the same time.

After a torturous pause, her curiosity won out.

She tapped the mail icon and closed her eyes.

CHAPTER

23

Ember

EMBER AND THORNE were strolling on the beach in front of his house when the notification popped up on her dashboard.

"Oh my God," she breathed, stopping abruptly. "It's here."

He lowered himself onto the sand. "I don't know if I'm ready."

She sat beside him. Dark sunglasses shielded his eyes and made him seem distant, almost unreachable. She yearned to say something comforting, but a false platitude would only annoy him. He despised anything other than the truth. And the truth was that she, too, was petrified.

Instead, she grabbed his hand and brought it to her lips. The waves lunged toward them, hurling white water at their feet. They scooted backward out of reach. Thorne shivered. The sky was a sheet of endless gray, and the chill in the air had scared away the sunbathers. Only a few surfers in wetsuits remained bobbing in the ocean, waiting for the angriest waves to show them a good time. Ember surveyed the beach. Not a soul in hearing distance; no one close enough to recognize him. But privacy didn't make the daunting task any easier.

"We need to just rip the Band-Aid," she declared.

He didn't try to stop her, but he didn't encourage her either. He remained immobile, staring grimly at the horizon.

"Okay, then." She pinched her virtual dashboard with two fingers, to enlarge the green mailbox icon. Then she tapped it open gingerly, as though to forestall a blow.

Your LagunaLab Results Are Now Available!

"Do you want to see?"

"No."

The report was a single page. It contained three columns labeled "Locus," "Fetus," and "Alleged Parent." Under "Locus" was a list of genetic markers with random names, like TH01 and D21S11. Under "Fetus" and "Alleged Parent" was a list of numbers indicating their respective allele sizes—each one's own particular flavor of that stretch of DNA. Ember skimmed all the letters and numbers in a hurry, zeroing in on the verdict at the bottom:

Probability of Parenthood: 0 percent. The alleged parent is excluded as the biological father of the tested fetus. This conclusion is based on the non-matching alleles at the loci listed above.

Ember's head snapped up at the sound of a scream. She realized it was her own. Before she knew what was happening, she was on top of Thorne, tackling him onto the sand, her lips on his. He kissed her back enthusiastically, making a sound in the back of his throat that was either a laugh or a cry, or both. She ripped off his sunglasses to find him teary-eyed.

"Is this for real? I'm free?"

"Free as a fucking bird. As I said, I'm good at my job."

"Thank God." He cupped her cheeks with both hands and kissed her again.

She pulled away after a moment. "It was a wake-up call, though. We can never take your safety for granted again."

"I know." His face darkened. "But what about the baby shoes?"

She waved it off. "As I suspected. Just a stupid prank."

"And Quinn's client? She said he was obsessed with me and the Vault?"

Ember bit her lip. "They've got nothing on you as long as I'm around."

* * *

Later that night, after a steak dinner followed by candlelit sex in the bathtub, Ember closed her eyes in bed and saw the usual knife. It was sharp, gleaming, and deadly.

The same fantasy often popped into her mind, which she had at first resisted and now allowed as a source of gruesome pleasure she would never admit to anyone. She let her mind play the familiar loop.

Nighttime. A dark and quiet house. The smooth handle of the knife in her palm. Gripping tightly, stepping inside. Shadows abounded. She knew the way to the man's room, up the stairs. No one ever stopped her from reaching the door. Finding him alone, he was always alone. Sleeping. Unaware. Vulnerable.

Creeping closer into the hushed room, raising the knife. His eyes would open in time to see the blade before it sank into his flesh. She liked to dwell on this moment, stretching it out, imagining the terror in his face, the recognition of her victory. Game over.

She didn't care to envision blood or screams or escape. None of that thrilled her. Only the knowledge of her imminent brutality reflected in his eyes. The drawn-out fear of his own suffering, payback for the suffering he had been inflicting on others without hesitation or remorse.

Under the covers next to Thorne, her right hand clenched into a tight fist, as though the knife were really there. Her pulse quickened as she imagined pressing the silver blade against the man's throat, keeping him in suspense about the agony in store. How else to stop the metastatic cancer the Vault had become? It had deteriorated so far from its original incarnation as the vigilante justice operation the two of them had started in secret together.

Making embryos from the tissue of unsuspecting "desirables" was never the business they had agreed on. It was capturing DNA from the unsuspecting *villains* of society—the lying politicians, the hypocritical corporate bigwigs, the democracy-killing judges—and listing their sequences for sale on the Vault to the highest bidder. Intensely private information could be deciphered and exposed through a person's genome: their health risks, biological relationships, ancestry, inherited personality traits. Enough for any target to feel grossly violated. The point was supposed to be anonymous citizen revenge against the country's most corrupt power players.

But then her cofounder had gone rogue, seeing an opportunity to increase profits with a new "market opportunity" in targeting famous desirables for their DNA, instead of famous villains—and then taking it a chilling leap further by selling their lab-made sperm and eggs to parents who would stop at nothing to give their future kids an edge.

Despite Ember's ferocious opposition, her partner had started chasing the cream of the crop instead of rock-bottom evil. Legendary singers, Olympic athletes, Nobel Prize winners—all prime targets, all naive to the threat they suddenly faced out in public. Their used coffee cups, tissues, and straws became a liability practically overnight, ripe for the taking. The pioneering of a new market in human history had catapulted the Vault to a new level of infamy, scrutiny, and cash—and obliterated every principle Ember held dear.

But it didn't matter. Her partner didn't need her anymore. By then, they both knew all about running a lab and manipulating human DNA. With all the cheap DIY tools available, it was scarily easy anyway, even though they were both professionally trained scientists.

Trying to stop him had horribly backfired. The trauma of their final confrontation lived close to the surface. The snap of celery while making dinner would remind her of the pop of her bone breaking. Grout between tiles would trigger her memory of being facedown on the bathroom floor. She was lucky to have escaped with her life.

Of course, she couldn't actually go back and kill him now. Nor could she go to the authorities. If she tipped off the FBI, he would know it was her. The Vault was their shared secret. Then he would blow up her new life so fast, it would vanish like a mirage in the desert. So they were locked in a stalemate of mutually assured destruction. She did whatever she could to thwart him from a distance while he continued to wreck lives and profit off innocent people. It was like getting away with murder, except he was getting away with births.

Thorne's touch pulled her back to bed. He rolled on one side to face her, draping his heavy arm across her chest. He propped up his head and eyed her sleepily.

"What's up? You look stressed."

She sighed. "I'm fine."

"You sure?"

"Yeah."

"I hope so. 'Cause we have nothing to worry about now."

Nothing she could control, anyway.

Let it go, she told herself. *Don't let him ruin any more of your life than he already has.*

Thorne's serenity was a balm. She gazed at him, overcome with an immense wave of relief. They had dodged a nightmare with Quinn. The past would only hold her back if she let it.

"Let's make a baby," she declared, surprising herself.

He grinned. "Right now?"

"No, silly. Next week. I'll make an appointment at the clinic."

"But what about the wedding?"

"We don't have to get pregnant yet. We can make the embryos and do Selection, and then implant after the wedding. What do you think?"

"You're ready for a baby?" He raised his eyebrows with a smile.

"*Our* baby? Absolutely."

"Just ours. A family no one else can ruin."

"Exactly." The warmth of a hundred suns lit her up from inside. "There's nothing I want more."

"As long as he or she inherits my rhythm and not yours."

She gave him a playful shove. "Fine. It's a deal."

They sealed it with a kiss. And just like that, what could have been the worst day of her life ended as one of the very best.

CHAPTER

24

Quinn

When Quinn shuffled out of the bathroom, Robert was sitting in the kitchen, with his hands folded on the table.

"Everything okay?"

She nodded. She didn't trust her voice. She wasn't sure whether to trust anything at all.

"You're not. I can tell."

"Hormones are making me crazy." She shrugged, fighting back tears. "They say it's worse the second pregnancy."

"Oh, sweetie." He pushed back the stool and came to her. "It's normal. You know if men had to have babies, humanity would go extinct."

She laughed in spite of the lump in her throat. "Fair enough."

His capable arms wrapped around her like a long-lost shelter. She leaned her head on his shoulder. Giving in felt good, in the rebellious way that smoking a cigarette or binge eating felt good. She ached for all the pieces of their relationship to fit exactly back together. Even though a little voice in her head warned her to be careful.

Oh, fuck off, she thought. Listening to her anxiety had gotten her all the way to . . . nowhere. Thorne wasn't the father of Bubala. Which meant Evan was. God, how idiotic she was.

She could only imagine what Thorne and Ember were saying about her right now. *"Total nutjob,"* probably. She wished she had a way to contact them, to apologize. But they had taken her number only and refused to give her theirs. Not that she could blame them. The kindest thing she could do now was leave them alone forever.

"Do you want to see more pictures of Evan?" Robert asked in a gracious attempt to set her mind at ease.

She shook her head. "It's okay. I'm sure it's hard for you."

"Enough time has passed now . . ." He seemed wistful. "Maybe I'll start putting some back up in the house."

"That would be nice for Bubala."

Robert crouched to speak to her stomach directly. "I hope you know how much your daddies love you." He palmed her belly with both hands, like a basketball.

Quinn gave her womb a gentle nudge. Bubala responded with an elbow jab.

"Ah!" Robert beamed. "I felt that!" He leaned in close and pressed his lips against the skin of her midriff. "Do you hear Daddy? I can't wait to meet you."

Bubala squirmed at the deep timbre of his voice.

"She's dancing," Quinn said. "She missed you."

"Me too." He rose to his feet and looked her in the eye. "Are we good now?"

She glanced at the floor. "I think so."

You still lied about the Vault, she thought. But if she said that, she would have to admit she'd been snooping through the Thorne chatbot. Robert's trust in *her* would be destroyed . . . and then what? It was a tad late to fire her. But he could insist on closer oversight, devise ways to make her life miserable. And she still had about six weeks to go before the due date. Might as well play nice.

He picked up her hand and gave it a kiss. "I'm so grateful for you." She was surprised to see his eyes glisten. "I hate to think I've upset you even by accident."

"It's fine." She laughed uncomfortably and withdrew her hand. "Just a misunderstanding, I guess." Was he faking sadness? It struck her as a tad over the top. Or maybe he was just awkward when it came to expressing emotion.

She turned around to retrieve a glass from the cupboard in order to escape the intensity of his gaze. Everything he said was correct and sweet, but his direct stare reminded her of being in the presence of one of those super-alert android animals. You could tell their algorithms were always whirring, calculating their next move. She sensed that something was deeply off, but she couldn't say exactly what.

She cringed when he touched her shoulder.

"Why don't you go lie down?" He took the glass out of her hand and filled it with water from the tap. She shuffled toward her bed on the other side of the studio, relieved at the excuse to get some space. A headache was brewing at the base of her skull.

Did it really matter that he had lied about the Vault?

She had lied about things before too. She was no saint. There was the time in high school she'd ridden her electric bike while blinking on social media, even though she risked getting a big fine for DDD (driving digitally distracted). Predictably, she'd crashed into another rider, hurtling them both to the pavement. Neither was seriously injured, but when a police witness came over to write her a ticket, she'd denied having been online. She'd claimed her tire had hit a rock. The cop lacked proof, so he let her go.

She remembered other evasive incidents. After college, when she'd moved back home to work as a waitress, she'd lied to her parents for a whole summer about the person she was dating. A friend she'd met at the restaurant had gradually turned into more than a friend—a woman she enjoyed experimenting with sexually. Her Irish Catholic mom would never have approved. So Erin became "Aaron" that summer, until eventually Quinn realized that she was more drawn to men and moved on.

But no one had truly suffered for her lies; that was what mattered.

How could she know if Robert's denial was a white lie—or a serious breach?

Maybe he was just embarrassed to admit he had a grim fascination with the Vault, a morbid curiosity with the dark web, which he hid to avoid judgment.

She could relate if that was the case. She remembered once pretending to agree with her posh college roommate that tattoos were ugly and low class, when in reality she had gotten the letters *TT*—Thorne's initials in his signature font—inscribed near her hip bone. She'd gotten dressed in her closet for the rest of the semester.

But what if Robert was hiding something much worse? What if—she shuddered as a heinous thought occurred to her—what if she *hadn't* been wrong about Thorne being the other parent? What if there was *another* surrogate who was currently pregnant with Thorne and Robert's baby, while she carried Evan and Robert's baby? But why would Robert want two kids as a single dad? More importantly, why would he go to the bizarre trouble of making a nonconsensual baby with a celebrity? It didn't make any sense. Unless he was some kind of monster using innocent kids as pawns in a bigger scheme? The phrase *human trafficking* came to mind. Her head throbbed. It was too sinister to contemplate.

More likely, there was no baby Thorne at all and no secret other surrogate, and Robert had denied knowing about the Vault simply because he didn't want her to think he was a creep for being curious about it.

She lay back against the pillow and closed her eyes, signaling to Robert that she was done hanging out. Fortunately, he set the water glass on her nightstand, promised to call later, and let himself out the front door.

When she heard his footsteps receding, she opened her eyes.

The truth was she couldn't ignore his lie.

Her love for Bubala was stronger than her craving to return to normal. She couldn't hand over the baby to a man who triggered her concerns. First she had to make absolutely sure he was safe. Hoping for the best was not a strategy. And she didn't have much time.

C H A P T E R

25

Lily

THE PLANE TRIP from Newark to California was only thirty minutes by supersonic jet. Lily barely had enough time to watch a short episode of a show before touching down at LAX.

It was Saturday afternoon, and her return flight was Monday afternoon, so she only had forty-eight hours to talk to Winnie and visit the prison administrator about her languishing FOIA request.

As the plane taxied to the gate, she was unnerved to find a rare email from Shane himself: *How's the article coming? S.*

Hmmm, she thought. *It's due in six days, and I still haven't been able to verify the main source's story—the story of the crime that wrecked my childhood—so you caught me on a last-ditch quest to nail down the details while my career hangs in the balance.*

Great, she wrote back. *I look forward to filing next week. L.*

She blinked off her dashboard, grabbed her backpack from the overhead bin, and marched off the plane in search of a carb-free blueberry muffin. She relished this stop whenever she arrived at LAX, because Winnie's very own bakery, Live

Free or Pie, had a franchise location right in the SonicAir terminal.

When she got to the front of the line, she smiled proudly at the cashier. "Guess what?" Lily pointed to the poster of a grinning Winnie on the wall behind him. In it, she was wearing a chef's hat over her curly auburn hair and stood with her arms crossed in front of a glass case of pies, cakes, and cookies. "That's my aunt."

Well, technically Winnie wasn't her blood relation, but she certainly felt like family. Ever since Lily could remember, they had shared a special bond.

"Wow," the young man said. "She's a legend."

"I know." Lily's heart quickened at the prospect of seeing her soon. They hadn't visited in person for too long. Work, school, and life had gotten in the way, as usual.

The cab ride to Winnie's home in West Hollywood took ages with the traffic, but at least Lily got to enjoy the most delectable *and* healthiest muffin in LA. Winnie's recipe was a secret, but Lily knew it had to do with synthetic molecules that tasted like sugar and acted like protein.

When her autonomous taxi pulled up to a pretty tree-lined street, she jumped out in front of an angular modern house with oversize windows and a row of fruiting trees.

Winnie opened the door before she had finished climbing the porch steps.

"You made it!" Winnie exclaimed.

They hugged without restraint. Lily inhaled the scent of her familiar citrus shampoo and felt a deep sense of calm wash over her. Winnie's embrace felt like home. When she had been little, living nearby in Beverly Hills with her dad, they had visited Winnie often, almost like seeing a supplemental mother while her own sat sidelined in prison. Their fierce affection for one another had never abated, even after her family moved to New Jersey for a fresh start once Mom got released. Not for the first time, Lily wondered if Mom had ever been jealous of their closeness, but she'd only ever expressed gratitude for the hole that Winnie had filled during those difficult early years.

Mom and Winnie had been close friends for decades, having met through a mutual friend before Lily was even born. *"She's like my little sister,"* Mom had told Lily. *"The sibling I never had."*

"You hungry?" Winnie asked. "I just made your favorite fig tarts with goat cheese."

"I am now. Even though I already had one of your muffins on the way."

Winnie chuckled as they entered the light-filled, quiet house. The usual loud male energy was absent. Lily shot her a questioning look.

"James is in New York on business and Cole went to Mexico with his friends, so it's just us."

Perfect, Lily thought. "Sorry to miss them."

"I'll tell them you said hello."

"Please do." Lily set her backpack on the console table, which stood beneath a row of gold plaques and framed stories about Live Free or Pie. The bakery had earned a cult following in the last five years, as Winnie was nearing fifty. Lily recalled a long stretch of time during which she had gone to culinary school, raised her son, and apprenticed with other pastry chefs before finally striking out on her own. She was the opposite of an "overnight success," even though people often called her that.

Staring at Winnie's accolades, Lily couldn't shake off the desire to nail her own success nice and early. If her article was a slam dunk, the doors to all the best media outlets would fling wide open. She wouldn't have to wait twenty years to break through.

"So how's work going?" Winnie asked, as if sensing her yearning.

"It's all right." Lily hesitated. She wanted to confide in Winnie, but not to the point of scaring her away from an honest discussion of her mom's criminal history. It was the one thing Lily desperately wanted to talk about, even beyond the purposes of fact-checking for the article.

Deep down, Lily knew the urgency of this trip was not really about impressing Shane or publishing a hit story, though those goals mattered too. The real heart of her mission was personal. She couldn't forgive her mother and gain closure until she understood exactly what had led Mom to accept a plea deal of a decade in prison . . . a deal that seemed a lot like giving up. Like abandonment. Their relationship stood to be forever transformed based on the knowledge she might glean from Winnie. And those stakes felt too important to screw up by blurting out something impatient. So she said nothing—yet.

On the patio in the backyard, they stretched out on chaise lounges beside the pool and ate the fig tarts while the sun dipped low in the sky. A privacy hedge of orange and lemon trees, flowering native shrubs, and succulents surrounded the pool, cozying them in.

"So how're you feeling about becoming a big sister?" Winnie asked after they had caught up on gossip about Cole (dating a new girl) and herself (no one interesting).

Lily poured herself a glass of sangria from the pitcher between them. "It was honestly a huge surprise. I had no idea they were making embryos."

"Good surprise or . . . ?"

"Sort of. I mean, yeah, I'm happy for them. It's just taken some getting used to."

"I'm sure."

"I don't even think they celebrated Conception Day. Or at least, they didn't tell me." Conception Day marked the occasion of visiting a fertility clinic with your partner for epithelial cell sample collection. Lily had researched it for her article. After collection, molecular biologists would chemically coax the cells to grow into eggs, then join them with sperm in petri dishes to form embryos. Cultural norms dictated that couples enjoy a romantic date on Conception Day to celebrate their first step toward parenthood. It was meant to be a cherished time for fun and intimacy before the stressful milestone of Selection Day.

Winnie shrugged. "Did you ask them if they did anything?"

Lily shook her head. "It's none of my business."

"Maybe they just wanted to be sensitive to you. I know they've wanted another baby for a long time, but they waited until you were all grown up."

"That's what Mom said."

"She felt it wasn't fair to force you to share attention . . ."

After everything. Lily's mind filled in the words that Winnie didn't need to speak.

"You're still angry with her." Winnie spoke softly.

Lily didn't bother to deny it. "I want to let it go. I really do. But there's still a lot I don't understand." *Like why she won't ever talk about it.*

Winnie nibbled on a fig tart. "Have you asked her?"

"Of course. But she basically shuts down and so does my dad. It's like they're traumatized or something."

"Well . . ." Winnie paused. "What have they already told you?"

"Just the basics. Some guy broke in when Mom was pregnant with me, she shot and killed him with a ghost gun, and then she got hammered for illegal possession."

Winnie sipped her sangria. "But . . . you're still upset with her?"

Lily cocked her head, eager to seize her chance. "How would you feel if your mother had literally *killed* someone? I mean, who was that guy? Was he threatening her? Did she *have* to kill him?"

Winnie didn't answer right away. When she did, her manner was solemn. A note of awe inflected her tone. "It was him or you. She made her choice and paid the price."

"So you think she did the right thing?"

"Without a doubt."

"Then why did she go to jail for ten *years*?" Lily's voice rose. "It never made any sense."

"That was the plea deal." Winnie shook her head as if in agreement that the punishment was too harsh for the crime.

"Did she fight it at least?" Lily asked, heart pounding. "When they were trying to get her to take it?"

How badly Lily wanted the next words to be: *"Oh my God, did she fight. She threatened to burn everything down if they took her away from you for that long. She had to be dragged away from you, kicking and screaming, but there was no way to stop it."*

Winnie shrugged and looked away. "She couldn't."

"Couldn't?" Lily demanded. "Or didn't bother trying? Was too afraid to?"

"It was impossible. But hey, it's really not my place to talk about this. You should ask her directly."

"Right." Lily snorted. "Because that's been so successful."

"Oh, spare me." Winnie's eyes flashed with an intensity Lily had never seen. "Your mom is a goddamn hero, okay? She saved your life. And not only yours. That's all I can say."

* * *

At nine o'clock sharp on Monday morning, Lily was first in line to speak with the records clerk at the Federal Women's Correctional Institution of Los Angeles. The imposing prison took up an entire city block in a gritty part of East LA. Its gray cement facade and steep front steps immediately brought back strange memories of visiting with her dad as a kid. She remembered the way she used to swing from the railing and make a game of stepping around the broken bottles and burned-out cigarettes that littered the climb up to the heavy steel gates.

Inside, past the security columns, bag check, and retinal scan that confirmed her identity as a citizen in good standing, she approached a double-paned glass window and smiled at the records clerk.

"Hi, I'm a reporter with *Vanguard*, and I'm here to follow up on a FOIA request I submitted about a month ago."

The clerk sipped coffee. "You got the request number?"

"Yep." She blinked a few times to navigate to the confirmation receipt on her dashboard, then read out the number to him. "It's regarding former inmate F1CD5," she added, to make his job easier. "I'm looking for her case records. I never got a response through the system."

The clerk stared at his own invisible dashboard and tapped rapidly on his desk. "What did you say the inmate's number was?"

She repeated it and waited hopefully. With a single command, he would be able to transfer the records directly onto her dashboard. She planned to spend the flight home reviewing every word.

"Oh," he said. "Sorry, that case is sealed."

"What? What does that mean?"

He lifted a shoulder. "Means it's sealed. I can't see it, and neither can you."

"But why?"

"The offender must have requested it."

"And there's nothing we can do?"

"Nope." He looked pointedly past her at the next person in line.

She muttered thanks and walked out in stunned confusion. Of all the possibilities for this trip to California, she had never considered returning home with even more questions than before.

CHAPTER

26

Ember

THE HELICOPTER LIFTED off with only Ember and Thorne inside. She grabbed his knee as it soared over the ocean, toward Catalina Island. The clear glass bottom and floor-to-ceiling windows gave her the dizzying sensation of levitating in thin air. From their height, the water appeared as still and glassy as a mirror, reflecting their briskly moving shadow. Thorne chuckled at her white knuckles and tightened his arm around her. Of course, he was no stranger to private autonomous flights. But this one was special even for him.

The gravitas of what they were about to do stoked a tingling throughout her body, despite her nerves. It was Conception Day.

Ember would have been keen to walk into any clinic like any other couple, give their samples, and go home, but Thorne had surprised her that morning with the Platinum VIP package from the fanciest clinic in Orange County: an afternoon on a private beach twenty-two miles off the coast to collect their samples in total seclusion.

The package was not new to her. Ads regularly appeared for it in the holoverse, billing it as "the most intimate and exclusive conception experience offered in the state of

California." Its sleek footage portrayed a cloudless sky and a pristine shoreline, where a nameless couple walked, smiling, hand in hand beside the clinic's logo and the pitch: *"Make your baby in paradise."* Whenever the ad popped up, Ember would roll her eyes at the cringey commercialization of a once-private act.

But now that she was living it, the word that popped into her mind was *surreal.*

"Look," Thorne pointed down below. "There it is."

The whir of the rotors overhead drowned out his voice in the cabin, but she heard him perfectly through her headphones.

The helicopter began smoothly descending toward rocky cliffs that rose up from the sea like jagged sentries. The reddish outcroppings were instantly recognizable from the ad. At the base of the cliffs, accessible only by boat or air, lay a cove of white sand. As it grew larger, Ember squeezed Thorne's hand and felt an awakening deep in her pelvis. She wondered if he felt it too—the primal vestiges from the old days of baby making.

First things first.

When they gently thudded down, the door automatically opened, and a row of narrow steps unfurled to the sand. They undid their seat belts and eagerly descended the stairs onto their very own beach. A warm breeze wicked the sweat away from their ears, where their headphones had been tightly pressed. Ember spun around in awe and kicked off her sandals. The powdery sand felt like hot sugar. Unlike at home in Laguna, there was no debris of seaweed or litter, just a stretch of untouched beach. At their backs, the cliffs towered high. Succulent plants abounded up on the ridge, along with an exuberance of yellow wildflowers. At their feet, subdued ripples lapped at the shore. The water glittered in a kaleidoscope of reflected sunlight.

It was the most beautiful place she had ever seen.

"Are we really here?"

"I knew you'd love it." Thorne hoisted her up at the waist, but she swatted him away when he brought her low for a kiss.

"No saliva exchange until after, remember?"

"Oh God. Imagine if they got my cells out of your mouth . . . "

Ember groaned. "You'd have a baby with yourself."

"At least then she would sing on key."

"She?" Ember raised her eyebrows.

"Don't you want a girl?" His teasing face grew serious. "I figured that's what you would choose."

"I thought you'd want a boy?"

"I'm cool with whatever you decide. As long as it's ours."

"Fine, then. A girl."

"I knew it!"

She laughed. "I hate being so predictable."

"Don't. I love knowing you better than anyone."

She turned away before he could see her wince.

Something colorful in the distance caught her eye: a picnic table covered in a peach tablecloth, the clinic's trademark color. It sat in the shade of a cave, beside a large cooler. They jogged over to it, leaving the helicopter on the sand until it was time to activate their return trip.

Thorne opened the cooler. "They said there would be instructions in here."

Inside were two separate compartments. One side contained collection tools like vials, swabs, cups, and bags. The other side was filled with food: baguettes, smoked salmon, wedges of gouda and brie cheese, peaches and figs, a platter of sliced veggies, and chocolate chip cookies. A chilled bottle of champagne lay at the bottom, along with two glass flutes. Ember's stomach rumbled. She couldn't wait to dig in.

Thorne pulled out a sealed envelope embossed with their names in gold.

He read aloud from its card: *"Happy Conception Day! We at Precision Reproduction Associates congratulate you on starting your family here with us today. Please follow the instructions precisely before you enjoy your picnic and special time together on ReproBeach™. Blink twice on this code to begin. Enjoy!"*

Thorne double-blinked and stared at his dashboard. "Ah, here's the instructions." He squinted as he read the steps. "Maybe you should take the lead, since you're the scientist."

"Sure." She brought up the instructions on her own dashboard and read them carefully. "It's pretty straightforward. Should I go first?"

"Please."

She swallowed a few times to dredge up some decent saliva. Her mouth felt dry; she hadn't been allowed to eat or drink for two hours, to avoid any cross contamination. "I just have to take a cheek swab and put it in the vial."

She tore the long cotton swab from its plastic wrap and handed it to Thorne. "You do it. Scrape it around my cheek really good for thirty seconds. And then . . . I'll get you back."

She opened her mouth wide. He did as she instructed, making sure the swab rubbed for a little longer than necessary to pick up all the cells it could. She closed her eyes and tried to imagine their daughter: Would she be tall, with hazel eyes and dirty-blonde curls like him? Or short, with light blonde hair and green eyes like her? Wondering was fun while it lasted. Of course, they would decide those things in a few weeks, on Selection Day.

When Thorne was done, he handed the swab to her. She plunged it into the collection vial, then pushed a lever in the cap to release a clear liquid into the sterile environment: a culture medium that contained stabilizers and a chemical accelerant to prompt the cells to quickly multiply into a useful layer.

Later that evening, at the clinic's lab, the staff scientists would manipulate the cells with chemical growth factors to revert them to pluripotency, allowing them to regain the potential to become almost any type of human cell. Then the staff would follow the Nobel Prize–winning protocol developed by Japanese scientists to trigger those stem cells to grow into perfect quality eggs, ready to be fertilized. The process was seamless. It took exactly sixteen days to go from Conception to Selection: three days to revert the cells, five days to grow mature eggs, one day to fertilize, five more days to grow several dozen embryos (at which stage they would be frozen), and then two more days to analyze a single cell from each embryo and determine polygenic scores. Then the Selection Counselor would call with the results, and the hard decisions would begin.

Ember took a deep breath and chided herself to stay in the present; she was always jumping ahead to the next situation, the next problem to solve, then blaming herself for missing out on the moment. Her anxiety was an inherited flaw, one she was determined not to pass on to their daughter if she could help it.

"You're done," Thorne said. "How does it feel?"

"Great." She tenderly laid the vial of her cheek cells in a padded shell inside the cooler. There was no great rush; the culture medium would keep her cells stable until the clinic's staff initiated the protocol.

Ember smiled and dropped to her knees in front of Thorne. "Your turn. Doctor's orders."

"Yes, ma'am." He dug his fingers into her hair as she tore off his pants and began to massage him with a tantalizingly light touch. When he moaned for more, she took him into her mouth and increased the speed and pressure the way he liked. She felt herself getting wet, but that would have to wait. It didn't take much longer for him to climax; she read all the signs and pulled back a few seconds early to lift the sample cup to his tip. His semen arced into it, filling it up more than halfway. He'd had to hold back for the last seven days to make sure enough live sperm was ready to go. Judging by the quantity, they had nothing to worry about.

She tightened the cap securely and deposited it into a thermoregulating bag that would preserve it at 68 degrees until it reached the lab. Then she placed the bag in the cooler next to the case containing her own sample. Thorne was still catching his breath when she turned back to him.

"Ready to go home?" she joked.

He kissed her in response and slid his hands into her shorts. "Take these off."

Soon all their clothes lay crumpled on the sand, and they had no further instructions other than to enjoy each other. The sun was flirting with the horizon, casting a pink glow across their bare skin.

"Wait," she said. "Only one thing could improve this day."

"What?"

She slid out her contact lenses and flicked them into the ocean. "There. I'm all yours."

He gawked at her in surprise. Going dark almost never happened; smart lenses were designed to be worn 24/7. Sure, you could turn off notifications, but even in "sleep" mode, they continued to receive and transmit data. Physically tearing them off your eyeballs was as radical as walking around naked, and it felt damn good.

"Fuck it," he said, and did the same.

They marveled as his clear little discs disappeared under the water. Now nothing could threaten their giddy solitude. No pings, no onlookers, no fans near Thorne requiring her hypervigilance. They were completely alone—for today.

Before long, they would be a party of three.

Ember was prepared for parenthood to bring many ups and downs—all the ordinary, extraordinary dramas and delights of raising a child. She felt *ready for the challenge*, a phrase she would recall as a sadistic understatement.

But the last thing she expected was for that child to shatter everything under the sky—and then later become the glue that held the stars together.

CHAPTER

27

Quinn

QUINN FURTIVELY GLANCED around the front porch as she climbed the steps to Robert's Bel Air mansion. It was a Tuesday afternoon, two weeks after his unexpected arrival at her apartment. His impromptu visit—and her uneasiness—had prompted the idea for her own surprise visit to his place. Except in this case, he wasn't home.

His car wasn't in the driveway, and all the lights were off. She knew he worked in an office somewhere far away. He'd told her where at some point, but she couldn't remember . . . downtown or on the east side? In any case, given traffic, he wasn't due back for at least several hours.

She also knew the code for his front door. It's not like she was breaking in. He'd given her access around Christmas, back when they were closer than ever. She could hardly believe that just four months ago, they used to spend whole days together, going to her doctors' appointments in the morning, shopping for maternity clothes in the afternoon, and cooking together in his glorious kitchen at night.

"Come over anytime," he'd offered in those days. *"Swim in the pool when I'm at work. Take a nap, whatever. Mi casa es su casa."*

Then her suspicions (paranoia?) had dug out a chasm between them, and she wasn't sure she could cross back. Bubala was due in four weeks. Four weeks! Time was encroaching like a wildfire, a force of nature that had to be reckoned with. Soon, Bubala would be a tiny person in her arms, and Robert would take her away forever. Unless Quinn found a solid reason to defy their contract and hold her back.

She punched in his four-digit code, and the lock discharged. Quietly she stepped inside.

The whiteness of the space assaulted her eyes. White marble floors, white sofa, white walls, absent any personal accents except a few generic photos of the Santa Monica pier and the New York City skyline. It suddenly occurred to her that Robert might have bought the house staging and all.

Who the hell *was* Robert anyway?

She cycled through the details she'd gleaned over the months, seeking any clues she might have missed. He was a crypto futures trader. His family lived back East. A brother he rarely mentioned. Parents she'd never met. Not many—any?—close friends she knew of. A deceased husband, if that story held. She thought of the photo he'd shown her with the guy he called Evan. That guy could have been anyone or no one—a deep fake. It proved nothing.

She desperately wanted to find something unequivocally reassuring about Robert, something *real.* He was kind and generous, but that didn't mean good and honest. People could put on a front to curry favor or inspire trust. Getting a handle on Robert felt like trying to hug sand. The more she scrutinized him, the more he slipped away.

The house was very still. Through the curved glass sheet that served as the back wall, the view stretched all the way out to the ocean, a blip of blue beneath the amber haze.

She stood in the foyer, listening for any sounds of his presence. All she could hear was the thrumming white noise of the air conditioner. No footsteps overhead in the bedroom. No clinking in the kitchen, no toilet flushing. All clear.

Out of habit, she left her Birkenstocks by the door, where several pairs of his shoes were lined up in a neat row. One indisputable fact about him was his allegiance to order. He relished total control over his environment, down to the way he arranged his closet (color coded) and the precision with which he organized his fridge (multiples of each item facing the same direction).

She hurried to the guest room to locate the Thorne statue. If she asked it more questions, she might be able to uncover more about Robert's interest in the Vault and whether it was indeed a harmless fascination or something serious, something that might cast doubt on his fitness to raise Bubala.

But when she entered the room, the nightstand was bare. She checked all the drawers, in the covers of the bed, and in the bathroom, but there was no sign of the friendly chatbot. She ran out to the living room to check under the coffee table and the couch, then proceeded to scour the kitchen drawers and cupboards, to no avail. How was she supposed to find out anything without it?

Upstairs, she made her way nervously to his bedroom, a place she'd never gone alone. The duvet cover was pulled tightly over the mattress. Blackout shades were drawn across the windows. His chest of drawers revealed stacks of folded clothes, but nothing else. In the closet, suits hung in a pressed row, ties draped over their own hangers. His faint cologne lingered in the air. The only criticism she could lodge was how *perfect* everything seemed—almost as though he didn't actually live there. She ran her fingers over his satin pillowcase, searching for creases from frequent usage. It was smooth as stone.

But so what if he was a neat freak? That didn't exactly give her grounds to withhold his own child from him.

She paused in Bubala's nursery, which was finally complete. A jungle mural covered one wall, featuring lions drinking out of a river and monkeys playing on tree branches. A cozy sheepskin rug lay at the foot of the crib. Above it hung a mobile of colorful birds. There was a matching changing table, dresser, and white bookshelf, all carved with the same elegant curves. Several dozen board books and a colorful rattle sat on the low shelf, waiting for little fingers to discover them. In the far corner, a rocking chair awaited many long nights of cuddles.

As much as she hated to admit it, the nursery was perfect too.

Standing there, the idea of keeping Bubala to herself struck her as ludicrous. Where would she even put a crib in her crappy studio apartment? How would she support a child with no future source of income? Robert was so much better equipped in every way.

Back downstairs, Quinn stopped in the guest bathroom to pee (her bladder tolerated an hour, tops). She was considering giving up and going home when she noticed the narrow steps that led down to the home gym. She'd forgotten about the lower level because they'd never hung out down there.

Gripping the railing, she carefully walked down to the finished basement area, where the temperature instantly seemed to drop ten degrees. What she found was disappointing: a modest room with white walls, a rubber floor, and some boring workout equipment: a treadmill, a rack of weights, and a rock-climbing wall.

Suddenly she heard the front door open.

Shit.

There was no way out, other than back up the stairs. And nowhere to hide.

Her throat seized up. A cold sweat broke out on her forehead as her gaze ricocheted around the windowless room. Deep in her womb, the baby writhed around in its cramped quarters.

Robert's heavy footsteps descended the stairs. He knew exactly where she was. He must have known all along. Oh God. Her mind spun, angling for what to tell him, how to explain—play dumb, make excuses, tell it straight? She had no time to decide, no time to think, because he was already coming, rounding the corner, striding toward the gym.

And then they came face-to-face. He stopped six feet away and stared at her with quiet fury, his mouth a stern line. His rage was the opposite of explosive. No shouting, no cursing. Just preternatural calm. Quinn was reminded again of those cunning android animals whose sharp eyes and blank expressions concealed a complicated world of invisible calculations. Like them, Robert was totally inscrutable, which made her feel all the more off-balance.

He crossed his arms. "What are you doing here?"

"You—you gave me the code, remember?" Her voice shook, but she forced herself to act normal. "I just felt like coming over."

"And snooping on me? I saw you on the cameras."

Her heart plummeted. "I'm really sorry." She realized she was backing away when her left heel hit the wall.

"What exactly are you looking for?" He smirked. "Maybe I can find it."

"Oh, never mind. This is all just a misunderstanding."

"You have those a lot."

"I'm sorry," she repeated. "I just . . ." her voice trailed off. There was no way she could accuse him of misleading her without proof. All she had was an unshakeable gut feeling, and that wasn't enough. "I've just been stressed lately."

He frowned. "You know, I keep kicking myself that I never required you to undergo a psych eval. That was my mistake."

"What? I'm not crazy."

"Quinn." He said her name as though she were a petulant kid denying an obvious fact. "You're suffering. And your paranoia is only getting worse. You have to let me help you now."

"Stop!" she cried. "You're gaslighting me."

"Oh, hon. This is what I'm talking about." He shook his head in frustration. "Look, I already spoke to Dr. Qua, and she said you can take up to twenty milligrams of an antipsychotic without harming the baby."

"Are you serious?" Quinn had been cowering, but in a moment of indignation, she straightened and made a beeline past him toward the stairs.

His hand shot out and closed around her bicep. "Where do you think you're going?"

"Home," she spat.

"It's time for you to stay here. So I can keep an eye on you."

She yanked her arm out of his grip. "You can't force me. I'll call the police."

"You're carrying my child. Didn't you read the contract? If you have a health crisis, I become your power of attorney. Remember?"

Her body sagged with the weight of his words. He was right. As long as she was pregnant, she was trapped. And they both knew it. A risky plan erupted in her mind like a thorn.

"Fine," she conceded slowly. "I'll stay."

Her about-face appeared to catch him by surprise. "You will?"

"On one condition."

"What?"

"That you pay me an added bonus for my trouble." Her mind raced to come up with a deal that would convince him of her compliance. "Five thousand bucks. Half now and half on delivery."

He rolled his eyes. "For God's sake, Quinn."

"You can make this easy or hard," she bluffed, as if she were negotiating a real transaction and not a clever diversion.

"Fine," he agreed. "But you live here now."

"Only until the baby is born. And only with a half dose of the meds. Nothing that will knock me out."

His eyes burned with triumph. "Of course. It'll be for the best. You'll feel much better."

"But first," she said matter-of-factly, "I need to go get my clothes, toothbrush, and pregnancy pillow. You don't have any of my stuff."

His gaze narrowed. "Home and back?"

"Home and back."

"Share your location with me," he instructed. "I'll wait."

She grudgingly pulled up her dashboard and pinged him her signal.

"Thanks." He paused. "I'd hate for you to get lost on your way back."

A chill wafted over her neck. "I won't."

"Good. Then I think we'll make it through just fine."

CHAPTER 28

Lily

THREE DAYS AFTER Lily returned from her LA trip, she nervously approached her mother's room. Shane was expecting the article tomorrow—and it was still missing two major things: first, Mom's permission; and second, documentation to back up her story. The only way forward now was to come clean.

The door was open. Lily walked in to find her sleeping; her eyes fluttered open at Lily's footsteps.

"Oh, sorry—I didn't know you were taking a nap."

Mom sighed and pushed herself up on her elbows. "I was just resting. This baby is sucking away all my energy."

Lily noted the purplish semicircles under her eyes and the sallow tone of her skin. Apparently pregnancy at age sixty-four didn't come with its promised glow. Lily remembered that Mom had also given up her regular cellular reboot to reverse wrinkles because it wasn't pregnancy safe. In a strange parallel, she was starting to show her age just as she was literally starting to show. Dad still told her every day she looked beautiful, but the dramatic changes seemed to be overwhelming her.

"I can come back later," Lily offered, even though she really didn't have time to wait. She started to backtrack, when Mom patted the bedspread.

"It's fine—stay."

"Are you sure?"

"I can tell something's on your mind. What's up?"

"I don't want to stress you out."

Mom snorted. "Now you have to tell me."

Lily hesitated. "So . . . remember last month when my editor assigned me the story about fertility clinics and how they have too much power?"

"Of course. I was sorry not to help you."

"Well . . . funny enough, you still can."

"How so?"

Lily's heart was beating fast. "Okay, look, I wrote you into the story—*anonymously*."

Mom's eyebrows shot up. "Why the hell would you do that?"

"Because you're the perfect example. It wasn't fair how they turned you away. My sources say it probably happens all the time to people who don't fit the mold of being the 'right' parents, but nobody talks about it because it's taboo, so it's been impossible for me to track down another anecdote."

Despite the awkwardness of confrontation, Lily tingled with excitement whenever she thought of holding Big Repro to account and making a name for herself in the process. Like the journalists she idolized, she might actually change the system for the better.

Mom gritted her teeth. "I was very clear about not participating."

"I know, but you're the one who holds the story together. What if I just read it aloud, and then—"

"No."

"Why *not*? I changed your name!"

"I don't care. Write me out of it."

"But you're the lead."

Mom paused. When she spoke, her voice was very low. "Were you going to file this story without my knowledge?"

"Of course not! I was always planning to show you first. And anyway, I need your court records for fact-checking. *Vanguard* won't publish an anonymous source without backup."

Lily tried to deliver this information casually, as though she hadn't already gone all the way across the country to the prison, only to find the records sealed. She was dying to know what was in there, and no one else could grant her access.

The briefest flash of fear crossed into her mother's eyes. "You know what? Just kill the story."

"Mom, please—"

"No. I'm extremely disappointed that you lied to me."

"And you haven't?"

Mom inhaled sharply. "What's that supposed to mean?"

"I don't know. Why don't you tell me?"

They eyed each other with mutual frustration. Lily waited for her to acknowledge that some mysterious thing remained unsaid between them. Something as vague as a distant star, whose light needed to be sharpened into focus.

But all Mom said was, "I think you should go."

"Fine." Lily jumped off the bed and hurried back to her own room.

Something was buried in those records. Something her mother had gone to great lengths to hide. If Lily were braver, she might have said so. She might have pointed out that in all her research, no other ghost gun conviction from the last twenty years had resulted in a decade-long federal prison sentence. What made her mother's case so different? Had she actually done something much worse?

Dad's fervent declaration rushed back into her mind: *"She didn't deserve what she got."* And Winnie's emphatic agreement: *"Your mother is a goddamn hero."*

How to square their support with Mom's secrecy?

In any case, the story was dead. Lily crawled into bed and buried herself under the covers. She had failed. Shane was going to be furious. And now Radia would score the job at the end of their fellowship.

As she wiped her eyes, she couldn't help feeling like the real story was just beneath the surface, if only she could figure out how to reach it.

CHAPTER

29

Ember

Ember couldn't stop checking her dashboard. It was sixteen days after Conception Day, which meant the report from the clinic with their embryos' genetic analyses was due at any time. Then, unless they got very lucky with an obvious finalist, the tricky process of Selection would begin.

Ember hoped they could get through the process as painlessly as possible rather than devolve into a fighting mess like some couples did. The clinic had offered Pre-Selection Counseling as part of their VIP package to prepare them for the high emotions and high stakes, and they had diligently practiced strategies for compassionate disagreement. But until the real scores arrived, it was impossible to know how they would each process the information.

Thorne was fooling around with his guitar in his studio to distract himself. Ember heard a catchy riff float into the living room, where she was staring at her empty inbox and willing the report to materialize. His nervous excitement would probably manifest as a new hit single. Maybe he would dedicate the song to their child. Their little girl.

What would they name her? In recent days, Ember had discovered her own bottomless fascination with baby names.

Their meanings, origins, and trends consumed delightful hours of research. She had already settled on the perfect name but was keeping it to herself until they got through Selection. She whispered it aloud like a good-luck charm; its simple poetry filled her with joy.

Smokey's gruff barking interrupted her reverie. He hopped off the couch and scampered to the foyer. Someone was approaching the house. She jumped to her feet at the sound of an official *rap, rap* on the front door.

She eyed the peephole and felt her stomach do a double take. Two stony-faced men stood on the stoop, wearing black suits and ties. Their jackets were embossed with the yellow letters "FBI."

She stumbled backward. Smokey barked with unrelenting fervor. Thorne's guitar chords continued to ring out from his studio. With his soundproof headphones, he must not have heard the commotion.

Were they here for . . . her?

No. This couldn't be happening.

The room tipped. Smokey circled her legs, batting his bushy tail against her ankles with a little whine. He seemed to sense she was in distress.

"Hello?" one of the men called, ringing the doorbell. "FBI here."

The piercing chimes echoed through the house. Ember froze. She couldn't bear to open the door. She tried to steady herself, but her body had begun to shake.

Thorne emerged in the foyer with a perplexed expression. "What's going on?"

She motioned to the door. So this was how it happened. Right here in their living room. Her whole life destroyed. There would be nothing left—no husband, no daughter, nothing. The magnitude of the pending loss left her unable to speak.

Thorne walked past her and opened the door a crack. "Hi, can I help you?"

Ember shrank away, out of sight, as the men flashed their badges. "Noah Heller and Rick Pearson, FBI. Can we come in?"

"Heller . . . We spoke a few weeks ago about the Vault?"

"*Spoke* is a nice way of putting it."

"I remember," Thorne said coolly. "You're in charge of the investigation?"

"Yes, sir."

"What are you doing here?"

"My deputy and I wanted to come in person to present an idea," Heller said. "We think you can help us take it down."

Thorne opened the door wider. "In that case, come in."

It was only after the men entered that they noticed Ember near the stairs.

"Oh, hello ma'am," Heller said politely. "Didn't see you there."

So they weren't here to arrest her after all.

She stared at them in stark relief. Heller was an imposing man who possessed an air of authority; his buzz cut and beefy build gave away that he was ex-military. Pearson was younger and leaner, with a sharp, dispassionate gaze. Ember's arm hair prickled. She would not want to confront these men on hostile terms.

"Gentlemen," Thorne said proudly, "this is Ember Ryan, my fiancée."

"Pleased to meet you," they chimed, taking turns giving her stiff handshakes.

Ember attempted a smile but was pretty sure it came out like a grimace.

Thorne led them all into the living room, where the agents sat in wingback chairs, and Ember and Thorne faced them on the couch. Smokey hung out at her feet. She stroked his silky fur, feeling her panicked breathing gradually return to normal.

After waving off Thorne's offer of something to drink, Heller got right to the point: "We want to launch a sting operation. And we need you to be the lure."

Ember felt the color drain from her face. But they weren't looking at her.

Thorne cocked his head. "I'm listening."

Heller looked at Pearson to explain. "Are you familiar with the Vault's gametes on demand?" Pearson asked.

"I think so," Thorne said, turning to Ember. "Isn't that where someone can custom order another person's sperm or egg?"

She cleared her throat. "Yeah."

"Ember is my bio-guard," Thorne explained to the agents. "Her job is to prevent any of my cells from being stolen for those assholes to exploit."

"We'd hate to put you out of work," Heller said to her, with a smile that showed he would love nothing more.

"Oh, that would be just *fine*," Thorne said on her behalf. "We could finally stop worrying about this once and for all."

Ember clenched her jaw. "What exactly would he have to do?"

"It's pretty simple." Heller leaned forward in a conspiratorial manner. "We custom order your gametes from the Vault as an anonymous customer. The current market price is five million bucks. We wire them half up front in crypto, plus a premium for expedited delivery. It stays in a locked digital escrow account until they deliver the goods. Then they'll be incentivized to obtain your sample as quickly as possible. The rest of the money only comes when they make good on the order. So we'll make it easy for them—"

"Wait," Thorne interrupted. "How would you know if they sent you my gametes or someone else's? Couldn't they just pocket the cash and con you with any random person's sperm or egg?"

Ember already knew the answer, of course, but she wasn't about to speak up.

"Every order the Vault delivers comes with a file containing the entire decoded genome of the target," Heller explained. "Plus instructions on how to cross-check their DNA with the National Library of Genomes, the publicly searchable database containing the genomes of every US citizen. Remember the Healthy Genes, Healthy You program that launched back in the 2020s?"

"Not really," Thorne said.

"At first it was an opt-in program to amass a large library of people's DNA to study genetic diseases. But once Medicare went all ages, it became mandatory for everyone to join. It was a cost-saving measure for the government so diseases could be caught and treated earlier, when it's cheaper. You might remember your doctor drawing a dab of blood for the program—this was, like, twenty years ago. There was a big public health campaign: Sequencing Saves Lives."

Thorne was nodding in recognition. "Wasn't there a whole fuss about it?"

"Yep. A bunch of people resisted, but then they started getting fined or kicked off the national health plan until they came around."

Ember sighed quietly. That era when she was a teenager brought back memories of all the hand-wringing around privacy, autonomy, and government overreach. Many people, including her parents, had been outraged at the mandate to join the program. But it was a moot point now. The erosion of privacy—both technological and biological—had been steadily occurring for decades. No one bothered to oppose it anymore.

"So the client gets this file of the target's genome," Heller was saying, "the raw sequence of all twenty thousand genes, and is instructed to upload it to the national database. The search function only works in that direction—you can't type in a person's name and get their DNA, but you can upload a complete DNA sequence and find a match. It's the Vault's key to authenticating their product. Pretty ingenious, I have to say."

"Evil geniuses," Thorne mused. "What a concept."

"So, back to the sting," Heller went on. "We'll have you announce a surprise gig at a venue we choose, where we'll have our surveillance all set up. Until then, you stay absolutely hidden in your house—don't even walk the dog. Don't give them any way to target you in public without us watching. And then on the night of the gig, we have eyes on anyone who might try to take your used water bottle or Kleenex or whatever. We give them the perfect opportunity—Ember, you'll suck at your job that night—and then we intercept whoever tries to sneak off with your trash."

She crossed her legs. "I don't know . . ."

"Why not?" Thorne demanded. "This is a no-brainer, sweetie."

Her stomach churned. There was no logical reason to oppose them—other than the one she couldn't say. She felt utterly torn: if they failed to thwart the Vault, desirables like Thorne would continue to be targeted, leading to wrongful births. But if they succeeded, *she* would face the consequences for unleashing a force that had spiraled beyond her control.

"You'll be in great hands," Heller said confidently. "Top-notch security both in and outside the venue. We'll pack the place with plainclothes officers."

"I'm in," Thorne declared. "How do we get started?"

"Hang on," Ember interrupted. "Shouldn't we take some time to think first?"

"We'll be fine." He put his arm around her and shot the agents a smile that said, *"She's just a worrier,"* as though she were overthinking the obvious.

"Great!" Heller exclaimed. He leaned over to confer with Pearson just as Ember's dashboard lit up green with an incoming call. It was the clinic.

She leaped off the couch and raced out of the room: "Hello?"

"Ms. Ryan? This is Molly Mandel, one of the Selection Counselors at Precision Reproduction Associates. Do you have a minute?"

"Of course!"

"We have your embryos' scores back."

The woman spoke gently—too gently.

"And?"

"And some of them have inherited a serious genetic disease. We thought you should know as soon as possible."

CHAPTER 30

Quinn

"I'D HATE FOR *you to get lost on your way back.*"

Robert's veiled threat hung in Quinn's mind as she ambled to her car on the curb. He stood in the front window, watching her leave, his face obscured in shadows. She concentrated on making her movements as unhurried as possible: climbing into the passenger bay, adjusting her seatbelt over her giant belly, and programming her home address into the control panel. When the autonomous vehicle lurched forward, she waved goodbye as though they were friends parting for the afternoon.

It wasn't until she was halfway down the block that she fully exhaled.

Time was short. He was no doubt tracking her location via her lenses and timing her return. Once he caught any whiff of suspicion that she was deviating from their agreement, he would call the police and accuse her of fetal abduction—and by then, she needed to be getting the hell out of California.

Because what could she say if she had to defend herself? That she didn't trust him?

She still couldn't point to hard evidence to support her misgivings, but she knew one thing for sure: she wasn't crazy. There was no way she could hand Bubala over to him now. Not after he'd threatened to drug her and keep her captive in his house. *"For her own good,"* he would surely tell the authorities if she accused him of anything sinister. It would be his word against hers, and she'd already shot her own credibility by sneaking into his house. The only move left was to get to a state that wouldn't recognize her surrogacy contract.

The perfect destination materialized in her brain: Arizona. Her parents still lived there in her childhood home. Arizona state law forbade surrogacy, which was why she'd decamped to California upon getting hired by the agency. She remembered explaining to her parents at the time why she needed to move:

Whoever gives birth in this state is seen as the mother. So I have to leave if I want the job.

Now she wondered if the law would actually work in her favor. If she gave birth in the same hospital where she'd been born, in Phoenix, she could sign the birth certificate as Bubala's mother. There would be no other parent in the picture. Her heart swelled with certainty: it was the right thing to do, even if it meant that she could never return to California as long as she lived. Even if she had to hide from Robert and delete all her social media and completely start over. She put her hands on her belly and felt Bubala kicking away happily, ignorant of the peril they both faced.

But how to confess everything to her parents? Would they accept her with a baby who wasn't really hers—a Selected baby, no less? Would they let her stay there until she could get back on her feet somehow? If they shut her out . . .

In a desperate bid to reassure herself, she called her mom. They hadn't spoken in over a week. Mom's disapproval of her line of work had made their recent conversations feel forced. In the earlier months of her pregnancy, they had mostly avoided the topic and kept up their usual chatter. But that was no longer possible now that Quinn's days consisted of suffering through Braxton-Hicks contractions and waddling to the bathroom every twenty minutes.

As the car darted in and out of traffic, Mom's voice filled her ears: "Hey. Everything okay? I was just worrying about you."

"You were?"

"Of course. I'm your mother."

That word, with its sudden new relevance, made her throat tighten.

"I'm in trouble, Mom. I need to come home."

"Then come." She sounded lovingly firm.

"Do you want to know why?"

"It doesn't matter. We'll sort it out when you get here."

"Are you sure? I'll need help with the baby after I—I give birth . . ."

Quinn heard the shock in her voice. "You're keeping it? Is that allowed?"

"I have to, Mom. Trust me."

"All right. Just come. We'll figure it out."

"Thank you," Quinn whispered. "I love you."

"I love you too, sweetheart."

"Even when you're mad at me? Like, really mad?"

Mom snorted as though all the rage in the world couldn't dent the ferocity of her affection. "Even when I can't stand you, I love you. More than all the stars in the sky."

Quinn smiled, recalling their old bedtime patter. *"More than all the sand on the beach."* "I'll be there tonight. I'm going home to pack, and then it's a five-hour drive."

"Your father and I will be waiting."

* * *

Thirty minutes later, as Quinn willed the car to move faster, an unexpected call lit up her dashboard.

It was from an unknown number.

Had Robert already sicced the authorities on her under some bullshit pretense of her mental instability?

The dashboard blinked on and off, on and off, waiting for her to respond. As long as she wore her contact lenses, he still knew exactly where she was. She couldn't go dark yet. Not until she was all packed up and hightailing it to Phoenix. Ignoring the call would only heighten suspicion.

"Hello?" she answered reluctantly.

"Quinn?" came a terse woman's voice. "This is Ember Ryan."

"Ember?"

"Something's come up and I need to see you right away. In person."

"Sorry, this just isn't a good time—"

"It can't wait. Where should I meet you?"

"Um, I'll be home in half an hour, but—"

"Ping me your address. I'll see you there."

CHAPTER

31

Ember

THE DRIVE FROM Laguna Beach to Riverside took one hour, during which Ember tried to reason her way out of a massive panic attack. But anxiety never cooperated with logic. Instead, unspeakable questions tore through her mind, leaving her palms tingly and her breathing shallow. Thorne didn't know where she was going. Better to spare him from her nervous freak-out, if that's all it was. She was doing him a favor by saying she was going for a long hike in the canyon to process the bad news about their embryos.

Before she left, he'd pulled her in for one last hug. "Sure you don't want me to come?"'

"Yeah. I just need some time."

Time to figure out what the fuck is going on.

Quinn's apartment was a third-floor walk-up in an old brick building across the street from a permanently closed barbershop. A crushed beer bottle and napkins littered the front entrance. Inside, the carpeted hallway smelled like wet laundry that had been forgotten overnight. Ember raced up the steps two at a time, panting by the time she arrived at unit 3B.

An extremely pregnant Quinn opened the door. She looked flustered and sweaty, clutching unfolded shirts in one hand and a toiletry bag in the other.

"Hi," Ember said. "Sorry to interrupt . . . Can I come in?"

"Um, okay, but—" Quinn motioned to her suitcase on the floor. "I'm actually about to leave."

"This won't take long." Ember stepped around the open suitcase, which was already filled with sweatpants, underwear, and framed pictures.

Quinn quickly closed the door and returned to packing. "What's up? I really don't have much time."

Ember remained standing. "Thorne and I made embryos a few weeks ago. We're about to do Selection, but the clinic called earlier with some bad news."

"Sorry to hear that," Quinn said distractedly, emptying her drawers of pajamas.

"It's the male embryos. Some of them inherited a rare X-linked disease."

Quinn tossed her PJs into the suitcase. "And?"

"And I remember you told me that you're carrying a girl . . . because the boys in the batch had inherited a—"

"A rare X-linked disease, yeah," Quinn finished impatiently. "There's like hundreds of them."

Ember forced out the question. "Was it hemophilia A?"

Quinn's busy hands froze. "How could you know that?"

"My father had it."

Quinn looked startled. "That's a weird coincidence."

"Did you know that it only affects one in five thousand guys? And it's passed down through the egg? *Only through the egg?*" She spit out the last part, her heart thrashing against her ribs.

"Right . . ."

"Who hired you?" Ember demanded. "The gay guy you said was obsessed with Thorne?"

"His name's Robert Roy."

"I need to see a picture."

"Oh, he's not on social. He doesn't like pictures."

Ember frantically searched her own dashboard for a certain photo from her personal library and then projected it onto the nearest wall in shared mode. It was a picture of a good-looking guy with an impish smile, standing on the Santa Monica Pier.

Quinn gasped. "Oh my God. How do you know Robert?"

"Robert?" Ember rolled her eyes. *Mason, that devious motherfucker.* But divulging his real identity would only blow up her own. "I dated that scumbag for way too long. The night I dumped him, he broke my arm trying to stop me from leaving."

Ember recoiled at the memory of the last time they'd seen each other, almost nine months ago. When he'd showed up on her doorstep in Silver Lake after drone stalking her. That kiss. Oh God, the kiss. She remembered now the way he had aggressively thrust his tongue into her mouth. Trolling for her cells to spit into a tube and take straight back to their lab she had abandoned—just as she'd abandoned him.

"What do you mean?" Quinn stared at her in alarm. "What's going on?"

Ember gazed at her near-bursting belly.

"It was never his baby with Thorne. It's his baby with me."

PART 3

CHAPTER

32

Quinn

EMBER WAS STILL saying something, but Quinn heard only buzzing. Her hands flew to her stomach.

"His baby with me."

Bile spiked into her throat as she dug her nails into her abdomen. So Bubala was a nonconsensual child after all. A crime scene in her womb. Equal parts innocence and horror. And the phantom Evan? Nothing but a pretense, as she'd long suspected. Now she finally understood why.

"I knew he was a fucking liar."

"Oh, you have no idea." Ember averted her eyes as though the sight of Quinn's belly was obscene. She slumped against the wall, drawing her knees up to her chest.

"But why? Why would he do this to a *child*?"

"To trap me." Her hands shielded her face. "He obviously wants to destroy my life with anyone else."

"But this is—" Quinn paused, unable to come up with a word that captured the intensity of her disgust.

"Psychotic?" Ember suggested. "Evil? Insane?"

"Yeah. I just can't believe anyone would go to these lengths out of jealousy."

"Then you don't know him very well. He's probably telling himself some story about how this is what I always wanted, and he's finally giving it to me, so it's somehow justified." She shuddered in horror. "A long time ago, we used to argue about having a kid. I can't believe I used to want one with him."

"Jesus." Quinn rubbed her temples in a daze. "Now I feel like I don't know anything about him at all."

"You probably don't." Ember bit her lip. "How many weeks are you?"

"Thirty-five and a half."

"So the baby could be born anytime!" Her tone evoked the pitch of someone realizing a nuke was hurtling toward touchdown.

"Theoretically. But . . ." Quinn hesitated, considering how much to confess, and then decided what the hell, everything was on fire anyway. "I was going to raise her myself, actually."

"You were?" Ember stared at her, aghast. "Why?"

"I thought she had nobody else. That's why I'm packing to go to Phoenix, to be with my parents . . ."

"But what about . . . *him*?"

"Fuck him. He threatened to keep me hostage in his house and drug me. He doesn't deserve her."

Ember didn't seem entirely surprised. "And you didn't go straight to the cops?"

"I want to, but I'm worried they won't believe me. He's already told my doctor I was having paranoid delusions, and I did just break into his house and snoop around . . . so I have to either run away or go along with him until I give birth."

"So run. Far."

"But wait, why don't we just go to the cops together now?" Quinn spread her hands excitedly. "We can tell them everything, and they'll listen to you!"

"No!" Ember cried. "Not yet. I mean, we have to prove I'm right first, or they won't take us seriously. You know the blood test you did? We need the lab to repeat it with me."

"But there's no time. He's expecting me back in a few hours."

"Then the cops will have to wait." Ember's voice was strangely firm. "First let's get you out of here."

"Fine." Quinn yanked open her sock drawer with renewed urgency. "Let me finish packing, and then I can hit the road."

"You're driving?" Ember frowned. "I don't think so. I'm sure he's drone stalking your retinas. You need to fly there if you want to lose him."

"Seriously?" Quinn squeezed her eyes shut. The thought of her retinas being tracked in the atmosphere without her knowledge made her heartburn return with a vengeance. "But I was going to turn off my lenses so he couldn't track my signal. I shared my location with him earlier."

Ember wrinkled her nose. "Another pretense. He's usually a step ahead."

"But a plane ticket will be super expensive. Plus I would need to go to the airport this minute."

"I'll buy you one and take you myself." Ember seemed to perk up at the thought. Energy seized her fingertips as she began typing rapid-fire on an invisible keyboard.

Quinn studied her for a moment, sizing up her pale face, mussed blonde hair, and creased forehead.

"Are you just trying to get rid of me?" she blurted. "I mean, not like I would blame you."

Ember lifted her eyes. They appeared as green and clear as sea glass.

"Not at all. I just want to protect you. Not let him get a chance to do to you what he did to me . . ." She extended her right arm and pointed to the underside of her elbow, where Quinn saw two pink scars the size of cigarette burns. "From the surgery I had after it broke. I needed pins inserted."

"Holy shit."

Ember seemed to push away the memory, still typing, while Quinn tossed the last remaining clothes she owned into the suitcase, no longer caring if anything was folded or organized. At the touch of a side button, the automatic zipper deployed and traveled the perimeter of the bag, securing her belongings inside.

Soon Ember glanced up with a sigh of relief. "Okay, I got you a ticket on the 6:20 PM flight to Phoenix out of LAX on SonicAir. We can make it if we leave right now."

"Then what are we waiting for?" Quinn grabbed the bag's handle. "Let's go."

CHAPTER

33

Ember

"LET ME TAKE that for you." Ember dragged the suitcase down three flights of stairs as Quinn struggled to keep up. Then they burst out into the harsh sunlight and hurried to her car, a used black sedan that she'd bought in the aftermath of her breakup. Ember heaved the suitcase into the trunk and opened the door for Quinn, who was nervously blocking her face from any invisible drones.

"Wait," Quinn said before stepping inside. "Should I cancel my location sharing now? I don't want him to track me to the airport. But then he'll know I'm going back on our plan."

"Yes. You have to. And lie low in the car." Ember squinted up at the cloudless blue sky. "No looking out the window. Those sensors are scary good."

"What if it finds me in Phoenix? Can it do that?"

"I'll order you the thing I have." Ember pointed to her own eyes. "He was tracking me too, but then I had my lenses treated with a biometric shield that masks my retinas. It's not available to consumers, only security professionals. When you get to Phoenix, stay inside until I send it to you."

Quinn stared at her gratefully. "You would do that for me?"

"Of course. I'm going to help you until this nightmare is over—for you, anyway."

"Thank you so much." Quinn tapped a few times on her dashboard. "Done. Now he can't see my GPS."

"Let's go."

They climbed into the horseshoe-shaped passenger bay, and Ember commanded the car to head to LAX, optimizing for back roads as much as possible to escape freeway traffic.

"We should be there in a little under an hour."

"You think I'll make the flight?"

"There's a good chance."

As the car swerved onto the road and sped out of the neighborhood, Quinn lay her head down on the empty area between them and shifted heavily onto her side, grunting at the effort.

Ember glanced away from her massive stomach spilling over the edge of the seat.

My baby.

Those two words did not fully compute.

Apparently she had been naive to think she could ditch her past and start a whole new life with Thorne. The irony of their pairing did not escape her. If she hadn't joined him on tour, publicly appearing as his biosecurity guard, Mason might not have found her and sicced the drone on her. Then he wouldn't have showed up at her house and thrust his disgusting tongue into her mouth.

What the hell was she supposed to do now?

The right thing would be to take responsibility somehow. First she would have to prevent Mason from taking custody. If Quinn gave birth in Phoenix, and he didn't know, Ember could swoop in and claim her baby. And then . . .? Maybe place her for adoption to a loving home. Thorne clearly had enough money to put in a trust to safeguard the child's future. But adoption hardly ever happened anymore now that people could so easily conceive their own children. She wondered if any of those old agencies still existed.

Or surrender her to the state? Drop her off at a police station in a blanket, and drive off into the night? Ember tried to imagine herself with a newborn baby in her arms, a baby who was her own flesh and blood, and then literally turning her back forever. Reclaiming her life with Thorne as though nothing had changed—except the guilt that would demolish her whole. As much as she hated Mason, the child wasn't at fault. It seemed cruel to saddle the poor thing with a lonely and fractured upbringing in foster care. Ember imagined her growing up unloved, a burden on the system, shuffling between caregivers. The product of a heinous crime, her life stained by pity, gossip, and abandonment.

No. There had to be another way.

Ember snuck a peak at Quinn sprawled beside her, eyes tightly closed. Copper ringlets surrounded her pudgy face, making her seem younger than her twenty-something years. Quinn was practically still a child herself, eager and innocent. What if . . . what if Ember let her take the baby, as she'd been planning to? The idea was tempting. But Mason would eventually track her down, whether it took him a week, a month, or a year. Ember's life would be spared, but Quinn's would be destroyed. He'd press charges for fetal abduction, and then Quinn would go to prison, and the child would be forced to grow up with him as a father—all because Ember had sought the easy way out.

She rested her head against the window, digging her nails into her palms. The nuclear option would be to call Heller and Pearson at the FBI. She could blow the cover off the Vault, turn Mason in, protect Quinn and the baby. But then she'd have to turn *herself* in too. Thorne, her freedom, her future —all would be lost. The possibility made her clutch her throat; a cold sweat broke out on her hairline. Of course, Mason was counting on her not to go that route, knowing her self-preservation instincts were as keen as his own. She realized he'd wanted to share the news with her, in his own evasive way—the baby shoes on *her* doorstep, not Thorne's.

She wondered what he was planning to do after the baby's birth. The message from the shoes seemed all too clear: he wanted to throw a massive wrench into her life. He would try to use the baby to wreck her happiness with Thorne, confident that he was acting with impunity. He was too smart to think their relationship could ever be salvaged. No—this was pure nihilism. He would prefer that she hate him forever, as long as she was miserable—as miserable as she had made him by leaving.

Think. There had to be some other way to salvage her life that didn't compromise Quinn or the baby. But what if there was no solution? Real life didn't conform to desires, no matter how desperate. Innocent people suffered. Often there was no satisfying end, just a string of painful traumas and immeasurable grief. The thought of telling all to the FBI—and never seeing Thorne again—cleaved her heart in half. No way.

Quinn's voice interrupted her thoughts. "How will we get the DNA test done? I can't *wait* to go to the police."

A bolt of pain shot through Ember's jaw. She realized she was grinding her teeth so hard, she'd hit a nerve. "We'll have to wait until I can visit you in Phoenix," she said slowly. "More important right now is for you to get there safely."

Quinn peered up to catch her eye. "Can you come out soon?"

"I'll try."

"Because once we get the results back, he's toast. I can't wait to see him arrested."

Except we can't go to the cops, Ember thought. *Because if we do, he'll tell them about me.*

She pinched her shirt off her collarbone. The fabric was soaked with sweat, as though she were running a race that had no finish line, just a never-ending series of blind turns and dead ends.

"There's something I don't understand." Quinn was furrowing her brow. "Isn't he worried you'll report him as soon as he tells you about the baby? I assume he's planning to tell you at some point, right? If it's your kid?"

Ember shrugged. She wished she could share how their mutual stalemate had trapped her in a powerless hellscape.

"Shit." Quinn blinked several times. "Speak of the devil. He's calling me right now. He must have seen me go dark."

"Don't answer it."

"He's going to freak out."

"So let him."

"There." Quinn winced. "I blocked his number. He's gonna lose it."

Ember pressed her nose to the window. They were flying down Freeway 105 in the carpool lane at breakneck speed. Of its own accord, the car activated its blinker and seamlessly crossed multiple lanes toward their exit. Traffic backed up as the airport neared.

"We're almost there," Ember said. "You're going to make it."

Quinn's face looked as white as the faux leather seats. "What if he finds me?"

"He won't. But if he does manage to reach you, do *not* tell him I'm helping you, okay?"

"Of course not."

"And you'll let me know when you get there?"

"For sure."

Before long the airport came into view, with its towering parking garages and crisscrossing monorails and thunderous jets landing overhead. As traffic slowed, the car stalled in the departure lane for SonicAir. They were still a good mile away from the drop-off point.

"It'll go quick," Ember said, more confidently than she felt. "You'll be out of here in no time."

Quinn drummed her fingers on her knees. "Maybe I should get out and make a run for it . . ."

"You could barely get down the stairs. I was thinking of putting you in one of those automatic wheelchairs."

"Fair enough." Quinn opened her mouth to speak, then closed it again. She seemed to be having trouble getting the words out.

"What is it?"

"Are you going to take the baby?"

Ember cringed. Every time she thought of the child forged out of her own cells, without her consent, by the person she most despised, a fresh wave of disgust walloped her. How could she ever be a mother to such a kid, even if she forced herself to try?

"I don't know," she admitted.

"Because, to be honest . . ." Quinn hesitated. "I think I love her."

"You do?"

"I know I'm not supposed to. But I'm the one bringing her into this world, and I can't help wanting to protect her."

Ember pursed her lips. Quinn's earnestness was touching—and a grave strategic error. She had no idea whom they were up against and how far he would go to crush his opposition.

"I would take her—if you want," Quinn added, mistaking Ember's silence for an opening. "Even just, like, temporarily, while you figure things out."

Just then, a traffic light turned green, and they accelerated toward the drop-off curb. The car pulled into an open slot and parked beside a busy sidewalk. Travelers from all directions were scurrying toward the rotating glass doors and disappearing inside.

"We'll see," Ember said. "But first, you need to get on the plane."

CHAPTER

34

Lily

"WHAT DID YOU just say?" Shane Hart cocked his head at Lily in front of the entire *Vanguard* staff at the Monday pitch meeting. The veteran reporters eyed her with mostly sympathetic expressions, though there were a few annoyed scowls. Everyone sat around the long glass table in the conference room, their faces darkened by the low clouds outside brewing a summer thunderstorm. Lily wished for the sky to erupt with a violent clap just to buy a short distraction. But the stillness was unrelenting. She had never felt more alone in a roomful of people.

"My piece fell through," she mumbled. "I'm really sorry."

She stared down at her hands in her lap as her cheeks burned. Then, astonishingly, Radia's voice rescued her from Shane's silence.

"So did mine. My source ghosted me. It really sucks because I loved my idea." Radia caught Lily's eye across the table. "And yours."

"Thanks," Lily said. A buttery warmth spread through her. Emboldened, she lifted her chin to Shane. "We really did try our best."

Now it seemed clear that neither of them would land the job at the end of the fellowship, and this understanding came as a surprising relief. Selected people failed like anyone else. What could be more human? Lily exhaled as the last sliver of envy toward her genetically superior friend melted away. If they had to disappoint the boss and humiliate themselves before their idols, better to do it together.

Before Shane could respond, Radia cleared her throat. Her eyes flashed at Lily with a strange excitement, and inexplicably, she grinned. "Good thing we have another idea."

We?

"And what's that?" Shane demanded. He did not look amused. "The holographics team is already working on packaging for the next issue. Now we have *two* holes to fill."

"Lily and I want to do some old-school immersive journalism," Radia announced. "Are you guys aware of the new law that Congress passed about Selected kids? It didn't get a lot of press because of the Europa moon landing."

Shane shook his head as he tipped back a can of seltzer. A few drops trickled down his goatee and soaked into his silk shirt. Today's design showed a parade of endangered elephants clasping trunks and tails in a row across his chest.

"What's the new law?" he asked.

Lily widened her eyes at Radia with curiosity. She hadn't heard of it either. But maybe Radia was about to redeem them both with a byline after all. *Go for it,* she thought. *I'll write about anything.*

Radia spoke with confident eagerness, as though she knew the idea was a slam-dunk. "So this totally flew under the radar, but it's a big deal. As of last week, Selected kids who are eighteen or older can, for the first time, access our own embryonic medical records from the national database. Previously, the records were only included in our parents' files, but after a bunch of lobbying from frustrated folks whose parents wouldn't or couldn't share the information, Congress agreed to grant access." Radia stared meaningfully at Lily. "So you and I can go and see what our scores were before we were Selected. *And* we can see the scores of all the other embryos from our batch who were *not* chosen."

Lily chuckled uncomfortably. "Oh, that's okay. I . . . already know mine," she lied.

"And the *other* embryos too?"

"Oh, well, not that. But who cares?"

"I do," Radia insisted. "Because I would finally be able to understand my parents' choice in Selecting *me*. It's not only about seeing my raw scores and predictions, which obviously I want to see for myself. But haven't you also wondered, like, what made *you* stand out above all the others?"

"Not really."

Radia pursed her lips with visible irritation.

"I mean, sure," Lily added. "Sort of." She glanced at Shane to see how he was taking the pitch. To her chagrin, he was rubbing his beard.

"Could be interesting," he allowed, which basically qualified as a rave response.

"Thank you." Radia flashed Lily a smile. *We got this.* Lily forced one in return.

"But," Shane said, "we need to mine it for conflict and drama to make it feel big. How do you plan to do that?"

Radia thought for a few seconds. "The drama will probe the meaning of personal identity, in the zeitgeisty context of precision reproduction, genetics, and choice."

"Oh, cut the crap. This isn't English class. How will you make this *story* interesting to people who don't give two shits about hyper-privileged Selected kids?"

She reddened. "I guess people could hate-read it."

"Now you're talking. We need to get those blinks up. But what will make them share it?"

"Well, we could lean into shame and stigma. For example, I'll be super open with you: I think I have a genetic predisposition for depression. I've been treated, but I've always wondered why my parents chose me if they knew that going in. All they've told me is that I was Selected to *be successful.* So it's like, at what cost? What responsibility do parents have to their future kid during Selection? That's something I would find out about myself and explore in my piece."

Shane's impatience appeared to soften. "Next month is mental health awareness. We could do a tie-in."

"Absolutely."

"So," he turned to Lily, "what about you?"

"Oh, I'm good." Lily shrugged. "It's Radia's idea. She should run with it."

"Why not go bigger, though?" Radia suggested excitedly, spreading her palms flat on the table. "Our generation is coming of age now with access to more information than anyone like us has ever had. Why not make this a capital-M moment and run a series of first-person essays? It's *so* on brand. We could call it 'The Reckoning of Generation Gamma: Selected Kids Confront Their Embryonic Pasts.'"

"It's not kids, though, right?" Shane asked. "Because then we'd need a legal review, and the attorneys are anal as hell."

"No, but 'Selected people' doesn't have the same ring."

He waved a hand. "Something for the copy editors to figure out."

Lily hoped no one noticed her slinking lower in her chair.

But then Shane blasted the heat of his attention back on her. "If we do a series, we need more voices. What's your angle?"

"Um . . . I don't have one."

"Yet," Radia said quickly, trying to come to her rescue. "We need to do the reporting first. Why don't we go pull our records together?"

Lily wrung her hands under the table. "But I was born in a different state . . ."

"It doesn't matter. All Selection records are stored in a central genomics database. We just have to go in person to the local health department for a retina scan to get access. It's not far—on Broadway and Chambers."

"I would need these pieces filed within the week," Shane said. "So I suggest going as soon as possible."

"For sure." Radia grinned at Lily. "In fact, why not go right after this meeting?"

"Great," Shane said before Lily could decline. What was she supposed to say? *"I'm Unforeseen! I don't have any Selection records!"* Plus, she thought dryly, stigma was already Radia's angle.

"Awesome!" Radia exclaimed. "Can't wait." As Shane moved on to status updates from other journalists, a text popped up on Lily's dashboard: *Our first Vanguard bylines coming in hot!!! Can you believe it???*

So pumped, Lily typed back. She didn't add: *Way to dig me an even bigger hole.*

CHAPTER 35

Quinn

QUINN HURRIED THROUGH the airport's revolving door as fast as her feet would allow. The plane boarded in thirty minutes. She tightened one arm underneath her enormous belly and tried to make a run for the security checkpoint, which ended up more like an exaggerated waddle. She had forgotten her pregnancy belt amidst her rush to pack and the shock of Ember's arrival. No matter. Once she arrived at her parents' house in Phoenix, she would stay put until the birth.

Other travelers zipped past her toward the line much more quickly, and by the time she took her place in the back, her hopes sank. It snaked around at least two long ropes. She checked the time. Only twenty-four minutes until boarding. Cutting it close was an understatement. What would she do if she missed the flight? Wait in the airport on standby until the next one? Sleep in a chair overnight? She wondered if that was even allowed. Going back to her apartment was *not* an option, now that she'd ditched Robert for good.

Thinking of him sent ice through her veins. She didn't want to imagine how enraged he must be at this very moment. But after what he had done to Ember, satisfaction prevailed.

He would not take this baby. He didn't deserve her and never had. Despite his repeated attempts at gaslighting, her own gut feeling had been correct all along. Once Ember visited her—hopefully soon—and they completed the maternity bloodwork, their case against him would be rock solid. The police would arrest him, and Bubala would be free to grow up far away, in a home where she would be treated with love, and not weaponized as a pawn in some sick revenge ploy.

Quinn wondered whether Ember would step up and raise her with Thorne in their seaside mansion, with all the luxuries and burdens of fame, so foreign that Quinn could hardly picture what such a childhood would look like. Flying on private jets to far-flung shows? Growing up with nannies and chefs and security guards? Attending private schools and mingling with other rich and famous kids, an evergreen topic of tabloid fascination?

Or maybe not. Maybe the crime of her existence would deter Ember, understandably, from upsetting their lives to take her in. Then Bubala might wind up with Quinn in Phoenix, living a quiet life in her parents' modest two-bedroom bungalow. They would have to make room in their hearts and home for a child who had nowhere else to turn. Eventually, she would learn to call them grandma and grandpa, and the four of them would share the single bathroom until Quinn saved up enough money to move out. Bubala would attend public schools, wear secondhand clothes, and go on the same family vacations Quinn had taken as a kid, camping in Monument Valley and boating on Lake Havasu.

Someone tapped her shoulder, and Quinn jumped. She hadn't realized she'd reached the front of the security line—and just in time. The guard directed her to look into an eye-level camera that served as the identification portal. At the same time, she blinked on her dashboard and transferred her ticket into the system.

Up ahead, the baggage screening area was moving swiftly. People were hauling their suitcases up onto the conveyor belt and marching through the infrared scanners in a steady stream. Excitement bubbled up in her stomach. She was going to make the flight as long as she didn't get chosen for one of those awful random suitcase inspections.

The machine scanning her retinas suddenly flashed red and blared a horn, and out of nowhere, two TSA agents in uniform appeared. She glanced behind her to see who was in trouble, but then they each clasped her elbows. Their touch was light but jarring, and she stumbled backward in surprise.

They steered her out of line. "We need you to come with us."

"I can't!" she cried. "I'll miss my flight!"

"Sorry, this isn't optional." One agent grabbed her suitcase and rolled it for her while the other kept his hand firmly on her elbow. "We need you to answer a few questions."

"Am I under arrest?"

"No, but—"

"Then I should be free to go." She shook off the man's grip and lunged for her suitcase, but he easily restrained her. A hysterical cry rose in her throat. People walking by stopped to watch the scene. She choked back her sob, embarrassed.

"Look," the other man said, "this will be a lot easier if you cooperate, okay? It shouldn't take long."

She pressed her lips together and nodded reluctantly. They marched her down a corridor faster than she could comfortably keep up with them, stopping before an unmarked white door. Inside, another man in uniform was sitting at a table under a bright light. The glossy black wall behind him appeared to be a one-way mirror. The guards motioned for her to sit in the empty chair facing him, and promptly left the room.

"Can you confirm your name and date of birth, please?" He narrowed his eyes at her belly.

"Quinn Corrigan," she said, trying to stay calm. "June thirteenth, 2030. I don't understand what's going on."

"Are you the gestational surrogate for Robert Roy?"

Quinn felt the blood leave her face. "Yes."

The man's tone was grave. "I'm sorry, but you've been placed on a no-fly list."

"What . . .?" Quinn sputtered. "I'm not a terrorist!"

"Mr. Roy has warned police and transit authorities that a fetal kidnapping might be underway. A statewide Amber alert has been issued."

She gasped. "Am I under arrest?"

"No, no charges are being filed, but since you're pregnant with his child, we can legally detain you here in the meantime."

"The meantime? Until when?"

"He comes to pick you up."

CHAPTER

36

Ember

"READY TO GO live?" Noah Heller asked. He sat across from Ember and Thorne at their glass kitchen table, all of them staring intently at Thorne's social media profile in draft mode. For the last half hour, they had finessed the language and the visuals that would announce his surprise new show—the lure the FBI hoped would smoke out the perp behind the Vault.

Hey, Thornies! the post read, alongside a picture of him strumming his iconic Strat guitar. *It's time to honor my roots, and I can't think of a better place than the legendary Troubadour, which helped kick off my career many moons ago. So come join me for an intimate show THIS SATURDAY NIGHT at 8:00 PM. Tickets are super limited so get yours now. Can't wait to see you there!"*

Thorne squeezed Ember's hand. "Good to go?"

She hesitated. "Sure you want to do this?"

"We have literally nothing to lose."

Except everything. "Okay."

With a rapid double-blink, Thorne published the announcement for his seventeen million fans and then leaned back with satisfaction. "Come at us, motherfuckers."

Heller whooped. "Game on."

Ember barely feigned enthusiasm. "Great, but how can we be sure the right person will get a ticket if there's only space for, like, five hundred people?" She wasn't sure if she was rooting for the sting to succeed or fail. Admittedly, her greatest desire was to sabotage the man who had viciously wronged her. She wanted to see him pay for the rest of his life—just not at the expense of her own.

Heller rubbed his thumb in circles with his pointer finger. "Moolah. This morning, we wired two and a half million in crypto to a locked escrow account for the Vault. It expires in seven days unless we receive proof that Thorne's cells were obtained."

Thorne uttered a disgusted sound. "You mean *stolen*."

Heller nodded. "So whoever it is will make damn sure they're at your show, even if they have to spend a fortune on the resale market to be there. Whatever it takes to be up close and personal with your sweat and spit and snot."

Ember wrinkled her nose. "Yum."

While Heller and Thorne launched into the details of the operation—the placement of the plainclothes agents, the hidden camera surveillance, the mobile headquarters they would set up in a trailer outside—Ember's mind shifted yet again to Quinn.

Almost twenty-four hours had elapsed since the airport drop-off. The flight to Phoenix landed uneventfully, but Quinn had gone dark. Ember checked her dashboard every couple of minutes, constantly distracted by the thought that *maybe now, or now, or now* a text would pop up, confirming her arrival at her parents' house. But as the hours passed without any contact, Ember's hope was beginning to fray. Few things in life were as frustrating as sheer helplessness. There was nothing Ember could do to find her if she didn't want to be found.

Probably took off her lenses to escape his harassment, she reassured herself. And now she was probably too scared to put them back on. Who could blame her? But in another day or two or three, she would surely get impatient with being cut off from the world and come back online to alert Ember to her whereabouts. After that, Ember had no idea what came next. Go visit her in Phoenix? Confirm her maternity with a blood test? Notify the authorities—or not? Take the baby after the birth—or not?

One thing was clear: she needed to tell Thorne.

But the timing couldn't have been worse.

"Look," Thorne remarked, pointing at his dashboard projected on the wall. "Over twenty thousand 'likes' already."

"Good," Heller said. "Word of the show will spread fast. There's no way they'll miss it."

"What else do I need to do now?"

"Stay put. I'm serious. It's only for the next four days. The show has to be the only time anyone will catch you out in public."

"So I'm basically under house arrest."

"Yeah, so the rest of your life can be free."

"*A*-men." Thorne's eyes sparkled, but Ember saw that an uncharacteristic crease cut into his forehead. It had deepened since Quinn's sudden appearance at the café, as the Vault preyed on his worst fears. Then the distressing news from the clinic about some of their own embryos had further rattled him. Now the Selection process would have to wait until after the sting. Ember wondered if he would still even want a baby with her at that point. If they did get through this weekend unscathed, then what?

She closed her eyes and tried to imagine a future in which they were raising their own loved and wanted child along with the nonconsensual one who never should have existed. No, that would be atrocious for everyone. It would have to be one or the other—or no family at all, if the sting doomed them first.

Thorne was pacing anxiously around the kitchen, listening to Heller discuss the hidden cameras he would wear onstage, in the bathroom, and wherever else he went inside the venue.

"Do you think I could get attacked?"

"It's unlikely. Our perp is looking to make a discreet move. And we're going to give them the perfect opportunity . . ."

Thorne chewed a hangnail as he listened to the plan, still pacing like a caged lion.

Four days to go.

Ember couldn't bear to break the news about Quinn and the baby just yet. He had enough to keep him up at night. She would spare him one less crisis while he geared up for what could be the most consequential gig of his career.

Because he was the prime target, and the show had to go on.

CHAPTER

37

Lily

"SO WHY DID your story fall through?" Radia asked after the editorial meeting. She and Lily were walking to the health department on Broadway and Chambers streets, ten blocks north of *Vanguard*'s headquarters.

Lily shrugged. "My source didn't want to cooperate."

"Same. Such a bummer. Mine was this housewife I tracked down in Texas, whose son is already on his third set of transplanted lungs from cystic fibrosis, and he's only sixteen. So sad, right?"

"That's nuts. All because she didn't want to do IVG?"

"She didn't, like, believe in it. And regrets it now but is too embarrassed to go on the record."

"I mean, to be fair, she would get a ton of hate. Can you imagine the comments?"

"Sure, but then the cycle in those communities just keeps repeating itself." Radia sighed. "Oh well."

A brisk wind whipped between skyscrapers and rattled their coats. Lily squeezed her arms to her chest and shivered. She was dreading their arrival at the genetics database for their new assignment. Talk about embarrassing. Was she going to just blurt it out? *"I'm Unforeseen! So sad, right?"*

"So why didn't your source come through?" Radia asked. "I thought Shane was going to let you offer anonymity."

"I did. But she freaked out anyway. Made me kill the whole thing."

"How annoying. What a bitch."

Lily stopped short. "She's my mom." As soon as the words escaped, her hand flew to her mouth. Radia's scorn had touched a nerve, but the admission felt surprisingly good. Like coming up for air.

"Your *mom*? Who's currently pregnant?"

Lily nodded. "The first clinic turned her away because of a felony in her past. She was in jail when I was little." Radia gasped as her large brown eyes grew even larger. Discovering someone else's scandal was like stumbling on a forbidden buffet.

"Holy *shit*. What did she *do*?"

"Honestly? I'm not really sure."

Radia snorted. "Come on. You can tell me."

"I swear. There's the official story my parents told me, but I've never been able to verify it. I even went to the prison on my trip, but her records are sealed."

"Why don't you just ask them directly?"

"Great idea." Lily rolled her eyes. "I never thought of that."

"And what do they say?"

"It's always the same song and dance about how she shot an intruder with an illegal gun. But then she went to jail for ten freaking years. And whenever it comes up, they both get super quiet and change the subject."

Lily could see the wheels turning behind Radia's eyes. "Sounds sketchy."

"I know!" Even if Lily never got to the bottom of it, sharing her frustration with Radia felt like a watershed moment. All throughout her teenage years, after her family had moved to New Jersey and started over, she'd kept her uneasiness to herself, never wanting to start rumors among her friends and teachers or, God forbid, leak to the press, given who she was.

But now, she finally felt enough like her own person—and not just *his* daughter or *her* daughter—to acknowledge the past out loud.

"So what are you going to do now?" Radia asked.

"Nothing. I think I just need to let it go and move on."

"That's no fun," Radia teased. "Were you Selected for maturity or something?"

"Actually . . ." Lily tasted the bitter words on her tongue but didn't say them: *I'm Unforeseen*. She pictured Radia's shocked horror. In New York society, such a confession was on par with saying she'd never been vaccinated or taught to read. Maybe Radia would overcompensate with a pointed show of tolerance. That would be even more embarrassing.

As they turned the corner, a lacquered black building came into view, a spiral feat of carbon fiber that towered elegantly over the old stainless steel behemoths in the neighborhood. Lily's pace dragged. It was the Justice Tower, the famous new building that housed all of the important city and state functions—including the health department.

"Actually what?" Radia prompted.

"Do you ever wonder what's really *you*?" Lily asked. "I mean, when you achieve something, is it because you were Selected to do it, or is it *you*, whatever that means?"

"Like where do my predispositions end and I begin?"

"Exactly."

"I think about it all the time. That's partly why I'm dying to see my scores. Like if I *wasn't* Selected for physical stamina, and I'm really good at running anyway, do I get to be prouder of myself? Or the reverse . . . If I *was* Selected for it, are my varsity championships meaningless?"

"Maybe it's sometimes better not to be Selected?" Lily ventured. "So there's no preconceived notions? Just a blank slate."

Radia gave a dismissive wave. "No one's a blank slate. We all come into this world with our own set of tools, whether your parents choose them or not."

"I'm just saying, maybe leaving it to nature isn't *always* so bad. It's not like Einstein was Selected."

"*'Nature is a cruel and fickle mistress,'*" Radia declared, parroting the words of a young biotech star who was the subject of a recent *Vanguard* profile—a total bro who took himself way too seriously and only wore clothes made of mushrooms.

Lily laughed in spite of herself. "I guess."

"He's a douchebag, but he's not wrong." Radia abruptly stopped and pointed. "Look."

Across the street, the gold revolving doors of the Justice Tower loomed.

They had arrived.

CHAPTER

38

Quinn

INSIDE THE AIRPORT's holding room, Quinn whipped around as soon as the lock unclicked. The door opened, and the man she knew as Robert Roy dominated the frame. A lock of hair stuck to his sweaty forehead, and his starched white Oxford shirt flapped open at his chest, as though he'd been running. Now an undercurrent of fury stiffened his posture, but he gazed at her with the perfect facsimile of concern.

She met his stare with stony hostility, apologizing for nothing. His eyes narrowed slightly, and then the briefest of smiles flashed across his lips. So there it was. Their new terms of engagement. No longer would they entertain a pretense of friendship. Her attempted escape was a declaration of war, and he would marshal all his artillery to win. He obviously expected to crush her.

Bring it on, she thought. Little did he know about her secret weapon. Once Ember's maternity was proven, it would be game over. He didn't stand a chance of taking Bubala. Her tongue itched to blurt out the accusation, but she made herself hold back. No point in firing her one and only missile too soon. Her credibility was already shot; he'd covered that base. But not for much longer.

Clock's ticking, motherfucker.

The police officer sat a few feet away, her temporary buffer of protection. He rose and walked around his desk to shake Robert's hand.

"Thank you for coming on such short notice."

"Of course," Robert said smoothly. "Sorry to trouble you. She'll be in good hands now."

Okay, she thought. *I'll play.* If he was casting her as the crazy surrogate, she might as well mess with him. She stood wearily, cupping her heavy stomach. "Oh my God," she moaned, doubling over. "Oh, shit."

"What's wrong?" the officer cried.

She squeezed her eyes shut and grabbed her lower back. "I think I'm having a contraction."

Robert rushed to her side. "But it's four weeks early!"

She sank to her knees in mock pain. "It's really bad. Oh God."

The officer disappeared into a back room and returned with a wheelchair. "Do you need to get to the hospital?"

"Yes! Can you take me?"

"I will," Robert cut in. "We don't need to trouble him."

She plopped into the wheelchair. "Take me now. Like, right now."

He pushed her frantically out of the holding room and into the airport proper, dragging her suitcase and leaving the worried officer in their wake. Once they were far away, weaving through hordes of travelers, Robert's rush slowed to a stroll.

"Nice try," he said.

"What? I had a contraction."

"I bet."

"I feel another one coming."

"Oh, please."

"If you want to stop my extremely loud and painful labor, I'm going to need a cheeseburger, fries, and an extra thousand bucks." Extorting him for Bubala's sake felt like poetic justice.

He actually laughed. "Wait—so you kidnap my child, and I owe you a bonus?"

"It was a misunderstanding," she insisted.

"Well, let me be perfectly clear. You're going to spend the next four weeks at my house, under my watch. I'm not letting you out of my sight."

She rolled her eyes. "I must have missed *hostage* in the contract."

He ignored her and held out his palm. "First things first. Lenses, please."

"What? No way."

"I'll tell the authorities you tried to hurt the baby."

"You wouldn't."

"Try me."

With a cry of frustration, Quinn peeled off her lenses. The two discs balanced on her fingertips like tiny saucers. A point of neon green pulsed at the center of each one—her dashboard glowing with notifications she would not be able to answer.

"Thank you," Robert said graciously, curling his fist around them. "Now, let's go find some lunch."

* * *

At first, she thought constantly about escape. From her bed in the guest room, she could see past the infinity pool and the shrub-dotted canyon, all the way out to the hazy strip of ocean in the distance. Confinement with a killer view was a strange irony. Her mind turned over different options, kneading ideas like dough. Make a run for it in the middle of the night, even though she could hardly walk? Scream loudly enough to alert the neighbors down the hill? Attack Robert without a weapon?

She knew he was watching her 24/7 through cameras. God only knew what else he was using to monitor her every move. But at least he wasn't hurting her in any way. In fact, quite the opposite. Winning their war—at least so far—had put him in a chipper mood.

On her first morning upon waking up at his house, he'd brought in a tray with organic berries, Greek yogurt, and a kale pineapple smoothie, along with a few old-fashioned paperback mysteries to pass the time.

"I'm not in the market to torture you. I just want my baby to be born healthy."

She wanted to spit on him and his fancy food. "The higher my blood pressure, the worse it is. You know that, right?"

He crossed his arms. "So what can I do? You see my dilemma, of course."

"Call my parents. They must be worried sick."

He nodded. "I'll tell them you're staying with me until you go into labor."

"And then? You're not going to make me attempt a home birth, right?"

"Relax, we'll go to Cedars Sinai."

"Good." She sat back on her fluffy pillows. The promise of a finish line—doctors and nurses at her bedside—gave her the strength she needed to keep going. She wouldn't be stuck alone with him forever. The medical staff would protect Bubala and ensure justice for Robert once she confessed everything in private. They would contact Ember to corroborate her story. Until then, she would just have to wait.

* * *

On Saturday afternoon, Robert marched in and tossed a long, flowy black dress with tags onto the bed. She pushed herself up on her elbows.

"What is that?"

"Get ready. We're going out."

"We are?" She hadn't set foot outside his property since their return from the airport five days earlier. "Where? Why?"

Robert's lips curled up. "Thorne's playing the Troubadour tonight, and guess who got tickets?"

Her mouth fell open. "Seriously?"

"Since I can't leave you here by yourself, consider it a perk."

She double-blinked out of habit, trying to summon her dashboard, but nothing happened. If only she could tell Ember, who would most certainly be there too. The possibility of getting to see her again in real life—tonight!—perked her up considerably. Maybe she wouldn't have to wait until the birth to get back on track after all. Ember would notice her by Robert's side and immediately understand the reason for her silence.

"Do we have good seats?"

"It's standing room only, but I got us VIP access, so we'll be first in line."

"Fantastic!" Quinn smiled at him. "You know how much I love Thorne."

"Oh I do."

"Too bad you can't go with Evan," she added sweetly. "I'm sure he would have loved to come."

Robert smirked and turned toward the door. "We're leaving in an hour. Don't be late."

"Don't worry. I wouldn't miss it for the world."

CHAPTER

39

Ember

Backstage at the Troubadour, Thorne's green room buzzed with a different kind of preshow excitement than usual. Ember sat on a velvet couch next to him and across from Noah Heller and Rick Pearson, both alert as hawks, muttering commands into their ear nanochips to confirm that all the undercover agents and surveillance systems were ready to roll.

Ember knew they had been setting up and running drills for the last twelve hours, since nine AM. By the time she and Thorne and his bodyguards had ducked through the back door around six PM, the venue had been transformed into a voyeur's dream, with hidden cameras mounted in every corner and crevice, onstage, in the pit, in the VIP boxes, backstage, in the bars, in the bathrooms. Nothing said or done tonight in pursuit of Thorne's cells would escape notice.

An assistant poked her head through the door. "Five minutes to go. That crowd is hungry."

The band was already onstage playing a musical prelude behind a nine-foot-tall hologram figure of Thorne that always riled up his fans in advance of his actual appearance. Their rising chants reverberated backstage louder than any sound system: *"We Want Thorne, We Want Thorne!"*

He waved the assistant away. "I'll be right there. But first"—he turned to their group—"a toast."

A chilled bottle of Grey Goose waited on the coffee table. He poured out a shot for each of them, and Ember held hers up shakily, hoping it would calm her nerves.

"To you," Heller declared, lifting his chin at Thorne, "for this opportunity."

Thorne raised his glass. "And to freedom."

They all tipped back their shots. Ember winced as the vodka burned her throat.

Thorne's hand rested on her knee. "You ready?" In some sense, she would be performing tonight too—pretending to overlook a biological sample he'd purposefully leave behind, when normally she would scrub away all traces of him down to the cellular level.

"Yep." She squeezed his fingers. In spite of her torn desires, her love for him remained unshakeable.

"Don't worry," he said, picking up on her anxiety, but not its cause. "I'm gonna be fine. These guys won't let anything bad happen to me." He thumbed at Heller and Pearson, who were getting ready to head outside to their command center in the trailer outside.

"He'll be more protected than he's ever been," Heller assured her. "This place is literally swarming with agents."

"Thank you," she replied.

Thorne pecked her on the lips. "See you after."

After . . . what? she wondered. How much she hoped they would end the night as they often did after he performed, partying until two AM backstage, drinking and eating with his team, all the audio engineers and lighting coordinators and hologram managers and assistants, all of whom would finally get to relax after the pressure of pulling off a live show.

Or the night could end very differently.

As they exited the green room, Thorne's assistant announced into her monitor that he was heading onstage. The back of the venue consisted of a narrow row of dressing rooms underneath a low ceiling, and a viewing area just off stage left. Ember, the assistant, and several other staffers followed Thorne right up to the edge, just out of sight behind the curtains, and watched as he slung on his guitar and ran out to the roar of the crowd.

The overhead lights immediately switched to a swirling medley of magenta, blue, and yellow spotlights as he launched into one of his classic hits, "Sugar Pill." Ember sang along under her breath from the side of the stage, admiring his handsome profile and the sexy rasp of his voice. The darkened audience shimmied and clapped along in thrall of proximity to their idol. Two tiers of concert-goers packed the house: a standing-room-only section at Thorne's level, where fans angled for intimate viewing of the stage, and a second level that hosted fans in a rear balcony. If she didn't know any better, Ember would have believed this show was the same as any other. There was no hint of the robust presence of law enforcement, inside or out.

She was just beginning to relax slightly when Thorne shouted, "What's up LA!" at the end of the first song, and the lights panned to the crowd, illuminating dozens of faces beneath a stark white glow. Near the front of the stage, an odd sight caught her eye: a young woman's beachball belly. In that split second under the floodlights, Ember noticed the woman's arms wrapped around it protectively, elbows sticking out. Tight copper curls bounced atop her shoulders, framing her girlish face.

It was Quinn.

CHAPTER

40

Lily

RADIA GRABBED LILY's hand as the revolving doors swallowed them inside the Justice Tower. The spinning doors spit them into a marble foyer with soaring ceilings, wide columns, and an expansive lobby.

This is it, Lily thought. *The end of the road.*

There would be no byline. No article. No future at *Vanguard.*

"Come on!" Radia practically jogged through the security check-in, tossing her purse and jacket onto the conveyor belt in the foyer. Lily followed reluctantly. A machine scanned their retinas to confirm their identities as citizens in good standing, and then a guard stepped aside to let them reclaim their belongings.

"Excuse me," Radia asked, "can you please point us to the office with the national genetics database?"

The guard grunted toward the gold-plated elevators at the far end of the spacious lobby. "Thirtieth floor."

"I—" Lily started, but Radia was already halfway there.

"Hurry up!"

Lily jogged inside before the elevator closed. It whisked them up with dizzying speed, and in what felt like two seconds, they were stepping out onto the polished black marble of the thirtieth floor. Lily rubbed her eyes. It was all happening too fast. She wished they could pause for a moment, get their bearings.

"This way," Radia said, making a left to follow the signs.

"I don't know if I'm ready."

"Oh, come on—it'll be fine."

A gold plaque on a white door read "Bureau of Genomic Statistics." Radia yanked the heavy door open for Lily to enter first. Lily shuffled in, feeling like she was being pushed by a current that threatened to drag her under at any second. Inside the empty waiting room, a man with perfectly smooth skin sat behind a wall of bulletproof plexiglass.

Radia marched up to him confidently. "Hi, we're here to pull our Selection records. We're both over twenty-one."

The ageless administrator nodded. "Lots of you guys lately, huh?"

"Yeah, with the new law and all."

"All right. The camera will establish your ID with a retina scan, then source your records in the national database. I'll be able to transfer them to you once you sign a consent form accepting the risks of learning sensitive information about yourself that you can't unknow."

"Well, when you put it that way . . ." Radia said jokingly, but she stepped up to a boxy white machine on the counter. A single lens rested in its center like a bullseye. Radia gazed into it, eyes wide, unblinking. After about five seconds, a green light flashed, and the receptionist told her to step aside.

"Your turn." Radia moved away so Lily could take her place in front of the camera.

Dread kept her rooted to the spot. "I can't."

"Go," Radia instructed, nudging her lower back. "You can't bail now."

Lily stumbled two steps forward in a daze.

She stared down the camera as though it were an enemy. Nothing happened. After a few seconds, she turned away, her cheeks hot.

"It's not gonna work."

"What?"

"My parents had me by accident. I didn't want to tell you."

Radia drew back sharply. "Wait, what?"

"I'm Unforeseen." Lily gave a tight smile. "But hey, I don't have any expectations to live up to, so don't feel too sorry for me."

"Very funny. She's punking me," Radia told the man. "We're doing a project together about this."

Annoyed, Lily turned back to the camera and sighed. "I'm not in the system because I wasn't Selected, okay?"

"Nice try," the man said, his eyes twinkling as though he were in on the joke. "I actually found your records right here."

CHAPTER

41

Quinn

SWEATING UNDER THE lights and half deaf from the speakers, Quinn reluctantly sang along to Thorne's final song of the set—her favorite hit, "Love So Holo." By all accounts, she appeared to be enjoying herself like all the other rowdy fans who kept accidentally jostling her. It's not as though she could cry for help in the middle of the show. *"I'm being held hostage!"* she imagined whispering to some random person in her vicinity.

"By him?" the bystander would ask in disbelief.

"Yes, him." The handsome, attentive guy who had bought her the hottest ticket in town. Yeah, right. People would think she was joking, or a lunatic—not to mention that the police already had a record of her breaking into his house and attempting a fetal kidnapping. Her predicament reminded her of those sailors who died of dehydration at sea.

Throughout the set, Robert kept his palm flat against her lower back, a subtle menace that made her squirm. By virtue of their VIP passes, they had been among the first fans granted access to the area right in front of the stage. At thirty-six weeks pregnant, though, Quinn was seriously starting to doubt whether standing for two hours still qualified as a perk. Her secret hope, reconnecting with Ember, now felt like a distant fantasy. Ember was nowhere to be seen.

Halfway through "Love So Holo," Quinn tugged on Robert's sleeve.

"Can we duck out now?" she asked, struggling to be heard above the rollicking drums and the fans screaming themselves hoarse. The sound was amplified by the neon lights pulsing overhead in time to the beat. "I really need to sit."

"Then we'll miss the encore."

Anger flared in her chest. "Come on. I desperately need to pee."

"No," he snapped, never taking his eyes off Thorne.

Thorne stood front and center, strumming his guitar, closing his eyes as he hit a high note. The crowd whooped and clapped as he sustained it with full power, his tenor range as rich and pure in real life as in the holoverse. Quinn had to admit he was electrifying. To be so close that she could see the sweat dripping down his face felt like witnessing a historic spectacle, something she would recount to Bubala one day, even if it was just a song being sung.

When he finished, he raised his arms up high in triumph, and the fans went ballistic, jumping up and down and screaming their appreciation.

"I love you, LA!" he shouted. He picked up a water bottle and downed it one giant gulp, and then he and the band jogged offstage together as the stage lights blacked out. When the house lights came on a moment later, the chaotic cheering morphed into a single chant: *"Encore! Encore! Encore!"*

Quinn gazed longingly at the "Exit" sign over the nearest side door. From their position at the front of the stage, it would be a battle to elbow their way through the packed crowd, but still possible. "Please can we just go?"

Robert's eyes narrowed at the darkened stage; the two of them seemed to be the only people not chanting at the top of their lungs. She followed his gaze and gasped. Ember had walked out from stage left, barely noticeable in the darkness, like a black cat prowling in the night. She moved nimbly across the stage, shining a tiny flashlight around the mic. Wearing latex gloves, she wiped down surfaces and collected Thorne's fallen bandana, used tissues, and whatever other debris had been shed in his wake. When some fans shouted at her to hurry up so Thorne could come back, she didn't acknowledge it, but she did appear to move more quickly.

Quinn yearned to catch her attention somehow, but how? Ember was in full-blown bio-guard mode, never once glancing at the crowd. And even if she did notice Quinn, what could be accomplished? Quinn still lacked her lenses; there was no way to communicate discreetly, out of Robert's sight. Quinn rubbed her eyes, wishing she could speed up time to the point of lying in bed alone, even if it was at Robert's house. At least she would only be trapped with him for a few more weeks. Giving birth would set her free.

Robert's hot breath tickled her ear. "I need you to do me a favor. See that?" He pointed to Thorne's used water bottle that had rolled to the edge of the stage beside an amp. Ember must not have noticed it. Her back remained turned while she examined the floor near the mic.

Quinn frowned. "Yeah?"

"Grab it for me."

"Why? It's trash."

"Just do it. Hurry."

A phrase fired into her mind like a gunshot: *the Vault.*

She recalled his feigned ignorance and illicit search history, and the fact that he'd somehow acquired Ember's cells to create embryos. It was bad enough to think of him as a potential customer of the Vault, but what if he was more involved? Why else would he want to claim something with Thorne's spit on it?

"Fuck you," she snapped.

He elbowed her hard between the shoulder blades, sending her stumbling forward.

"What the hell," she cried, though in the middle of the raucous crowd, no one really noticed or heard her. He grabbed her arm, ostensibly to stabilize her, but she felt the threatening clamp of his fingers.

"Don't piss me off or you'll regret it."

"Fine." She shook him off and wove her way through the half-dozen people standing between them and the stage. The lights were darkening again overhead, signaling Thorne's imminent return. The last thing she wanted to do was betray him. Instead, she planned to snatch the bottle and throw it high into the air, lost to the crowd forever, just to savor Robert's distress. He had no real power to hurt her after all—not if he wanted his own baby to live. And if he made her life miserable in the meantime, well, so be it.

"Excuse me, excuse me," she muttered, groping her way through the cluster of people. They parted with annoyance but complied nonetheless. She grabbed the edge of the stage, but the bottle remained a few feet out of reach. She would have to physically get onto the platform to snatch it. The lights were dark and the space empty. Ember had already disappeared backstage.

Quinn guessed she had maybe thirty seconds to grab the bottle before the lights came back on again and Thorne ran out. The thought of screwing over Robert with this one small gesture of insubordination prompted her to climb up the few steps to the stage, still in the pitch-black darkness. She cradled her belly as she scooted over to the amp and grabbed the bottle, squeezing the soft plastic and pulling her fist back. She was about to toss it like a football when all the lights blasted on bright white, and a stream of people rushed the stage from both sides.

Flustered, she dropped the bottle and scurried back toward the edge in embarrassment, thinking it was part of the encore act, but then a pair of rough hands closed around her shoulders, and another pair yanked her arms behind her back and slid cold metal cuffs around her wrists.

"You have the right to remain silent . . . " a man intoned.

"What did I do?" she cried. "Just for getting onstage?"

"Anything you say can be used against you in court," he continued as a swarm of strangers surrounded her, some of them in regular clothes, others in uniforms with guns. *Guns!* Quinn dropped to her knees, faint with shock. *This isn't happening.* She struggled against the cuffs, her fingertips starting to tingle. A scandalized hush fell over the crowd as hundreds of eyes gawked at her. She sucked erratic gulps of air into her windpipe, searching frantically for a way out, for help. Inside her belly, Bubala pummeled her ribcage.

"Stop!" yelled a woman's voice nearby. "Let her go!"

Quinn turned her head to the sound, as did everyone else.

Ember was jogging onto the stage with her arms straight out and palms up, wrists touching. Her face was white with terror, but her steely blue eyes looked resolute, like a daredevil undertaking a high-wire act without a net. She squared her shoulders and spoke at a normal volume, her voice matter-of-fact:

"It's not her you want. It's me."

PART 4

CHAPTER

42

Quinn

EMBER STRODE TOWARD Quinn on stage, wrists facing up as if she were demanding the cuffs. A uniformed agent, with a buzz cut and a jacket with the yellow letters "FBI," parted the crowd of plainclothes officers surrounding them. He stared at Ember in disbelief.

"What do you think you're doing?"

"Turning myself in."

"No!" Quinn cried, jerking against her cuffs. "She's just saying that to protect me. It's the guy I came with—" She peered out into the darkened theater, where an anxious urgency snaked through the crowd. A few shouts of *"Encore"* erupted here and there, but many people were already clamoring for the exits while others remained watching the stage, transfixed by the scandal unfolding before their eyes. There was no sign of Robert.

"He was just here!" Quinn yelled. "Tell them the truth!"

"I will. But first," Ember said sternly to the agent, "release her."

He drew back at her commanding tone. "Excuse me?"

"She's innocent. She has nothing to do with the bottle."

"But she went after it!"

"*He* forced me to," Quinn interrupted. "I've been a hostage in his house!"

The agent frowned. "Who's he?"

"My ex," Ember said calmly. "We started the Vault together."

The agent smirked. "Now you're just fucking with me. I don't have time for this." He grabbed Quinn's elbow and hoisted her up. "On your feet. Now. We're going to need to take you down to the field station."

Quinn rose heavily. Her brain had congealed like sludge around Ember's apparent confession. Could it be true? Her job was to *protect* Thorne from the Vault. How could she have helped usher in its existence? Reconciling the two was like a sunrise in the dead of night. Impossible.

As the agent clamped his hand around her bicep, Ember ran over and planted herself in his path. "Stop. I'm telling you, this poor woman is innocent. And she's pregnant with my child, so let her go."

The agent jerked back. *"What?"*

"I can't stay silent anymore. I'm prepared to fully cooperate now."

His smirk faded. "You're serious?"

She nodded. "Last summer, my ex stole my cells without me knowing, and hired her as a surrogate to carry our baby, to punish me for leaving him. I thought he was targeting Thorne, but it was me. And now . . ." Her voice trailed off as she glanced sidelong at Quinn's stomach, as though she couldn't bear to face it head on. Quinn felt herself prickle with defensiveness on Bubala's behalf. Yes, her existence was abhorrent, and yes, Ember deserved to scorn her, but even now, Quinn delighted in her baby's little shimmy as Bubala changed positions. The movement reassured Quinn that she was okay.

A surreal feeling of detachment suddenly washed over her. She watched herself as if from a distance, under arrest, on the stage, at the center of a national scandal. Somehow

Bubala's kicks still gave her comfort—and joy. Was this how it felt to be a mother?

The agent blinked. "This is insane. You were hiding this the whole time?"

"I only just found out myself. But you can run a blood test on us to prove it," Ember said.

That's when Quinn heard an icky sound somewhere close by. She glanced toward the wings in time to see Thorne retching near the curtains. He had apparently overheard everything. An assistant raced to his side with a bucket and rubbed his back as he fell to his knees, his face pale and glistening. So he didn't know about the baby. Quinn felt a conflicted sense of horror on his behalf.

"Are you involved with the Vault?" the agent asked Quinn point-blank.

"No. I swear." She tried to raise her palms in a gesture of innocence, but the cold metal restrained her wrists, its presence a fresh shock.

The agent appeared to hesitate.

"I can help you," she offered. "I know where he lives. I know the code to his door."

"All right," he said curtly. "But we'll need a full witness statement. Guys, escort her to the trailer so Pearson can do the intake."

"Am I still under arrest?" Quinn asked.

"No. Release her," he said to the officers. He muttered something into his invisible ear monitor and then announced soberly, "Ember, you come with me."

Ember smiled at Quinn as they unlocked her cuffs, but Quinn refused to meet her gaze. Her heart ached for Bubala, coming into a world of utter depravity.

A gaggle of officers led Quinn offstage, past Thorne's sour yellow puddle—he had disappeared into some private room—through the narrow hallways backstage, out a side door, and to an unmarked white trailer parked on the curb behind the venue. A youngish agent in an FBI jacket opened the door and held her hand as she climbed the three steps up into the trailer. He seemed to be expecting her.

He introduced himself as Deputy Agent Rick Pearson and welcomed her inside what appeared to be a mobile command center: half a dozen screens showing live footage of various vantage points both inside the venue and out. A hologram projection of Pearson's dashboard extended from floor to ceiling, accounting for every camera, agent, and live wire in the vicinity. He gestured for her to take a seat in one of the rolling chairs in the hub.

"Holy crap," Quinn breathed. "I had no idea it was a setup all along."

"I'm told you have some info on our perp?"

"I do."

He tapped a button on his dashboard. "Audio's rolling. Please state your name, age, and occupation for the record."

She did so and then proceeded to share every single detail she could recall about Robert, starting with their very first meeting at Thorne's concert the previous summer at the Hollywood Bowl, all the way through the development of their friendship and her agreement to serve as his surrogate, to her eventual suspicion and growing distrust, which had culminated in her trespassing on his home, his ominous threats, the ill-fated airport trip, and the last five days of captivity in his house, without her lenses.

"You have to find him ASAP," Quinn finished, her throat dry from her lengthy monologue. "I'm afraid he'll come after me for the baby. He knows where I live."

If Pearson was disturbed or upset, he didn't show it. "Thanks for all that. What we really need now is a visual hit for the facial recognition algorithms. I've rewound the footage to right before you got on stage. Check it out."

He pointed to one of the large screens mounted on the wall. She watched the soundless reel play in ultra hi-def resolution: her own figure pushing through the crowd toward the front of the stage. Her image had been captured from some hidden camera up above. It showed the top of her head, her auburn curls bouncing over her shoulders as she cradled the underside of her belly, leaning slightly back as a counterweight.

Pearson rewound the film several seconds; her figure reversed course in double time, flying right back to where she'd started beside Robert.

"There!" she exclaimed, pointing at his face.

Pearson zoomed in, then further in, and still further, until they could practically see the pores on Robert's nose—his viciously handsome nose. His stubble looked about a day old. He was clenching his jaw, his lips moving slightly—and then without warning, he shoved her between the shoulder blades, and she stumbled forward, though in the packed theater, no one appeared to notice.

"He was threatening me," she explained, relieved by the evidence of her lack of complicity. "I didn't want to go up there."

Pearson dropped a pin on Robert's face, then let the footage continue to play until the pin abruptly darted toward a side exit, as Quinn's arrest was happening on stage. Then the pin disappeared off the screen altogether.

"I knew it," Quinn said. "He ran."

"At least we have a solid image now."

"Are you gonna go to his house?"

"We'll get a warrant and have a look around, but you can bet he's not going back there now."

"I don't want to go home either. What if he's waiting there?"

"Do you have family nearby?"

"No. And it's past one AM. Where am I supposed to go?"

Pearson's hawkish gaze softened. "Look, you're a critical witness, and we need you close by. How about if we put you up in a hotel for a little while?"

She almost leaped up and hugged him, but the heaviness of her body kept her glued to her chair. "You would do that?"

He nodded. "But first thing tomorrow, you'll need to go get new lenses so you can get back online. We need to be able to reach you if there are developments."

She pointed to her purse. "I've got my wallet, but none of my stuff. It's all at his house in a suitcase in the guest room."

He typed something on his invisible keyboard. "When our team gets to his house, I'll tell them to retrieve it and drop it off at your hotel."

"Thank you so much! God, I don't know what I would do without you."

Pearson didn't appear to be one for sentimental reflection. He was furrowing his brow, back to business. "Anywhere else this guy likes to visit?"

"Not really. He's pretty much a homebody, as far as I know." The urge to yawn took hold, and she covered her mouth. "Sorry. I guess I don't really know very much about him."

He waved a hand. "That's okay. Let's get you to the hotel so you can get some sleep." He typed on his dashboard for a brief period, during which Quinn shut her eyes. "I just ordered your AV. It should be here in three minutes. Meanwhile, the hotel I booked you at isn't exactly a luxury resort, but it should do. It's the Sunrise Terrace on the corner of North Croft Avenue and Beverly Boulevard."

"Sounds great," she replied, which she would have said to any place with a bed and a lock.

Outside, the streets were deserted; the Troubadour had long since emptied out. The cool night air bit her cheeks and roused her alertness again. She wondered what was happening with Ember and Thorne. What would become of Bubala? But there was nothing she could do now to problem-solve the future. She glanced up at the sky as a drop of rain landed on her bare shoulder. Pearson pushed open an umbrella and held it high above them both until a black sedan turned onto the street and rolled to a stop in front of them.

"Take care of yourself," Pearson said, opening the door for her. "Here's my number if you need anything." He withdrew a pen from his front pocket and scribbled it on the back of her hand. "Sorry—I don't have any paper."

"Paper?" she joked. "What's that?"

"Seriously, call me if you need anything. We'll be in touch."

"Thanks so much again."

She climbed into the passenger bay and he shut the door. She closed her eyes for the entire seven-minute drive to the hotel. Her body was begging for rest. A clean bed. Nothing but sleep as long as she wanted.

When the car's motion ceased, she reluctantly opened her eyes. A quick scan of the neighborhood revealed a Goodwill next to a gas station and a liquor store. The hotel was a run-down two-story building at the corner of the wide Beverly Boulevard and a smaller side street. There did not appear to be a brightly lit lobby to welcome her, but rather a plain old front door. Not far from it, a homeless person was bending over at the waist in a stupor. Beside him, a metal grocery cart was piled with clothing or debris.

When she got out, the rain was coming down in a steady patter. The car sped away and a wave of loneliness overcame her. If only there was a driver like the old days, who could watch to see that she got in safely.

Several yards away, the homeless man began to pull down his pants and squat. She didn't want to wait around to see what happened next. Instead, she hurried toward the back of the hotel, banking on a rear entrance facing the quiet side street. She rounded the corner with high hopes as her hair grew soaked.

Just as she glimpsed a glass door with the sign "Welcome Guests," a gloved hand closed around her mouth from behind. She shrieked, but the sound was lost to the rain. A jacketed figure wrapped his other arm around her chest and held her firmly against him, no matter how angrily she tried to bite and squirm and struggle free. Then something sharp plunged into her shoulder and a scream tore out of her, but almost as quickly, her desire to fight melted away. She noticed her body relax against the will of her mind.

Her arms went limp and her eyelids closed. Now even her rage was fading, as though reaching her from the end of a long dark tunnel. It was hard to even remember why she was so angry, when everything felt heavy and far away. Incidentally, her heels began to drag along the grass, getting lodged in the mud here and there. She heard a groan as she felt herself being scooped up under the neck and knees. Her legs dangled and her head fell against the man's puffy jacket, bobbing like a doll's as he walked.

Then the rain stopped and a padded cushion took up the space behind her body. A belt clicked in over her lap. The floor jerked forward. Without much care, she realized they were in a car.

And they were headed somewhere fast.

CHAPTER

43

Ember

Ember faced Noah Heller across a wooden table in a windowless interrogation room. The overhead lights shone harshly on the concrete floor. On the left wall hung a two-way mirror, as inscrutable as the look on Heller's face.

He placed his folded hands on the table. Hers remained cuffed on her lap. Her confession was less than two hours old, and already she was accustomed to feeling like a criminal. The withering stares of the staff at the FBI field station had blasted a clear message as she submitted to being booked, photographed, and fingerprinted: *"You are not to be trusted."*

The world of entertainment, affection, and luxury—Thorne's world—felt as distant as the bottom of the ocean. Her stomach clenched at the thought of him. She hadn't even gotten to say goodbye.

"Let's get on with it," Heller said coldly, as though they had never met. "You're offering a voluntary and truthful statement for the record. Is that correct?"

"Yes, sir."

"What is your full name and date of birth?"

"Ember Olivia Ryan. Born November first, 2014."

"What is your educational background?"

"Bachelor's degree in molecular biology from UT Austin, doctorate in bioengineering from UCLA. Plus a postdoc there."

"Solid creds." Heller squinted. "So how did you wind up selling the products of people's skin trash? And a better question: *Why?*"

Ember drew a breath. Dread gripped her. This was the story she had been hiding for nine painful years, the parasite that had been feasting on her soul, but one her freedom depended on. The opportunity to release it came as both a catastrophe and a relief. There was no going back.

"Long story short, I ended up with the wrong guy, but I didn't know it at the time. And it proved to be the worst mistake of my life."

Heller paused. "A lot to unpack there. Who is he?"

"He's gone by various aliases over the years, but his real name is Mason Brown, born the same year as me. He goes by Robert Roy now. He's like a shape-shifter. That's the best way I can describe him. He knows what you want from him, and he becomes that person. But I don't think he has true feelings for anyone but himself."

"How did you meet?"

"At UCLA. We were both selected as postdocs to join the lab of a pretty important researcher. Mason and I hit it off right away. He was charming and funny, and by far the most talented scientist I'd ever worked with. He helped me get through a really tough time."

"How so?"

"I was grieving the death of my parents who had just died weeks apart, and at the same time, that postdoc was a huge opportunity. I didn't want to screw it up. There was major grant money behind us, and if we succeeded, nothing would ever be the same. We're talking Nobel Prize–caliber research. I almost quit because of the pressure, but Mason wouldn't let me. He walked me back from the edge, showed me more kindness than anyone ever had besides my parents. I remember thinking . . ." Ember swallowed hard. "It's embarrassing, but I remember thinking that he was the sweetest guy I'd ever met. And the smartest. And I couldn't believe my luck."

"What was the project?"

Ember recalled the enthusiasm of those heady days. The possibility of a breakthrough had burned in their hearts with the brilliance of a supernova.

"We were working on building a virus-resistant chromosome. It required making around four hundred thousand edits to the human genome, to remove DNA sequences that viruses use to hijack cells and replicate."

"Whoa. That sounds wildly ambitious."

"It wasn't just about ambition or prestige, though. It was personal. I grew up in the wreckage of Covid, and then my parents both succumbed to a bad strain of the flu. So when I heard about this project, I jumped at it. The idea was that if we could engineer this chromosome with all the necessary changes to make it virus-proof, then in theory, a drug could be developed for use in preventive care. It would be a one-time gene therapy infusion to circulate the upgraded DNA in the bloodstream. Then *bam*—no more pandemics. No need for vaccines or antivirals or anything."

Heller let out a low whistle. "So why haven't I heard of it?"

"Because of 2049."

"Oh." His tone turned somber. "Oh."

"By that February, we had been working on the project for two years already, and we were close to proof of concept in mice. The animals had been dosed, and we were tracking their responses, almost living in the lab. We'd already prepped some of the manuscript for the *New England Journal of Medicine*, and our professor had agreed to let us be listed as coauthors. But first we needed to prove that the mice had become immune to all viruses."

"And then . . . February hit?" Heller wrinkled his nose. Nobody on Earth wanted to recall February 2049, the onset of the worst pandemic in two hundred years. Henipavirus-7 had practically made people nostalgic for Covid.

"Yep. And you know the rest."

Heller nodded. She didn't have to tell him how society had shut down for over a year—how people suddenly ceased going out, full stop. Stores boarded up, cities emptied, airlines grounded entire fleets. All shopping went digital, with food and goods delivered by drone. The US government, in conjunction with Big Pharma, beat its own record on vaccine development, delivering a successful shot after only four months, but many closures persisted long after they were necessary. Partly it was collective trauma, but in California, the problem was compounded by irrational laws. Governor Shelton had refused to lift the state bans until a full year after the vaccine had become available.

"Our lab in UCLA was on public property," Ember explained. "So the whole campus stayed shut until Shelton lifted the order in the summer of 2050. By the time we were allowed back in, the mice were long dead. The grant money had dried up, the venture markets had cratered, and we couldn't raise any more funding to start again. The window of opportunity was gone, and we never got to find out if our experiment was successful or not."

Heller raised his eyebrows. "Ouch."

"We were devastated. And furious."

"I get that. But how is this relevant to the Vault?"

"In July of 2050, Shelton was campaigning for reelection. He was going after the Hispanic vote so hard because they had just become the majority voter bloc. Things got ugly. This was five years ago, so you might not remember what happened."

Heller scratched his chin. "Wasn't there some scandal?"

"Yes. Shelton claimed to have Hispanic heritage, but he looked as white as a lily. His critics were calling bullshit, but nobody knew for sure. Meanwhile, he seized every opportunity to pander.

"That July, we attended one of his rallies in LA so we could boo him. We felt that if he had made a reasonable exception for scientists to be allowed back in labs sooner, we could have kept the mice alive. Instead, we lost everything, as did many others. And because we had no published paper, we had no chance of landing other positions.

"At the rally, he repeated the claims again, sucking up to the Hispanic voters, and we booed. Afterward, he walked by us and the other protesters, and he stopped when he saw our sign—it was a cartoon of him jerking off into a sombrero. He spit on it before he got into his limo. I was horrified, but Mason was delighted. It was his idea to take the spit straight back to the lab and sequence his DNA, to see if he really did have any Hispanic heritage. And that's exactly what we did. It turned out he was a liar after all. He was Irish and Swedish."

"Oh man. I remember this now. He pulled out of the election."

"Yeah, after we leaked it anonymously to the press."

"That was you?"

"Yep. And that's how the Vault was born."

Heller sat back in his chair. "So . . . then what? You start looking for customers?"

"No, at first, we didn't think of it as a business. We just liked the idea of anonymously taking citizen revenge on corrupt officials. After the stunt went viral, we set up the Vault's website on our own servers, where we could post open-source DNA sequences, and we set out to find our next target. DNA was easy to get from stuff people left behind, like coffee cups, tissues—that sort of thing. You shed your skin and hair all the time."

"But you weren't selling eggs or sperm derived from their cells?"

"No, definitely not. Back then, we were just going after DNA sequences—and just for kicks, not cash."

"Who was next?"

"I had a personal beef with the former governor of Texas, Ruby Maroni. Back when she was governor, and I was a college student in Austin, I ended up in the ER hemorrhaging from a miscarriage. Even though abortion had just been made legal again, I was still harassed and investigated by her DA." Ember felt her face run hot at the memory. "She intimidated so many women in Texas, threatening them if they tried to seek medical treatment—who knows how many died?"

"So what did you do?"

"Mason and I took a road trip to Texas that summer, where we attended her talk at a veterans' memorial. Afterward, she went out to dinner with some other officials, and we followed. When they left, we took her fork. We'd come prepared with a test tube and a culture medium to stabilize cells, and we soaked her fork in it. Back at our lab in California, we had enough DNA to sequence it. Turned out she carries a gene associated with psychopathy, which we also leaked to the press. People freaked out. I like to think it stifled her political ambition."

"So you kept using UCLA's lab?"

"Only in the beginning. By December that year, our postdocs had officially ended, and we couldn't get into the lab anymore. Or get jobs. But we had started getting requests through our site—people who wanted to pay for the DNA of others, to blackmail them by threatening to expose their health risks and personality traits, biological relationships, ancestry—stuff like that. It was a mean business.

"But we had a simple rule: we only took commissions on targets who deserved it. Powerful people who had violated others. We began accepting payment in crypto. People weren't so much on guard in those days. It was almost too easy to take their abandoned items in restaurants, coffee shops, conferences, hotels. We started to make serious cash, enough to fund our own space and lab equipment. This was the heyday, about four years ago."

Heller was sitting up straight now. "Who else was involved?"

"No one. We never hired any staff because it was too risky. Only the two of us. We collected money through crypto and stored all the data through blockchain on our own servers, so nobody could shut down the site or trace the transactions."

"Who else did you target?"

"Oh man. There was so much demand, at first we couldn't keep up. Besides politicians, we went after corrupt CEOs, conspiracy theorists, medical quacks, lying pundits—you name it. Plenty of villains out there."

"And you authenticated sequences for your clients through the national genetic ID system?"

"Exactly. We sent customers the complete DNA sequences, which they could reverse check through the national database for confirmation of identity."

"Who were your clients?"

Ember shrugged. "We never required names. Just payment. Half up front and half on delivery. For a while, things were going well. We had money, we had each other. I was alone, and so was he. He came from a terrible family background. His father walked out when he was a kid, and his mom was an alcoholic. So we kind of clung to each other and our new purpose, and the secret brought us even closer. We did become pretty codependent, though, to the point where we had no life outside of one another."

"Sounds healthy."

"Things got worse when business slowed after a few years. Many of the potential targets became much more on guard thanks to all the bad press about the Vault, and it wasn't so easy anymore to pick off their abandoned stuff. I was starting to doubt the whole thing. Mason got paranoid, questioning whether I loved him, whether he could trust me. I knew we needed a fresh start, and that's when I suggested having a baby."

Heller's eyes narrowed. "Really?"

"I know, it sounds crazy. But I was in my late thirties then, and I was burned out, looking for something to give me hope again. I also deeply missed our old research, but I couldn't go back to academia with those gap years and no published papers."

"So what did he say?"

"Hell no, basically. He wanted to focus on rebuilding the business. But mostly I think he was scared. He'd never had a parental role model, and he was afraid he'd be a shitty dad. He's too obsessed with work, and he has no experience with kids. He's the younger of two boys, but his older brother got into drugs at an early age and was in and out of rehab. He saw how hard that was on his mom and how screwed up the world is, and he just said no."

"And you disagreed?"

"I thought we could do better. I thought he was too negative. I had wonderful parents, a happy childhood. I thought we could give a kid a good life. We could retire from the Vault and start a different business or go into teaching. Something decent . . ." Ember's voice trailed off as she shook her head. "Of course he never went for it. There's no power in that, no thrill."

"Where were you living at this point?"

"We'd moved out to Lincoln County in Nevada, where the land was still cheap and no one looked over your shoulder. But things kept going downhill. We fought about the baby idea and the Vault, and he started drinking too much, like his mom. We fought about that too. We began to resent each other, kind of quietly at first, and then openly. We got an android dog, Sparky, to try to turn things around, but it didn't really help. Mason just got jealous of how much I loved the dog. And then we got our very first request for the gametes of a desirable."

"When was that?"

Ember didn't have to think. She could remember the day perfectly—her own horror, in stark contrast to Mason's excitement, and her subsequent grasp of how deep his depravity ran. He never questioned his own willingness to cross the line. That had been the scariest part. She could still see herself sitting at their kitchen table, holding a cup of coffee, the sun streaming in through the shutters. The realization had shaken her faith in reality. It was like learning that the person she loved was an AI with no moral compass whatsoever.

"September fifteenth, 2053," she said. "Almost two years ago."

"What was the request? Who was it from?"

"A woman from China, that's all we knew. She was aware the Vault was famous for stealing the DNA of high-profile people. And since most upper-middle-class people were choosing IVG to reproduce, this woman wanted to know, could we obtain the cells of T. S. Chan and derive his sperm for her?"

"Who is that?"

"He's a brilliant young math professor at Stanford, a prodigy with a cult following. That year, he'd won the Fields Medal. This woman was obsessed. She was willing to pay handsomely if we could deliver his sperm."

"What did you say?"

"I flipped out. I told Mason absolutely not. I wouldn't do it for all the money in the world."

"Was it a big ask from a technical perspective?"

"No, not with the right sample. Deriving iPSC—that's induced pluripotent stem cells—from epithelial cells and then coaxing them to form gametes is standard procedure. For scientists with our training, it's very doable with saliva, mucus, blood, or hair plucked at the root. Just more time-consuming than sequencing DNA."

"What did Mason say?"

"He saw a whole new market open before his eyes. He wanted to *'stay relevant.'*" Ember pricked the air with disgusted finger quotes. "He craved money and the attention for the Vault in the press, no matter how negative, and the high of chasing a new target. This woman was offering us five times our usual price. And we were getting dangerously low on cash by then."

"But you disagreed?"

"More than disagreed. That was the last straw for me. I told him if he went through with it, I was done. He lost his shit. He claimed nobody would get physically hurt, and we could help the next generation be smarter and better. I told him he sounded like fucking Hitler, crossing a line. He said the line had already been crossed with Selection years ago, so we couldn't pretend to still care about ethics. Then I called him a monster, he shoved me against the wall, and I kneed him in the balls. He wrestled me to the ground and bent my arm so hard it snapped." Ember pointed to the pink scar on the underside of her elbow. "Still hurts when I move it sometimes."

Heller winced. "Then what?"

"I blacked out from the pain. When I came to, he had left me on the bathroom floor alone. I heard him swearing and drinking in the other room. I was scared to leave the bathroom, so I waited until I stopped hearing anything. Then I found him passed out on the couch. I packed up my stuff as fast as I could and called an AV to the hospital. Blocked his number and never went back. Of course, he proceeded to target desirables without me—including Thorne after I was gone, because he's one of the most lucrative desirables out there. I was appalled, but I didn't report him because I didn't want to go to jail myself. Instead, I started my own business last year to thwart him, and here we are."

"Was that fight the last time you saw him?"

Ember sighed. "There was one other time. Last summer. While I was in the midst of touring as Thorne's bio-guard. Mason must have seen the gossip about us and realized I had moved on and wasn't coming back. He drone stalked me, and showed up at my house in LA, saying he missed me and how sorry he was and how he wanted me back. He kissed me long enough to scrape my saliva into his mouth and get my cells to take back to the lab. Then out of spite, he hired Quinn to carry our baby without me knowing—and now she's weeks away from giving birth."

Heller pressed his lips together. "Of all the twisted shit I've heard in my career, this takes the cake."

"I know."

"Can you help us find him?"

"I'll certainly try. But first I have one request."

"Call a lawyer?"

Ember gave a bitter laugh. "It's a little late for that, don't you think?"

"Then what?"

"Let me see Thorne one last time to say goodbye."

CHAPTER

44

Lily

THE ADMINISTRATOR OF the Bureau of Genomic Statistics smiled wearily at Lily. "All right, enough kidding. Are you ready to view your records?"

"They—they must not be mine," Lily stammered. She turned up her palms at Radia. "I swear, I wasn't joking. I'm Unforeseen. I've never told anyone because it's so embarrassing."

Radia, flushed with curiosity, pressed her nose up against the glass that divided visitors from staff. "Are you *sure* they belong to my friend? Can the system be wrong?"

The administrator shook his head in alarm, as though he felt personally responsible for the confusion. "I've been workin' here eighteen years, and I never saw it mix people up, but I can scan her again just for the heck of it. Honey, can you face the lens?"

Lily stared into the dull gray bulb. A red light blinked. She waited five seconds, then rubbed her eyes and turned away. "It's useless—"

"Same file matched," the administrator announced. "Connected to Social Security Number 914-93-2171?"

Lily felt her knees go weak. "That's mine."

"All righty then!" He patted his desk with apparent fondness. "Tight ship here, always has been."

Radia nudged Lily's arm. "Aren't you gonna look at it?"

"I still think there must be some kind of mistake. It doesn't make sense."

"You heard the man!"

Lily stumbled a few steps away to catch her breath. *Think. Where did I go wrong? What the hell is going on?*

Mom and Dad. They would know.

She blinked open her dashboard and called her mom first. The tinny chime rang in her ears several times before going to voicemail. Ugh. She was probably napping or at one of her prenatal appointments. Dad was usually easier to reach, now that he was out of the limelight and spent most of his time at home, working on his nonprofit foundation. But his call, too, went to voicemail.

Were they avoiding her? No, that was crazy.

Yet this whole situation was crazy. She thought back to what she knew about her own conception. The story her parents had told her many times:

> *We were on vacation. It was a hot summer day, and we had a private oceanfront condo. The whole beach to ourselves. We ended up having one too many mai tais, and one thing led to another . . . we wanted a baby anyway, so as soon as we found out, we knew we could never . . . No matter how medieval it seems, we never looked back. We were prepared to love you just as you were. Like the old days.*

Radia sidled up next to her. "You okay?"

Lily nodded because she couldn't speak. Her existence was a paradox.

Who was she? *How* was she?

"Do you want to see your file?" Radia asked softly. "I'm going to get mine."

Lily nodded again. A giant lump was obstructing her voice. It took all her strength to calmly follow Radia back to the front desk without letting out a primal shriek.

"Ready, girls?" the administrator asked. He winked at Lily, unaware of her inner turmoil.

"Yup," Radia said on their behalf. Lily wished she had half the confidence of her genetically superior friend. Or—wait. Was that even true anymore if they were both Selected? Had they been on equal footing all along?

Jesus Christ. The room was starting to spin.

"Do you each consent to view sensitive information about your embryonic origins that you can't unknow, which may have the capacity to inflict emotional and mental pain?"

"I do," Radia declared.

"I do," Lily whispered.

The only way out was through.

The administrator tapped a few invisible keys to transfer their private files to each of their respective dashboards with a single electronic command. Lily saw and heard the whoosh of her inbox lighting up with incoming data.

"We're HIPAA compliant, so there's a security key built in as the password to open your file. It's the last four digits of your social."

"Great," Radia said. "Thanks so much."

"You can go into private viewing rooms if you like." He gestured to a hallway behind his station. "We offer them as a courtesy, first come, first served. There are a couple open rooms left at the moment. Numbers three and four."

"We'll take them," Radia replied. "Come on." Her own excitement was palpable, in stark contrast to Lily's numbness.

Lily followed her silently down the hall until they arrived at side-by-side white doors labeled three and four. Radia pushed hers open. "See ya on the flip side!"

Lily mustered up a weak smile and went inside. Her space was the size of a doctor's exam room. But instead of a sterile feel, it contained a black couch upholstered in shiny mushroom leather next to a coffee table. A few posters hung on the walls with promotional messages from the Bureau of Genomic Statistics: *"Did you know? Preimplantation genetic screening has prevented approximately ten million cases of pediatric cancers."* Another read: *"Friends Don't Let Friends Forget to A-T-C-G: Act To Catch Genetic Illnesses."* And: *"An Ounce of Prevention Is Worth a Pound of Cure. Selection Saves Lives."*

There were no windows.

Lily slouched against the couch. Across from her was a blank wall intended for the projection of her own private data.

She blinked twice on her new file and held her breath.

CHAPTER 45

Quinn

QUINN KNEW SHE should feel afraid. The car was racing through the slick, empty city streets in the dead of the night, but all she felt was a warmth oozing across her consciousness, as though someone had spilled a cup of soup inside her brain. Not that she particularly minded. Sleep beckoned.

As the car zoomed onto the freeway, she became gradually aware of the hooded man next to her. His woody cologne was familiar. So was the way he cleared his throat, like a nervous tic. He picked up her limp hand and pressed her wrist.

"Good," he muttered.

She tried to pull her hand away, but it barely budged. She tried again, imagining herself thrashing, flailing, putting up a wicked fight. Her fingers curled. She concentrated on not giving into the warmth. It felt like an enticement to surrender. But then from inside her belly, a subtle kick sharpened her senses. The baby. Oh God.

Her eyes fluttered. She opened her mouth to speak.

"Wha . . ." A cough rattled her throat. Her voice sounded thick and slow, like it was underwater. In her mind, questions crashed into one another, like a four-way stop gone wrong. She hardly knew where to start. “What—”

“You’re fine.” Robert’s impatient voice cut her off. “You got a low dose of Versed. It won’t harm the baby. It’s already wearing off.”

A firebolt of rage suddenly penetrated the warmth. But instead of cursing him out with every nasty word she knew, she heard herself grunting incoherently.

He chuckled. “Relax. We have a long drive. No use in getting worked up, or I’ll have to dose you again.” He crossed his legs, right foot across his left knee, and looked out the window with a sigh.

The freeway was mostly empty, and the sky a purplish black, like a bruise. Quinn caught sight of the car’s control panel. It was 3:44 AM. She had no idea which direction they were going in or even which freeway they were on. Her vision blurred; the green signs passed too quickly for her to read.

But her mind was becoming sharper, the cotton ball monopoly loosening its grip.

She coughed. “How . . .?”

He tilted his head while she struggled to eject the thought.

“How did I find you at the hotel?” he asked.

She nodded.

“Hon, I’ve been tracking your retinas since the day we signed the surrogacy agreement. Not that you ever go anywhere interesting. You could afford to get out a bit more.”

She felt her cheeks go hot with fury and embarrassment. Ember had been spot-on. All this time, he’d been violating her privacy. Watching her from the fucking *atmosphere.* It was sick. But it also made sense. There was that odd time he’d shown up at her apartment unannounced, somehow knowing she was home. And the time she’d trespassed at his house, only to have him arrive within the hour . . .

“Did you really think I could let you carry *my own child* without taking extra safety measures?” he asked, as if in response to her unspoken rebuke. “I mean, seriously. We had known each other for, like, a month when you got pregnant." He sighed. "And now it's all going to shit. The one thing I can't figure out is, how did you and Ember get in contact? You obviously have been, or else she wouldn't have thrown herself at the cops to save you." He shook his head in frustration. "But you shouldn't even *know* about her."

Quinn felt a tug of satisfaction. For the first time, Robert was stumped. Even if she had her full verbal powers, there was no way she was about to come clean, telling him about the chatbot that had revealed his seeming obsession with Thorne, her own persistence in tracking Thorne down at the Laguna café, meeting him and Ember, insisting on the paternity tests, leaving them her number. Followed by the unexpected call from Ember herself, who had inferred their connection. But Robert didn't deserve an explanation. He deserved to stew in his own confusion, with nothing but her insolence to comfort him.

"Where . . ." she managed to say. "Where are we going?"

He shrugged. "You'll know when you know."

Her breath quickened. "What about . . . the baby?"

"She'll be fine."

"Doctor's appointment," she eked out. The visit was in two days, for her thirty-seventh-week checkup. Surely he would be reasonable and allow her to attend to his own child's medical care.

He waved a hand. "So you'll skip it. You've gone to all the other ones."

Shit. This was sounding worse and worse.

"Why?" she asked hoarsely.

"Why what?"

She gestured wildly in an effort to boil her question down to its essence. There were a million *whys* she wanted to understand, like why he had targeted her in the first place to take on a sham job, why he had pretended to be a gay widow, and why he was obsessed with a woman who hated him. But most of all: Why create a child without the other parent's knowledge or consent? Why turn a kid into a crime scene?

She finally rested her palm on her belly. It rose up so high in front of her that it could have held a dinner plate. "Why do this? It's not fair."

"Fair?" He repeated the word with incredulous amusement. "You, of all people, should know better. You're just an Unforeseen failing to keep up with all your Selected friends."

She glared at him. He knew how to lob an insult below the belt. But he wasn't wrong. Maybe if she'd been Selected too, she wouldn't be renting her womb for a living.

"Fairness," he went on, "is a farce. There are those who get ahead and those who play by the rules. You can't do both."

Quinn frowned. For some reason, her mind filled with an image of her mother. It was an old memory ricocheting back in full color: the day her mother quit a lucrative job working for a boss whom she'd realized was making phony claims to customers. Mom's decision had left the family in a tough spot, but she'd never regretted it. She had always taught Quinn to do the right thing, even if their understanding of what that meant sometimes differed.

"What about good and evil?"

Robert laughed. "What is this, a fairy tale?"

"You don't mean that."

He stretched out his legs, nudging aside a small black bag at his feet, its zipper half open. The glint of a syringe caught the moonlight. Her insides went cold with fear.

"You're so innocent," he remarked. "It's why I chose you. People like you are easy marks."

She knew he was trying to rile her up, but she refused to give him any reason to dose her again. She said nothing.

"I knew after we hung out that you would be perfect," he went on. "Lonely, isolated, easy to impress. You actually gave me the idea in the first place, did you know that? When you told me at the Hollywood Bowl that you were a surrogate, that was my lightbulb moment."

"What?" Her mouth fell open.

"If Ember and I had a kid together, her perfect new pop-star life would be fucked."

"What about the *kid*?" Quinn demanded. "Did you ever think how *her life* would be?"

"I have enough money for anything she could ever need or want."

Quinn couldn't help making a disgusted noise in the back of her throat. "And you think that qualifies you to be a father?"

He shrugged. "Better than my own, that's for sure."

Keep him talking, she thought. It would distract him from the syringe. Her tone softened. "What did he do?"

"My dad? Who the hell knows? He left when I was four. I barely remember him."

She racked her brain for some response that conveyed sympathy without hatred. All she came up with was "I'm sorry."

"Yeah." He paused. "Talk about fair. My mom had to work three jobs to support us, but she was a mess. I pretty much raised my brother from the time I was in high school."

"Really? You never told me you have a brother."

"Had." Robert gazed out the window at the vast darkness beyond the highway. They were somewhere outside the city now, the lights far behind them.

"He committed suicide when he was twenty-three. He was depressed and I couldn't save him."

Quinn gasped.

"You saw him once. That picture I showed you when I was at my cousin's wedding? That wasn't my husband. That was him."

Figures, she thought. Everything she knew about Robert was a persona crafted for her benefit. She recalled the crisp pillowcases on his bed, as though no one had slept there. He was a master at covering his tracks. That was all she could say for sure.

He seemed lost in thought.

"It happened around the same time I lost my lab. Everything I cared about, just *poof.* Gone. Nothing left. Nothing but Ember."

Quinn said nothing.

"When I finally decided to stop being a victim, everything changed."

She glanced at the syringe again out of the corner of her eye. She wondered how much of the drug was left in the bottle, and if there was any way to snatch it from him. Better yet, to drug *him*. It was impossible, though. Any sudden moves would only ensure another jab. He was much faster.

"But now Ember's ruined it all. And for *you*?" He shot Quinn a scathing look. "I don't get it."

"Why are you telling me this?"

He shrugged. "It won't matter soon."

A chill ran down her spine. "Just promise me the baby will be okay."

"Oh, stop worrying so much," he responded irritably.

No such promise came.

CHAPTER

46

Ember

Ember jumped to her feet in the interrogation room as soon as Thorne appeared in the doorway. At first she was shocked to see him, especially so soon after she'd asked Heller for the chance to say goodbye, but then she realized Thorne must have been questioned as well.

He appeared pale and dazed, with purplish circles under his eyes and a deep crease between his brows. How different he looked now versus a few hours earlier onstage, when his charisma was on full blast for his adoring fans. Now he seemed shrunken down to size—deflated all the way through.

Heller tapped the doorframe. "You guys have ten minutes," he said before leaving them alone. Ember looked at the black wall. Of course, any notion of privacy was a sham. On the other side of the glass, they were still being watched.

Thorne slowly approached the table, narrowing his eyes in lieu of hello. Out of habit, she tried to reach for him, but both hands remained cuffed behind her back. She sat back down on the hard plastic chair. He stopped a few feet away, as though he couldn't tolerate coming any nearer. An awkward silence ensued. She cast about for what to say, something that would capture the depth of her devastation. Nothing came close.

"I'm sorry," she finally said. It seemed like a decent place to start.

He stared at her coldly. "So it's true then? It was you the whole time?"

"Yes and no." She sighed. "I did help create the Vault, yes. But only to punish bad people. My ex is the one who decided to go after desirables. I tried to stop him, but he assaulted me. That's why I left. Or rather, escaped. And as you know, he still tried to stalk me."

"So that's why you refused to call the cops." Thorne sounded detached. "You didn't want him to rat you out."

"I was trapped into silence. All I could do was try to stop him from afar. To protect people like you from the thing that had spiraled out of my control." She lowered her voice. "I guess I was naive to think I could start over. Obviously I don't deserve that."

"Do you know how much of an idiot I feel like? Thinking I knew you, and I had no fucking *clue*?" He curled up his lip in rage, but his eyes told a different story—one of immense hurt.

"I'm sorry. I can understand why you feel betrayed."

"Why didn't you tell me?"

"Because then you'd be culpable too. I wanted to protect you."

"You wanted to protect yourself. That's all you really care about."

"No." She looked him dead in the eye. "If that were true, I wouldn't be here right now."

He didn't respond.

"What I really care about," she continued, "is stopping him for good. Because now he's gone way too far."

"You mean with that pregnant woman? Who we thought was a crazy fan?"

Ember nodded. "He hired her behind my back. Stole my cells right out of my mouth. And now the baby is due in a matter of weeks."

"So it's really your baby? With him?"

"I'm afraid so."

"I can't—it's just—" Thorne sputtered, unable to grapple with it.

"I know." She tamped down her own disgust. "I came forward because that poor woman doesn't deserve to be caught in the middle. It's my doing, and now I'm going to help undo it however I can."

"But what's going to happen to the baby? And you?"

"I don't know." She smiled weakly. "But hey, at least you're free to walk away, right? You don't have to worry about it."

The sound of approaching footsteps interrupted them. Heller walked in briskly, agitated.

"We can't locate Quinn. She's gone off the grid, even though we just sent her to a hotel a few hours ago. The management says she never checked in."

"Shit." Ember sighed. "He's already gotten to her."

"No one's home at either of their addresses. His car is gone. We're scouring public cameras, but nothing yet. Any idea where they could be headed?" Heller frowned at her. "We could really use your help."

She felt Thorne's eyes on her as she spoke. "There is a place. But it's too risky for you to go there. If you do, it will trigger the Final Phase."

"The Final Phase?"

"That's what we used to call it. What we would do if authorities ever discovered the Vault's headquarters, where the lab and all the servers are stored." She touched her forehead to find it clammy with sweat.

"And you'd do what, exactly?"

"Bomb it. Rather than let all the evidence be discovered."

Thorne backed away as Heller's expression soured. "You have a bomb?"

"It's 3D printed," she admitted miserably. "If he and Quinn are both missing . . . he's probably on his way there now."

"Where?" Heller glanced at the glossy black wall, as if to ascertain that the agents on the other side were paying attention.

"In the desert north of Las Vegas. It's a remote bunker in the middle of nowhere. About three hundred miles from here."

Heller blinked rapidly. "So that's what—like, five hours away? And he's had a head start for the last two hours?"

"It might not be too late to try to stop him. But I have to do it alone."

Heller shook his head. "Too dangerous."

"It's Quinn's only chance—and the baby's. She knows too much."

"You think he's going to kill her, even though she's pregnant with his child?"

Ember swallowed hard. "I know how he thinks. People are just pawns to him. The baby was a tool to control me. But now that I've spoken up, he has no power over me anymore. He doesn't need the baby, and Quinn's nothing but a liability."

"Sick bastard," Thorne spat.

"And a coward," she added. "I'm guessing he wants to burn everything down with her inside, and then make a run for it. He's got multiple aliases and plenty of money. But it's possible he might listen to me."

"Why?" Heller demanded. "He already knows you came clean. That's why he fled."

"Because he's obsessed with me. I'll have to play it right. It won't be easy. But if I can get him to let me inside, then I at least have a chance of getting her out."

Heller paused. "We can stay close behind with backup. A SWAT team."

"But not too close. He has to think I'm truly alone. Otherwise, he'll blow us all up. He'd rather die than surrender."

"It's suicide!" Thorne cried. "You can't!"

The horror on his face laid bare all she needed to know: Even if they never saw each other again, he still cared. He cared deeply, despite the pain, and that knowledge was enough to rally her courage.

She turned to Heller and squared her shoulders. "We don't have much time. Let's go."

CHAPTER

47

Lily

In the private viewing room, Lily nervously stared at her dashboard on the wall. A jaunty command popped up: *Blink here to open your file!*

She blinked.

Her own name appeared beside her birthdate and social security number. It was startling to see her personal information in this strange place, and even more unsettling to realize it had been buried here all along.

A circle began to spin—her data loading.

Her whole life, she'd believed she was Unforeseen. She'd made up phony scores in high school when all the other kids were boasting about theirs. She'd pretended to be Selected for verbal ability, since she always got A's in English. The need to fib to be seen as normal had deepened her resentment toward her parents, on top of her bitterness about her mother's years in prison. Lily thought of the story—the *lie*—they'd told her: the Hawaiian getaway, the private beach, her mother's "accidental" pregnancy. But why would they saddle her with such an embarrassing taboo if it wasn't true?

Because there must be a terrible secret in my scores.

Was she destined to get Alzheimer's? Cancer? One of those terrifying illnesses that caused sudden death with no warning—an aneurysm?

Oh God. She thought of the administrator's warning: *"Do you each consent to view sensitive information . . . that you can't unknow, which may have the capacity to inflict emotional and mental pain?"*

Maybe she should just leave right now, before it was too late.

In that moment of indecision, her scores suddenly populated the dashboard. It happened all at once, like a car crash. She couldn't tear her eyes from the wreckage.

Three categories appeared: "Health Predispositions," "Personality Traits & Disorders," and "Physical Characteristics."

She quickly scanned the first category for any landmines. Her health scores—her inherited risks for a bunch of different diseases—were listed alongside the population averages.

Health Predispositions		
	Embryo's Lifetime Risk	**Average Lifetime Risk**
Autoimmune Diseases		
Psoriasis	2.1%	2%
Rheumatoid Arthritis	3%	3.6%
Systemic Lupus	2%	2.4%
Eye Diseases		
Primary Open Angle Glaucoma	2.1%	2.4%
Age-Related Macular Degeneration	7.8%	8.7%
Retinal Detachment	5%	0.1%
Cardiovascular Diseases		
Atrial Fibrillation	20.3%	21.6%
Coronary Artery Disease	52%	55.6%
Intracranial Aneurysm	5.7%	5.5%
Peripheral Arterial Disease	24%	21%
Venous Thromboembolism	9.1%	8.1%

Health Predispositions		
	Embryo's Lifetime Risk	**Average Lifetime Risk**
Endocrine and Metabolic Diseases		
Celiac Disease	1.1%	1%
Gallstone Disease	11.5%	13%
Lactose Intolerance	8%	12.1%
Type 1 Diabetes	1%	1.1%
Type 2 Diabetes	21%	24%
Neurological and Oncological Diseases		
Alzheimer's Disease	9%	12%
Migraine with Aura	11%	10%
Multiple Sclerosis	0.7%	0.5%
Parkinson's Disease	3.1%	3.7%
Basal Cell Carcinoma	13%	25%
Bladder Cancer	2.2%	2.3%
Colorectal Cancer	8%	4%
Gastric Cancer	0.8%	0.6%
Breast Cancer	7.1%	12.9%
Lung Cancer	4.5%	4.1%
Melanoma	1.5%	2.6%

Lily's eyes blurred with numbers and percentages as her heart raced. She forced herself to focus. When she did, one thing became clear: there was no major catastrophe lurking in her DNA. She did have double the normal risk of developing colon cancer but it was still pretty low, and she could easily get a liquid biopsy every year to find out if any bad cells were circulating before they amounted to a problem. And she had a slight propensity for a retinal detachment, but that too could be watched and treated preventively. In other words, she was pretty average. And average, in this context, was quite all right.

What a *relief*.

So what the hell was the big secret then?

She scrolled down to the next ominously named category: "Personality Traits & Disorders."

This time, various traits were listed beside her "polygenic score" results and each trait's "heritability." She quickly researched the terms to discover that the latter meant how important genetics was to a given trait. Some traits were highly dependent on genetics—that meant a heritability result close to a hundred percent, while other traits were more dependent on environmental factors—closer to zero heritability.

A "polygenic score" aggregated all the hundreds or thousands of an embryo's genetic variants to estimate the future person's chance of developing a given trait in real life. But the scores were not an exact science, the internet warned: *"Polygenic score predictions of behavioral traits are correlations, and correlations do not imply causation."*

Okay, Lily thought. *So take this shit with a grain of salt.* But still—this was her own self she was about to scrutinize, before she had been a self at all. Was there such a thing as a self-fulfilling prophecy if she learned something horrible about her own predicted behavior? Like, would she get depressed or go crazy if the scores said she might?

Oh, for fuck's sake. I am who I am.

She blinked out of the search bar and went back to the report.

Personality Traits & Disorders		
	Embryo's Polygenic Score	**Heritability**
Personality Traits		
Extraversion	23rd percentile	53%
Agreeableness	47th percentile	41%
Openness to Experience	35th percentile	61%
Conscientiousness	75th percentile	44%
Neuroticism	68th percentile	41%

Personality Traits & Disorders		
	Embryo's Polygenic Score	**Heritability**
Spatial reasoning	33rd percentile	50%
Verbal IQ	77th percentile	84%
Nonverbal IQ	52nd percentile	68%
Emotional intelligence	74th percentile	10%
Musical Ability	34th percentile	60%
Mathematical Ability	35th percentile	51%
High Energy	37th percentile	40%
Easygoing Temperament	32nd percentile	65%
Self-Discipline	63rd percentile	60%
Capacity for Creativity	70th percentile	49%
Persistence	80th percentile	50%
Educational Attainment	65th percentile	40%
Personality Disorders		
Major Depressive Disorder	15th percentile	50%
Bipolar Disorder	No variants detected	80%
Schizophrenia	No variants detected	79%
Psychopathy	No variants detected	49%
Attention Deficit/ Hyperactivity Disorder	16th percentile	80%
Autism Spectrum Disorder	No variants detected	90%
Obsessive Compulsive Disorder	32nd percentile	50%
Alcohol Use Disorder	11th percentile	55%

It was the strangest thing. This report from twenty-two years ago had predicted Lily spot-on. She *was* good with words, good with people, persistent, creative, bleh at math, so-so at music, a tad neurotic, on the introverted side. Clearly, she wasn't Selected to be exceptional at anything. With a twinge, she thought of Radia in the next room, who was probably an Elite—someone who had scored higher than the ninety-fifth percentile on a desirable trait. But at least

Lily wasn't at risk of becoming a psychotic drunk. So that counted for something.

She hugged her knees to her chest.

What did it mean? Why had her parents chosen her to be utterly normal and then covered it up her whole life?

Her dashboard abruptly flashed green. It was Dad returning her call.

"Hey," she snapped. "We need to talk."

"Can it wait? Mom's in the hospital." He sounded upset.

"Oh no." Lily's stomach dropped. "Is she okay?"

"She has a really bad headache for some reason. We're at St. Barnabas, waiting to be admitted."

"What about the baby?"

"I don't know. Can you come? Now?"

"I'm on my way."

Lily closed out of the report and jumped up. The riddle of herself would have to wait.

CHAPTER

48

Quinn

WHEN THE CAR stopped, Quinn rubbed her eyes, disoriented. She must have fallen asleep during the drive. Robert opened his door.

"Get out. We don't have much time."

"Where are we?"

He ignored her and climbed out.

She hauled herself to her feet with a groan. Her stomach felt like it weighed an extra fifty pounds, her hip ached where she'd been lying on it, her bladder was about to burst, and she was starving. What time was it? The air felt cooler than usual. The sky cast a hazy purple glow across the barren desert.

Wait, the—*desert*? Where the hell were they?

Without contacts, she felt disturbingly untethered.

Her sleepiness melted away as her senses sharpened. The landscape appeared remote and almost lunar, unlike any place she'd seen before. The ground was reddish-brown, littered with tiny rocks and some larger ones. There were no paved roads, no trees, no signs of life—literal or otherwise. Nothing except sparse rows of the weirdest half-built houses. Well, they looked more like facades than actual houses: steel doors inside of metal A-frames, with nothing attached to them except mounds of dirt. Quinn's heart lurched when their car scampered off over the crunchy gravel, stranding them.

"Hey!" she called, but of course it didn't stop or even slow down.

"It's fine," Robert said dismissively. "It's going to charge itself and come back."

He marched to the nearest partial house structure and placed his hand squarely in the center of the door, which looked more like a smooth hunk of metal without a knob. Quinn heard a beep. Then the hunk popped open a crack, and Robert beckoned her to follow him inside, though all she could see beyond the door was a pile of tightly packed dirt as tall as the frame.

She hung back. "I think I'll wait out here for the car."

"Come *on*. We don't have time to argue."

"Is this like a doomsday bunker or something?"

He sighed impatiently. "It's storage. I need to get a few things."

"How long are we gonna be inside?"

"Not long." There was a sharpness to his voice that evoked an image of the syringe in his bag. It hung from a strap over his shoulder, pressed close to his body.

"Fine." She stepped across the threshold into what appeared to be a primitive tunnel with a soft dirt floor and no lights. He pulled a flashlight from his bag and lit their path. It was chilly inside and smelled of dank earth. He led the way, single file, without hesitation, as though this was as normal as a walk in the park. She laced her fingers underneath her stomach like a support belt and struggled to keep up. Her groin pain was intensifying each day now, making even short walks difficult. If he noticed, he didn't bother to slow down. She detected a jumpy energy in his movements.

"I need to pee," she mumbled. "And eat something."

He rummaged in his bag and tossed her a protein bar. "There's a bathroom down there."

"Down?"

He stopped short. A dead end. He beamed the flashlight at a heavy-looking door in the wall, and when it opened, she realized it was an elevator.

He motioned for her to go in first. "After you." Numbly, she obeyed. She was no in shape to put up a fight. *But I'm still carrying your baby,* she thought. *So you have to keep me safe.*

The door sealed shut, trapping them inside, and the floor dropped faster than she'd expected. They were headed deep underground.

"Can you at least tell me what's going on?" she pleaded, trying—and failing—not to sound as terrified as she felt.

"I already told you." He stared straight ahead without making eye contact. "We're gonna get my stuff and then go."

"Go where?"

"Away. Somewhere safe."

She didn't like that he refused to look at her. He was lying, but about what, she didn't know. Maybe they were going to try to flee the country. After all, Ember had admitted in front of all those FBI agents to being a part of the Vault with him. There must be a massive manhunt underway now. The thought of it made her nearly light-headed with hope. But how would anyone find them? She didn't even know what state they were in. Maybe Arizona or Nevada, if she had to guess. Her parents' faces flickered across her mind's eye. Did they know she'd been kidnapped by her own client? Was she all over the news? They must be absolutely ravaged with worry. The agony of being unable to contact them was more painful than childbirth.

As soon as the car returned to pick them up, she vowed to plot her escape. She'd remain docile until the next town they drove through. Then, when he wasn't looking, maybe she could roll out at a red light without warning . . . or signal to someone for help . . . or fake contractions so he'd be forced to take her to a hospital . . .

But any possibilities seemed terribly far away as the elevator opened. The space she stumbled into was nothing like the cramped garage unit she was expecting, filled with crap on shelves. It was shockingly large and pristine, the size of a spacious classroom, with tall ceilings, built-in overhead lights, and a clean white laminate floor. She gasped when she saw two microscopes on a counter beside a pair of safety goggles, a fat cylindrical machine, some kind of hood, and other complicated equipment she couldn't name. A wide stainless steel freezer stood along one wall, its silver handle gleaming under the bright lights. Across the room were several dozen black machines, each about the size of a suitcase, stacked high on top of one another. They filled the air with a low whirring noise.

"Wait." Quinn spun on Robert. "Is this—the *Vault*?"

"Quite literal, I know. But it doesn't matter anymore." He gave a bitter shrug and pushed open a panel in the wall. It revolved and he stepped through it to the other side.

Mystified, she followed him into an adjacent space. It appeared to be a studio apartment. There was a bed made up with a comforter and pillows, a couch across from a wall of bright salad greens growing under a white light, a bathroom, and a kitchenette stocked with a fridge and with the latest model 3D food printer. On the floor, lying at their feet, was a pudgy Black lab with velveteen ears, coarse fur, and the sweetest brown eyes she'd ever seen. He didn't budge when they walked in. And then she understood: he was switched off.

She was about to say something when she caught sight of the framed photograph that Robert had paused to stare at. It was a picture of him with Ember; yes, despite how incongruous it seemed, it was definitely her in a greenish-blue tank top. They were both beaming at the camera, her arm draped around his neck, blonde bangs falling into her eyes. It must have been at least five years ago, back when mood-sensing shirts were all the rage. Robert was gazing at the photo with a strange mix of nostalgia and ire.

Quinn noticed that he hardly resembled his giddy younger self. His handsome tan was gone, replaced by sallow skin, an overgrown beard, and greasy hair. His eyes, once full of brightness and humor, now looked clouded and sullen.

After a moment, he shook off the trance and tore open a closet door, ignoring Quinn.

"You used to live here with Ember?" she asked.

"Only when we worked late. It was a crash pad." He crouched low in front of a safe rooted to the floor.

"But you guys are both supersmart. I feel like you could have done a million other things?"

He ignored her as he punched in a code.

"Like, why *this*?" She swept her hand over the space, even though he wasn't looking at her. He gathered an armful of watches, gold bars, and cash and stuffed them into his shoulder bag.

"Did you know in China, there's like ten different Vaults all competing? But here, I'm the only show in town."

She wrinkled her nose. "Maybe because America is better than that."

He snorted. "America is as fucked up as every other place. We're no different from the countries that treat their people like shit. Which is most countries, by the way."

"So then why bring a baby into this world?" It was a pointed question, and they both knew it. Quinn was in no position to antagonize him, but indignation bubbled out of her. She felt compelled to assert that the lively child in her womb was no tool—nor a weapon nor a ploy. She was a human being who deserved what all humans did: unconditional love and respect.

Robert went very still, as though he was trying not to spook her. A chill ran down Quinn's spine as they locked eyes. Behind his cold expression, she saw something that bordered on regret. And then she understood: she would not be leaving with him. She would not be leaving at all. She knew too much. She had become a liability. He would have to sacrifice the baby—and sacrifice *her*—to protect himself.

Abruptly she spun on her heel and broke into a run, sprinting through the revolving panel door, careening across the lab's squeaky floor, back to the elevator, where she jabbed the call button over and over, praying for the door to open and swallow her up. But of course she was too slow and too heavy, and there was nowhere else to run when his strong arms tightened effortlessly around her neck from behind, like a vise. She shrieked, kicked in vain, clawed at his forearms, as her breath shrank away, the fuzzy edges of blackness crowding her sight.

He dragged her across the floor. "I was going to make it easy, but now you've left me no choice."

She sputtered and spit, but the pressure on her throat choked off her voice.

He hauled her back to the living quarters, her legs sliding across the floor, and threw her on the bed with a grunt, easily holding both wrists with one hand as he slid on a zip tie and fastened her to the bedpost. He tightened the strap hard, so her arms were twisted painfully behind her head. Then he stepped back to assess his handiwork.

She was panting heavily, submerged in a feeling of unreality, incoherent with terror.

"It'll be quick," he promised.

"Please," she begged hoarsely. "At least—let her live."

"It's too late. I have to go. They're coming."

"Just let me come with you! I won't cause any trouble!"

He started to turn away.

"No, wait! What if you just left me on the side of a road? I won't talk. I'll say I can't remember anything!"

He shook his head. "Too many loose ends."

"But they'll find my body down here! With your lab and all your fingerprints on everything! They'll know it was you!"

"Actually, they won't find much of anything. Except ashes."

Her body went rigid. "What?"

He crouched down in front of the safe again, but she couldn't strain her neck far enough to see what he was doing. He came back into her view holding something ominous: a piece of metal pipe surrounded by wires inside a clear plastic casing. He slid his thumb over a small red switch on top.

"I'll have ninety seconds to evacuate. And then everything'll be toast."

"No!" She yanked her wrists as hard as she could, but the zip ties didn't budge.

He backed away.

"Wait!"

"I'm sorry. I get no pleasure from killing you or destroying everything I've built. But I don't see another way."

A shrill noise suddenly rang out from an intercom in the wall. A doorbell.

He nearly jumped. Quinn watched his face drain as he pounced on it, still clutching the pipe bomb. "Who's there?"

An unmistakable woman's voice pierced the room: "Hey, it's me. I'm alone. Can we talk?"

CHAPTER

49

Ember

THERE WAS NO answer at first.

Ember pressed her palm on the door, but her touch didn't work like it used to. He had cut off her access. The heat of the desert was already rising off the land in shimmering waves despite the early morning hour. Rows of mud domes—the deceptively primitive cover for the underground bunkers—blighted the reddish gravel like an alien settlement. She wiped the sweat from her brow and concentrated on her goal.

"Try again," hissed Agent Heller's voice inside her ear, where a discreet, flesh-colored bug transmitted noises to his trailer a half mile away. A SWAT team was waiting in another trailer for his command to infiltrate the bunker, but she had convinced them to let her try diplomacy first.

"I know you're down there," she said softly to the camera above the door, hoping to evoke the intimate tones they had once used with each other. "And I really need to see you."

"Fuck off."

His voice sent a shiver over her arms. The brutality it called up—the pain.. . .

But it confirmed his whereabouts. Maybe she wasn't too late to save Quinn.

"Please. Can we at least talk?"

"Bitch, you flipped."

"No, I didn't tell them about you. Only me." She paused to let the lie settle, hoping to gain a foothold.

"Bullshit. I'm not an idiot."

"I'm serious. If I did, wouldn't there be, like, a bunch of FBI people out here?"

She looked around, knowing he was watching her through the camera, and shrugged. There was no one in sight, as usual. It was why they had picked this remote location to hide the lab.

"Maybe they're waiting somewhere close," came his disembodied voice.

"Right." She snorted as if he'd said something ridiculous. Then she turned and shouted across the barren land, pockmarked with rocks and snake holes and the occasional cacti. "Come out, come out wherever you are!"

"Now wait," Heller whispered in her ear. *"Play it slow."*

She stood still. Nothing happened. She fought the urge to keep talking, to protest too much. After a minute, he spoke again, still wary.

"Why aren't you in jail? I saw you turn yourself in."

"I'm out on bail," she lied. "It killed my savings."

"What are you doing here? And why didn't you tell them about me?"

She mustered the finest acting skills in her power, picturing the dreams she'd once nursed of a life with him. It was impossible. She was no actress. All she felt was revulsion.

"Easy does it," Heller instructed.

"Because," she said quietly, "I can't let our baby grow up alone."

"How the hell did you even find out?"

"Quinn and I crossed paths . . . and I put it together. I was furious at first, obviously. I couldn't accept it. But I also can't turn my back on my own flesh and blood."

She stared at the ground, resisting the urge to scream.

His astonishment came through loud and clear: "So you actually took the hit for both of us?"

Every fiber of her being resisted what she had to say next.

"It was either that or take us both out of the picture and leave the baby without any parents. I couldn't let that happen." *In fact,* she thought, *letting the baby grow up with literally anyone but you would be a triumph.*

"But I thought you hated me . . ."

"Reassure him," Heller directed.

"We've both made mistakes," she said vaguely. "But that doesn't matter anymore. We have to put everything else aside. Isn't that what parents do?"

"Perfect," Heller whispered.

The truth was, she still had no clue what to feel toward the baby, her nightmare incarnate. But as she spoke, she realized that her last words were genuine. Why *had* she put everything aside to burst out on that stage and demand to be handcuffed? To save Quinn from injustice, yes, but there was more too. A subconscious driver she hadn't acknowledged even to herself: the desire to save her own daughter from the monster who had created her. Ember was surprised to find that beneath her horror, some part of her really did care about the baby. It wasn't love. Not even close. But it was something. A sense of solidarity, perhaps, in having both been deeply wronged by the same man.

The speaker crackled to life again with his hopeful voice: "So no one's coming here?"

"No one. They think I did it all by myself. Sorry," she added, risking a lighter tone. "I'm pulling an Orgeldick." It was what they used to call their awful old professor, Orgelding, who had been known to take credit for his postdocs' research.

A mild huff emanated from the speaker. She imagined him smiling, his left cheek marked by his one and only dimple. God, she hated that she knew him so well.

The sense of dissipating tension emboldened her.

"I want to see you," she declared. "Can you let me in now?"

"But Quinn is here." He said her name like she was an invasive species. "I don't trust her."

"It's okay. I have an idea. But can you just let me in please? It's like a hundred degrees out here."

The lock unclicked.

She pushed open the door with a mental fist pump. *I'm coming for you, Quinn.*

But before she started down the familiar tunnel, she slid her chunky gold bracelet off her wrist and left it as a wedge in the door, propping it slightly open behind her.

* * *

Unbeknownst to Ember, Thorne was watching the screen inside the FBI van. A drone beamed footage of her disappearing inside the mud dome, her svelte figure swallowed by darkness. Agent Heller leaned back in his chair with his hands behind his head.

"I can't believe she got in."

Thorne stared at the gold cuff in the door, which the drone captured in high resolution from its elusive vantage point in the sky. It was the bracelet he'd given her for Valentine's Day a few months ago, before they had ever encountered Quinn and her unthinkable pregnancy.

He felt a sharp ache in his chest. It was the same feeling he used to get when he first started going on tour, sleeping on a bus and performing in strange cities: homesickness. Except this time it was for a person, not a place. And now she was out of sight.

But did he even know her?

All this time, she had hidden the truth about her past—to protect him. Did that make it okay? Did that mean he could stumble in his heart toward forgiveness? It was too soon to tell. The betrayal still felt so stark, so sudden, like a nail ripped clean off.

All he knew was that after their final goodbye at the FBI's field office, some powerful impulse had overtaken him. In the parking lot, from the privacy of his own car, he'd watched Ember climb into the van behind Heller and Pearson, to hunt down the man who had ruined their lives. She was still handcuffed but holding her head high, in defiance of fear.

He wondered if it was the last time he would ever see her. His fiancée.

And then, as the van backed up and turned onto the road toward the interstate, he hastily reprogrammed his vehicle to follow them. He had no one to go home to anyway. Even Smokey wasn't there; he was staying in the doggie hotel he always slept at whenever Thorne had a late- night show.

Somewhere along the drive, he'd fallen asleep, but the car kept going. It was early morning when he jolted awake to discover that he was in the middle of absolutely nowhere, with the car bumbling over rocky Mars-like terrain, still fairly close behind the FBI van. The van stopped at a seemingly random spot in the wide open dirt, with no landmarks to visually orient him. So he stopped too. A few minutes later, Ember climbed out alone, this time without handcuffs, and broke into a mysterious jog, her destination unknown. It didn't seem like any actual destination existed around here.

Once her figure receded into the distance toward some strange-looking mud hills, he'd approached the van and sheepishly presented himself.

"We saw you behind us hours ago," Heller told him. "Don't know why you didn't just hitch a ride if you wanted to come that badly."

Thorne had felt himself redden. "I don't know what I'm doing here."

Heller gestured for him to come in. "I do."

Now, after having listened to Ember's entire interaction with that sick motherfucker, his stomach was roiling with anxiety and disgust.

And rage. This was the man who had forced him to live in a perpetual state of paranoid vigilance; who had broken Ember's arm; stalked her with a drone; blackmailed her into silence; stolen Thorne's own cells and extorted ransom; and stolen Ember's, to make a baby behind her back.

There seemed to be no limit to his capacity to inflict pain—and no telling what he would do next. He was a pernicious virus in human form. A parasite engorged on the innocence of others. Thorne wanted nothing more than to wipe him off the earth.

But Ember was about to come face-to-face with him underground. Alone.

Thorne's head pounded at the base of his skull. He realized there was one thing he wanted even more than to see that barely human scum destroyed.

He wanted her to make it out alive.

CHAPTER

50

Lily

THE EMERGENCY DEPARTMENT at the hospital was buzzing with crises when Lily arrived. Her gaze swept over the waiting room, taking in a sobbing kid clutching his arm, a young woman doubled over in pain, and an elderly man whose forehead was dripping with blood.

Her mother was nowhere to be seen.

Lily rushed up to the administrative counter, where a woman sat behind a glass shield.

"How can I help you?"

"I need to see my mom. She's here somewhere, maybe admitted?"

"Name, please."

Lily told her impatiently, peering through the window in the door beyond the reception area, in case her parents happened to walk by.

The receptionist pointed toward where Lily was staring. "She's still in triage. Down that hallway, to the right. Room Eight." Then she buzzed open the heavy door separating the waiting room and the triage area, and Lily called a grateful thank-you over her shoulder.

She flew inside and nearly collided with a nurse pushing a gurney. On it lay a patient who was barely conscious; drool leaked out the corner of his mouth. A machine with his vital stats was beeping frantically. Lily looked away so as not to stare. Why, now, did the universe have to remind her that not everyone who came to the hospital made it home?

But her mom would. Of course she would. *Right?*

Around the corner, Lily stumbled onto a row of holding rooms, each granted a modicum of privacy by a thin blue curtain on a metal rod. She jogged past the numbers until she stopped at eight, just outside the curtain, listening to make sure it was the right room. A man was speaking intently:

". . . antihypertensive medication as a first-line treatment, though I have to warn you that the most effective drug carries unpleasant side effects for certain women. Since you've never had preeclampsia and never been pregnant before—"

"Yes, she has," Lily interrupted, sweeping the curtain aside. "Hi, I'm her daughter."

Mom, lying in bed, gasped. Dad's eyes widened in what appeared to be horror. Lily's heart seized with fear. Hadn't they summoned her here?

"Oh, hello." The doctor seemed confused. He glanced back at Mom. "I thought you said this was your first baby?"

Mom faltered. She shot Dad a searching look.

Lily's fingertips started to tingle. "Um, sorry, but what the hell is going on?"

After a drawn-out pause—during which Lily could sense her parents holding a silent negotiation—Dad gave a slight, pained nod; Mom closed her eyes. When she opened them, they were wet. She addressed the doctor.

"It is actually my first pregnancy."

"What?" Lily stared at her mother as if seeing her for the first time: her bright green eyes and perky nose, her messy blonde hair and downturned lips. It was a face as familiar as her own. "Are you . . . not my real mom?"

"I am, but I guess it's finally time to tell you."

A lump bloomed in her throat. "Tell me what?"

"You are mine. But—I wasn't the one who gave birth to you."

C H A P T E R

51

Ember

EMBER STEPPED OFF the elevator, a hostage of dread. The lab was eerily quiet.

She had never expected to set foot here again. In another life, this room they had secretly created and financed together was a gleeful victory over the powerful bad actors in their crosshairs. She peered around at the two microscopes and computers on the counter along the far wall, exactly as she remembered, sitting beside the DNA sequencer and laminar flow hood, the liquid nitrogen tank and the centrifuge. Nearby stood the freezer and the stack of private servers holding all of the Vault's data. The accomplices of a different era.

Now it felt like returning to a family of mutinous strangers.

She tightened her arms across her chest and shuffled across the laminate floor toward the attached living quarters. Dread erupted into terror when she heard a muffled shriek beyond the door—

And then a chilling silence.

She sprinted across the lab and through the door to discover Quinn, red-faced, on the bed, with both arms and legs fastened to the bedposts, a rag stuffed into her mouth. She was arching her back and lifting her round belly into the air in a futile attempt to break free. The man Ember loathed most in the world hovered beside the bed. He seemed to be deploying a syringe into a tube of clear liquid.

"Wait!" Ember cried, rushing between them. "Don't hurt her."

He looked up at her blankly. "It's just to relax her." The lack of emotion on his face sent a shiver over her neck. For years, she had eaten, worked, and slept beside this man—yet his indifference now made him seem like someone she had never met. How had she failed to discern his inner darkness for so long? Unless her presence had kept it in check, and without her it had eclipsed him.

Now he was almost unrecognizable. A thick, coarse beard had grown around his mouth and chin. His cheeks appeared sunken, as though he had hardly eaten for days. She remembered how his stomach would shut down whenever he was stressed. Red veins crisscrossed the whites of his eyes, betraying his exhaustion.

She kneeled gingerly beside him: an ostensible gesture of peace.

"Try to de-escalate," Heller whispered, still in her ear. *"You got this."*

She wasn't alone. She could say the code phrase anytime: *"I'm feeling dizzy."* Then the SWAT team would kick into high gear and swarm the place within minutes.

But once he caught wind of them barging in . . . She glanced at the screen on the wall near the door, which streamed live video of the outside of the bunker from three vantage points. All the images now appeared still and silent, just reddish dirt and blue sky in every direction. If he saw a SWAT team approaching, they were all as good as dead.

The bomb. Where was the bomb? Her eyes flew to the closet, whose door appeared to have been hastily thrown open. The safe inside was also wide open—and empty. *Oh no.*

Beyond her own whooshing heartbeat, a snuffling noise caught her attention: Quinn's muffled sobs. Quinn raised her eyebrows pleadingly at Ember, who followed her gaze to the loveseat. There, lying casually on a pillow, was the football-sized bomb he had 3D-printed ages ago, its wires and powder naked with destructive potential.

Back then, his stunt of printing it had seemed to be the point more than ever deploying it. She remembered laughing nervously when he'd shown it to her, with the reassurance that it would stay locked up in the safe, a weapon meant to destroy the evidence if the Vault ever needed to self-destruct.

Which he apparently believed was right about now.

She never should have come down here—

Quinn whimpered, and Ember's attention snapped back to the syringe. He had just finished loading it up with the clear liquid. Oh God. Was he going to knock Quinn out and then blast them all to pieces?

"Wait," Ember interrupted. "Why do you have to drug her?"

"So we can talk privately. Isn't that why you're here?" The question was rhetorical; he raised the plunger.

"No," Ember said. "This is why."

She seized his face with both hands and kissed him on the lips—hard. It was the only thing she could think of to buy time.

Still kissing him, she pushed him down, climbed into his lap, and wrapped her legs around him.

"Whoa, whoa," he muttered, falling backward, still holding the syringe. "What are you doing?"

"Don't tell me you don't want it too." She kissed him the way he liked, sliding her tongue alongside his, deepening the pressure and sinking her fingers into his hair. His rigid posture relented as he started to kiss her back, somewhat tentatively. It took all of her self-control not to pull back in disgust and jam her knee into his balls.

She hoped Quinn understood.

When she felt his erection under his jeans—God, he was always so easy to turn on, it was pathetic—she sat back on her haunches with a little smile like the old days, when they would make each other ache for it.

"Fucking tease," he panted.

She laughed. If they had any hope of getting out alive, she had to act like she wasn't afraid. "Come and get it."

He narrowed his eyes. "Aren't you dating, like, the world's sexiest man? Plus you hate me . . ."

She waved a hand and word-vomited what she knew he wanted to hear. "Thorne? Total narcissist, and honestly a bit dull once you get past all the hype. I was going to leave him anyway when I found out about the baby, and it was like, holy shit—this is the missing link. What you did was so fucked up—don't get me wrong—but also the craziest grand gesture of all time."

Lies, lies, lies.

"You're—happy about it?"

"It's the one thing I've always wanted."

She forced herself to look him in the eye, to assess his grade of her performance.

His thick brows furrowed. It was impossible to tell if he was convinced.

"But you're going to jail," he said flatly.

"You need his help to flee," Heller interjected.

"That's why I'm here . . . I need your help to leave the country so we can raise our kid together. Not the future I ever envisioned, but still . . . it would be kind of full circle, right? Just us against the world . . ."

His face soured as he shot a glance at Quinn, who was watching them in fearful disbelief. "Us and *her*."

"Right," Ember said, as though they were fellow conspirators. "So what do you propose?"

They locked eyes. "Unfortunately, she knows too much."

Quinn's arms and legs flailed against her zip ties. With a grumble of annoyance, he strode over and plunged the sharp needle into her shoulder as if it was nothing more than a casual poke. Ember cried out and jumped to her feet as Quinn's eyes rolled back in her head. She went deadly still.

He scoffed at Ember's panic. "It's just a tranquilizer."

"What about—what about the baby?"

"It's fine. Short acting."

She turned away to hide her horror. He came to stand beside her.

"You okay?"

"Yeah." She sank to the floor and hugged her knees to her chest.

He paced the room the way he always did when he was overwhelmed. "God, I can't wait to be done with her. Caused me nothing but trouble lately."

"Isn't she due any day?"

"Yep. I'm talking about after."

"After she gives birth?"

"I've got morphine. She won't suffer."

Ember concentrated on not running straight at him with whatever sharp object she could find. "I see," she said slowly. "And then?"

"We dump her body in the river. It'll decompose pretty quick."

"And how do we get away?"

He thought for a few moments. "Can't drive over the border—too many cameras with facial recognition."

"Right . . ."

"But I have a ton of cash in crypto. I could charter a jet to come to the small private airport in Mesquite, about a hundred miles from here. It could take us and the baby somewhere warm, somewhere that doesn't have an extradition treaty with the US. Like the UAE. We could live like kings there."

"Wait, are you saying we wait for her to give birth *down here*? Like, not go to a hospital?" She widened her eyes in obvious displeasure.

"Of course. She would open her big fat mouth."

"Try to smoke him out now," Heller commanded.

"But she could carry for days or weeks. I don't want to wait that long. I want us to go now."

"And what, bring her with us on the plane?"

"Yes," Ember said eagerly. "If she gives birth overseas, she can get medical care there. It's safer for the baby."

"Oh come on, you know that won't work. No pilot would fly with her at nine months pregnant."

"It's worth a try," she insisted. "We could leave tonight."

"No." His tone took on a hard edge, one she remembered well from their frequent disputes. He hated to be contradicted. Even worse, he had the rations to stay underground in the bunker for months. Filtered water flowed through the pipes, and they had always kept a store of dried food and protein gel for the kitchen's 3D printer in case doomsday struck aboveground.

"Keep trying," Heller urged. Ember resisted touching the tiny device glued inside her ear.

"Fine." She paused. "Well, how about if you and I go take a walk and figure this out? I could use some fresh air."

He shot her a look of irritation. "It's hot as balls outside."

She sighed, unsure what to do. That's when she noticed Sparky, their old android dog, lying motionless on the floor near the kitchen. She sauntered over to him in a desperate bid to calm her anxiety. When she clicked the button under his armpit, his eyes sparked with instant recognition, and he lifted his head off the ground to greet her.

"Hey, buddy!" she squealed. He wagged his tail and sat up to lick her face with his dry leathery tongue, lacking any hint of saliva.

A hand closed around her shoulder. She jumped to her feet and turned around. His eyes bore into hers, heavily lidded with desire. With a sinking feeling, she realized what was coming next.

"We finally have some privacy now."

* * *

Inside the FBI's van a half mile away, Thorne leaped out of his chair. "You have to send help! Now!"

Heller looked stricken. "But she hasn't said the code."

"So you're going to leave her trapped?"

"He has a bomb," Pearson pointed out. "We have to be strategic—"

"He's going to *rape her!*" Thorne gestured wildly at the live audio of Ember's voice streaming into the van, her voice distant and strained.

"I'm not sure I'm still in the mood . . ."

"Come on, Em, don't be like that."

White-hot fury engulfed Thorne, making his entire body quiver with rage.

"That's it," he announced, acting on a sudden impulse. "I'm going if no one else will."

He charged down the steps and burst out of the van into the dry heat of the desert.

"No!" Heller yelled after him. "Hey, wait!"

But he was already sprinting toward the bunker, remembering the direction Ember had jogged—and the door she had propped open with her golden cuff.

* * *

Ember flinched as Mason slipped a hand inside her shirt, feeling for her bra hook. She shivered with repulsion.

"I'm feeling . . ." *dizzy*, she wanted to say. But that screen on the wall, it was too close. A quick turn of his head, and he'd notice a stampede of uniformed agents descending on the bunker. Then his retaliation would be swift and violent, and she would pay the price.

"Feeling what?" he breathed near her ear. He started to climb on top of her, but she quickly rolled out from under him, like she was escaping a moving car.

She gave a self-deprecating wince. "Sorry, I think I'm getting a migraine." Sparky sidled up next to her with his ears back. She petted his silky fur, wondering if his programming allowed him to detect fear the way a real dog could. He wagged his tail, seemingly oblivious.

Mason's face darkened. She remembered how jealous he used to get over the damn dog. How carefully she'd had to calibrate her attention to reduce the volatility of his moods. He could wield oppression in a glance.

Now, he stood up and crossed his arms. "This is all bullshit, isn't it." He said it as a statement, not a question.

Her pulse quickened. "What? No."

"You show up, make out with me, then go cold?"

"It's just . . . a lot." She peered across the room at Quinn, who was still passed out on the bed. "Not exactly a turn-on, you know?"

"Fine, then let's get out of here."

Her heart lifted. "Yes! I'm dying to take a walk, I know it's hot, but—"

"No," he interrupted, grabbing her hand and leading her out of the living area. He pulled her into the adjacent lab, with its sterile white floor and frigid air-conditioning and low hum of the servers buzzing in the background. Their twin microscopes perched on the counter next to the metal stools where they had spent countless hours sitting side by side, deciphering the secrets of other people's stolen cells.

"In here. Where it all began."

He shoved her against the freezer and pressed his lips against hers, thrusting his erection against her leg. She pushed him away more forcefully than she'd intended, and he uttered a grunt of surprise.

"What the hell?"

"I told you," she said, "I'm not in the mood."

He stepped closer again, so close she could smell his sour breath. Her gaze swept around the lab, frantically looking for a way out, but there was only the elevator in the corner.

She'd never make it there before he intervened. But now, she realized with a shock of relief, the screen with the security footage was in the other room. He would never see the SWAT team coming. She just had to keep him distracted for a couple more minutes.

"I'm feeling dizzy," she announced loudly.

"It's just us," he said, rubbing his torso against hers. "Relax."

He tucked a strand of hair behind her ear, his face inches away. She was bracing herself to endure another sickening kiss—*just a few more minutes*—when he jerked back out of nowhere, as though he'd been scalded.

"What the fuck is that?"

He was staring in horror at her right ear. Instinctively her hand flew over it. She realized a moment too late that she'd made a terrible mistake. His lips curled into a furious sneer.

"You stupid bitch. I knew it."

She opened her mouth to protest, but he scraped her flesh as he ripped out the tiny bug and hurled it across the room. The plastic shell bounced against the far wall with a little thud and fell to the ground.

"I didn't—" she began, but he smacked her hard across the face. Tears sprang to her eyes, the sting of his hand lingering. She touched her cheek as the memory of his last assault rushed back to her, his fists raised above her then as now.

"They're coming, aren't they? Aren't they? Answer me!"

She raised her arms over her face, but he reared back and punched her in the stomach instead. She doubled over with a gasp as the breath left her lungs.

"Fine," he seethed. "Let them. They'll find nothing but ashes."

Leaving her curled up and moaning, he ran back into the living quarters.

"No!" she screamed.

She rushed after him, stumbling and coughing, her ears ringing with panic. When she caught up to him, his back was to her; he was lifting the bomb off the couch. Quinn was still fast asleep a few feet away, blissfully unaware.

"Wait!" Ember cried. He turned around right as she lunged at him headfirst with all her might, slamming into his chest and knocking the bomb out of his grasp. It skidded a few feet away as they both crashed onto the couch. Livid, he immediately wrestled her onto her back and pinned her down with his arms and knees. She kicked and flailed, but it was no use. She was completely at his mercy.

But even then, she wasn't going to submit. She drummed up some saliva and spit in his face. It landed on his cheek and dribbled over his lip. The veins in his temple popped as his face went purple. When she looked into his eyes, she saw nothing human left, only hate.

His hands closed around her neck.

He squeezed too hard, too fast; there was nothing she could say or do. The edges of her vision grew fuzzy; a disturbing noise emerged from her throat; and she realized that she was choking. Her sight blackened and sounds dimmed as the pain in her neck ratcheted up, his grip unforgiving, the pressure unbearable—

She was fighting not to give in when her mind conjured a bizarre hallucination out of the last molecules of oxygen left in her brain: the impossible figure of Thorne storming in, swinging one of the metal stools by its legs like a baseball bat.

Except the vision was flying toward them in a frenzy of outrage, railing at the top of his lungs: *"Get off her!"*

The pressure relented for a blessed moment as Mason, dumbstruck, craned his neck to find Thorne towering over him, brandishing the stool. He didn't even have time to shield himself before Thorne brought it crashing down on the top of his skull with an ear-splitting thwack. Mason's head swayed as he attempted to regain composure, but Thorne brought the stool down again, his forearms bulging with all the force he possessed. Metal made contact with bone in a singular crack, like a gunshot. This time, Mason slipped off the couch and crumpled to the floor.

She peered down to see the deep gashes in his broken skull. Dark red blood seeped over his hair, already pooling beneath him.

Thorne. Thorne stood above him, panting. He set down the stool with shaky hands.

Ember froze, unsure how any of this could be real.

"How . . .?" she managed hoarsely. She touched her sore neck, where she could feel bruises forming.

"It doesn't matter." He scooped her up off the couch like a rare and precious bird. "You're okay. Right? You're okay."

He pressed his forehead to hers as she sank into the safe harbor of his arms. The reality of what had just transpired hit her in rolling waves.

Mason was dead. The bomb, undetonated.

Thorne had saved her. He knew her treacherous past, and he'd still thought she was worth rescuing. Still, maybe, worth loving.

She was going to live. And Quinn?

An abrupt clatter of shouts and footsteps filled the lab next door, Sparky barked, and soon a stream of uniformed agents entered the room, wearing black vests, helmets, and combat boots, with large guns strapped to their bodies. Agents Heller and Pearson stood at the front, leading the charge.

They quickly took in the scene: Ember in Thorne's arms, Mason's bloodied head, Quinn unconscious and tied up on the bed, the bomb lying on the floor.

Heller approached them, giving Mason's body a wide berth. "You guys all right?"

Thorne nodded. "I—"

"He was too late," Ember said quickly. "I killed him."

She felt his chest expand in surprise. But there was no recording and no witnesses. Nothing but her words to cover for him.

Heller frowned. "We lost contact about nine minutes ago, so we'll need a full recap once you clear out of here . . ."

"It's pretty simple, he forced himself on me so I bashed his head in with the stool, and then Thorne came in."

"All right. We gotta get to work defusing the bomb and getting forensics in here. You'll give Pearson your statement outside and then stay in the van until we determine next steps."

Next steps. She thought of the mountains of data stored on the lab's servers, dating back to the very beginning. A prison sentence would surely follow, but maybe she could strike a plea deal for cooperating, and avoid a humiliating public trial. Still, she'd be put away for years.

"What about him?" she asked, touching Thorne's arm. "You're not going to detain him, right? I mean, he didn't do anything wrong."

Heller's mouth hardened. "Besides trespassing on an active crime scene . . . but no, we're not going to bother with charges. We have enough to deal with here."

"What about Quinn?"

Across the room, several SWAT team agents were cutting her zip ties and trying to gently rouse her. Ember was relieved to see her eyes flutter open as they checked her pulse.

"Someone's gotta take her to a hospital to get her checked out," Heller said. "The sooner, the better. I'll call an ambulance now."

"I'll go," Thorne volunteered.

"Thanks, man." Heller wandered away toward the bomb lying on the floor and began blocking off a radius around it with caution tape.

Ember sighed under her breath. She and Thorne didn't have much longer to be together, only another minute or two until Pearson came to escort her back into her handcuffs, and Thorne departed for the nearest hospital. There was so much she wanted to say, yet no words sufficed.

So instead, she leaned into his chest, memorizing the rise and fall of his breath. His return would power her through the rest of her days, in more ways than one. And he would go back to being the adored superstar that he was, but free from the shackles of dread.

He bent his head low to hers. "Thank you," he whispered.

She smiled at the irony: though she was destined for prison, her heart had been set free. "Just promise me one thing. Make sure Quinn and the baby are okay? I guess that's two things."

He kissed her forehead. "You have my word."

CHAPTER

52

Quinn

STRANGE DREAMS BROKE across Quinn's mind. There was sloshing, then sirens, tense voices murmuring, more sloshing and nudging and many gloved hands, like a giant organism carrying her into the mouth of a cave. Except the cave shone with bright white lights. Seconds passed or maybe hours. More hands, more lights, the whir of wheels, some shouting, the screech of shoes against the floor, a painful prick in her spine, and then blackness again.

* * *

When Quinn finally opened her eyes, all was quiet except for the beep of a blood pressure cuff tightening around her arm. She looked down to find herself lying in a bed, underneath a white sheet. A whiteboard hung on the wall, and someone had scrawled out her medications (IV oxycodone), pain level (question mark), and nurse on duty (Pam).

She tried to sit up, but a searing agony ripped through her belly. In deference to the pain, she lay back down and felt for the baby the way her fingers had grown accustomed to doing.

Instead, she touched a row of stitches along her deflated stomach. With a cry, she threw off the sheet, panicking, but a gentle hand on her arm stopped her.

She was so disoriented that she hadn't realized anyone else was in the room.

She looked up and gasped. Thorne—*Thorne?*—was holding a baby.

In total disbelief, she stared at him without a word, struggling and failing to make sense of the picture: the baby was sleeping peacefully in his arms as if she belonged there, tightly swaddled in a pale pink blanket. None of his typical entourage of security guards surrounded him. She glanced around the small, sterile room and discovered that they were alone.

The scene defied comprehension. When had she given birth? Where was Robert—and Ember? Why Thorne? She hadn't seen him since the night of his disastrous show—though the timeline was fuzzy. Had it been last night—or last month? And yet, here he was, cradling a baby, the baby she must have just delivered . . . ?

"It's okay," he said softly. "You've been through a lot, but everything's all right now."

"The baby . . ." she croaked out.

"You had an emergency C-section late last night. Her heart rate was dropping, but you got here in time. She's doing really well. You both are."

Quinn tried to recall how she had ended up in the hospital, but it was like grasping at the wind. There were odd bits and pieces—a long descent, a pervasive sense of fear—but nothing solid broke through.

"Don't worry about it now," he said. "It's more important to rest. They say you've got a good six weeks of recovery ahead of you, but then you'll be back on your feet."

She leaned forward as much as she could to catch a glimpse of the baby's face.

"Do you want to hold her? She's the sweetest little thing."

Quinn nodded eagerly. She lay back against the pillows as he placed the baby against her bare chest. Bubala's eyes opened, and they looked at each other for the first time. Relief and joy overwhelmed her. The tiny face squinting up at her was scrunched and pink, with a furrowed brow, dark blue eyes, and puckered lips. Quinn lowered her onto her breast, where she immediately latched on and began to suck.

She was perfect.

Thorne was regarding her with awe.

"She's the spitting image of Em," he said wistfully. "Don't you think?"

As Quinn studied her face, the parallels revealed themselves: they shared the same perky sloped nose, almond-shaped eyes, full lips, and tiny cleft chin.

Yes, there was no doubt: she was Ember's child.

"Where is she?" Quinn asked.

He glanced down. "In custody. It's a long story, but she won't be around for some time."

"And . . . him?" She winced, reluctant to say his name or ever think of him again.

"Gone forever. You don't have to worry about him anymore."

"Good." She stroked the baby's downy hair. "But who's going to take her, then?"

"The hospital thinks we're the parents." He shook his head with a bewildered smile. "They already came by and asked for our names for the birth certificate."

"And what happened?"

"I explained that you're a surrogate, that her real mother isn't here." Quinn nodded sagely, though she felt a stab of disappointment.

"But then who will take her? Ember didn't want her in foster care . . ."

"I will," he said.

"You?" She widened her eyes in astonishment, as if he had just announced his intention to become an astronaut or run for president.

"We wanted a child. Now we have one."

"The child of a monster!"

"He's irrelevant now." Thorne gazed down at the baby, who was still suckling contentedly. "But look at her. She's incredible."

"You're already smitten."

"The second she wrapped her finger around mine, I was a goner."

"But you really want to raise a baby—*his* baby—by yourself?"

"She's mine now." When he smiled, Quinn felt a heaviness evaporate off her chest that she didn't realize she'd been carrying. The baby would be safe and loved by a good man, with all the comforts and protection money could buy. She would never suffer the outcast life.

And she herself was off the hook. As crestfallen as she felt, a smidge of relief also coursed through her. She was free to start over, free to go anywhere and do anything that would bring her joy. Now she just had to figure out what that might be. A kitchen flashed into her mind, stocked to the brim with butter and sugar and chocolate. Could someone make a career out of baking? It would be crazy to try, but no crazier than what she had already done.

The baby slipped off the breast, satiated, and closed her eyes for another nap. Thorne couldn't stop staring at her face. The way he marveled at her reminded Quinn of how unconditionally his fans admired him. She wondered if this was his first experience of profound adoration. She guessed that it was.

"What do you plan on naming her? Or have you not thought that far ahead?"

Thorne smiled, grateful to have been asked. "I want to use the name Ember's been saving for a daughter. For our daughter."

"Thank God I won't have to call her Bubala anymore. What is it?"

"I'm going to call her Lily."

CHAPTER

53

Lily

"WINNIE GAVE BIRTH to me?" Lily asked incredulously.

Both her parents nodded, the sorrow plain on their faces.

"And now," Mom said, "you know why we kept it from you all your life. We didn't want to burden you with the truth."

Lily stood perfectly still, as if the floor might rear up the second she moved. The doctor who'd stopped by earlier had excused himself as soon as he realized a family drama was unfolding, so the three of them were alone.

She glanced around the compact hospital room, with its drab wallpaper and blue paper curtain and the beeping machine hanging above her mother's head, which dripped a clear liquid into her IV. None of it seemed real. She felt like an observer outside of herself, watching for her own reaction. But nothing transpired. Only a strange whole body vibrating, like she had been plugged into a high-voltage socket. She became aware that she was quivering.

Nobody spoke. The air felt rife with anticipation.

Their anxious gazes remained fixed on her, waiting.

Finally, she lifted her eyes. "My whole life has been a lie."

She braced herself for them to deny it or make excuses.

Instead, they sighed sadly.

"It had to be," Dad confirmed. "There was no other way."

"Why not? You could have told me sooner!"

Mom grimaced, whether in physical or emotional agony, or both. "I don't know if we did the right thing. Either way, I'm sorry. All I know is we didn't want you to get hurt."

"But it was inevitable, wasn't it?" Dad ran a hand through his graying hair, and Lily noticed he seemed older and more weathered than ever. "We knew this day would come sooner or later. You don't know how long we've been dreading it."

Lily almost felt sorry for them, seeing how anguished they were by her pain.

Almost.

"And the whole ghost gun thing was a lie? You shooting the crazy guy?"

Mom pulled the white sheet up to her chin in bed. "The details were false, but the story was true. I was being threatened, and I tried to defend myself, but he died, and I went to prison for my mistakes."

"Except *I* was the one who killed him," Dad said with a sudden bite. "And your mother was the one who took the blame."

"It was the least I could do." Mom smiled wryly. "I was destined for prison anyway. As part of my plea deal, I had my records sealed so I'd be able to start over with a clean slate."

"A few weeks after you were born, before Mom went to prison, we got married, and I officially adopted you. I retired from touring to raise you out of the spotlight."

Lily struggled to put all the pieces together. "But I remember finding the ghost gun story in the news archives."

Dad nodded. "My publicist released that cover story to satisfy the media and leave us alone."

"Wait." Lily pressed her fingers to her temple. "So, let me get this straight. I was made from some of Mom's stolen cells, behind your back, out of revenge, by a psychopath who you ended up murdering before I was born?" The words felt divorced from meaning, entirely untethered from her life.

"That's right." Mom held her gaze. "No more lies. We're done hiding."

A cackle burst out of Lily at the sheer absurdity of it all, high pitched like a cry. She remembered how, for years, she'd felt embarrassed about her alleged natural conception, carrying the shame and stigma of being Unforeseen. That lie, ironically, was far more palatable than the truth.

"And he Selected me?"

"Yes," Mom said. "I had nothing to do with it, of course. But we received the report after you were born. He Selected you for good stuff, nothing bad. He had that much sense at least."

"But he was—evil." Lily touched her own face. "What about me?"

"You are *yourself,*" Dad said firmly. "You and only you."

"Exactly," she retorted. "What the hell does that even mean?"

Dad took a deep breath, as though he had been preparing for this moment. "You're the girl who started coming home and writing stories when you were five years old. You're the girl who wrote your mother a card on your own birthday, at age six, telling her not to cry, that you would always love her even though she missed your party. You're the girl who, at age nine, passed up a weekend at Disneyland with your friends to hang out with me after my knee surgery, so I wouldn't be lonely. You're the girl who stood up to the class bully at ten, who made friends with the new kid, who always gives people second chances when they mess up."

"Okay, okay." Lily held up her hand. "Stop."

"It's true," Mom said. "You turned out nothing like him."

Dad shrugged. "Your genes, your bloodline, it's all pretty much irrelevant unless you inherit a serious illness. But aside from that, it's not the big stuff. It doesn't control what you do or think or care about, or how you treat others, or how fully you love. All that's up to you."

A rush of anger swept in like a cold gust of wind. She had always considered herself lucky, not because her dad was famous, but because he was the ultimate parental role model, unfailingly kind and loving and wise. He was the constant in her life who had never let her down—not until today.

"That's great," she snapped, "but you're still not my real dad, and you never were."

"Of course I am," he said calmly. "I'm as real as they come."

"But—"

"I became your dad the second you curled your little fingers around mine, when you were five minutes old."

She started to cry. "I want it to be you. Not him!"

He opened his arms and she ran into them, sinking into his familiar hug. "Oh, honey. Don't you see?" He tipped up her chin. "All he gave you was a donor part. I'm your Daddy and I always will be."

She buried her face in his chest, and Mom scooted to the edge of the bed to stroke her hair. They all stayed in a quiet embrace while her sobs gradually ebbed.

"You guys could have turned your backs," she said after a few minutes, still sniffling. "But instead you gave up everything for me."

Mom smiled. "And we got so much more in return."

EPILOGUE

Eighteen Months Later

THORNE PICKED UP his guitar in the backyard and everyone let out a whoop. The summer sun shone overhead, unabashedly radiant. Even the thick foliage of the old oak tree couldn't stop the light from reaching the little party gathered under its branches.

Lily stood between Radia and Winnie while Mom bounced Annabelle on her hip. Lily smiled at the contrast between her sister's fancy velvet dress, covered with bows, and her chubby bare feet sticking out below. Her gummy smile, frequent hugs, and silly antics charmed Lily on a daily, almost hourly, basis. After her mother's complicated pregnancy from her advanced age, it seemed only fair that the baby was born exceptionally chill. Lily found it funny that she and Annabelle were practically the same age, in a weird biological way. Annabelle, after all, had been frozen for twenty-two years as an embryo, after Mom and Dad's journey to parenthood had gotten interrupted by Lily herself.

Dad strummed his guitar to warm up as Annabelle tried to stick a curious finger into the cake on the picnic table. Winnie had flown in from LA a day earlier to bake it at their house: maple-vanilla buttercream icing sandwiched between three layers of chocolate, topped by an edible crown of pink and purple flowers. It was sugar-free and nutrient dense, like all of Winnie's famous pastries. Lily half expected to eat it for breakfast, lunch, and dinner for the rest of the weekend.

Dad tapped a pretend mic in front of him. "This thing on?"

Radia hollered loudly, and Lily elbowed her. It was amusing to watch her best friend fangirl over her sixty-five-year-old dad, even if he was a legend.

As he launched into a soulful rendition of "Happy Birthday," she reflected on how far they had come since that fateful day in the hospital—the day she thought of as their family reckoning.

A fraught period had followed while she cycled through shock and anger, sadness and acceptance. Her parents gave her the space she needed, and she leaned on Winnie for extra support. Winnie listened to her vent, filled in her own side of the story, and gently offered perspective: "Your parents protected you the best they could. Never forget that we wouldn't be here without them."

Lily found that the most natural way for her to process her feelings was to wrestle them into a narrative. And so, with her Mom's blessing, she contributed a personal essay to the *Vanguard* series, "Generation Gamma Grows Up: Selected Kids Unseal Their Records."

Radia's piece about learning that she carried a version of the DAT1 gene that had strongly predisposed her to depression, and the ensuing cathartic confrontation with her parents, had performed decently for her first byline.

But Lily's piece had gone absolutely bonkers. Besides its vulnerable portrayal of confronting the past, it broke the news for the first time publicly about the anonymous duo behind the Vault, and her mother's role in shutting it down forever. At her parents' request, her dad got no credit. That was the official, legally consistent version of events; only the inner circle knew the real deal.

Upon publication, the overwhelmingly positive reaction stunned the family. Some commenters recalled the early years of the Vault with fond reverence for its mission of vigilante justice, bemoaning how, ironically, it had fallen prey to corruption itself. Many readers lauded her mother's bravery in owning her mistakes and facing the consequences. After two decades of hiding the truth, she was finally free.

And *Vanguard*'s blinks were way up, to Shane's delight, even beating the Escapes division. Soon the book world had come calling, offering Lily a deal to tell the whole history in depth, part memoir and part reportage. It would have been an easy foothold to a writing career, but Lily was surprised to find that she had no interest. It wasn't really her story to tell. She preferred to make a name for herself through her own ideas instead—starting with her job.

When the fellowship at *Vanguard* ended, Shane proposed that both Radia and Lily stay on to oversee a new vertical geared toward GenG. Shane realized that their blinks were the key to staying relevant—the secret sauce that would keep *Vanguard* cool in a world of legacy media dinosaurs. The job demanded all of Lily's creative energy, and she was just getting started.

Thorne strummed the final chords of "Happy Birthday," and everyone clapped. Annabelle squealed and Mom let her go straight to smashing the cake, skipping right over the candle part.

A tennis ball dropped on Lily's toe, and she looked down to see Sparky panting, his brown eyes gleaming with enthusiasm. After almost thirty years and a few replacement parts, he still never tired of playing his favorite game.

"Okay, buddy," Lily said. "Just for a couple minutes."

She threw the ball across the vast green lawn, and he raced after it. After a couple of rounds, she heard a tiny voice behind her saying, "LeeLee, uppy."

She turned to see Annabelle toddling toward her, stumbling like a drunken sailor. Then she plopped onto her butt and grinned, all pink gums except for two tiny bottom teeth. A smear of white icing decorated her cheek.

Lily blew a raspberry and her sister giggled. She was no longer a baby, but a little person now, an improbable presence in a world full of improbable people—all those who had beaten the competition to win the prize called life. The fun of it, Lily thought, was in not knowing what came next. The thrill of new experiences stretched before them, which no Selection could predict. Who knew when they might discover a passion, strike up a friendship, accomplish a dream, fall in love?

And yet the uncertainty was also the hardest part.

Sometimes Lily worried about her sister growing up to face the inevitable questions about how to be authentic and independent in spite of her established potential. A whole generation was already grappling with the same dilemma; maybe it would become a new teenage rite of passage. But Annabelle possessed an advantage that had nothing to do with genetics—a family who would love her no matter what.

She was teetering closer now, about to fall again, but this time Lily swept in and caught her before she hit the grass. Her dark blue eyes widened, mysterious as the ocean at night. Lily held her under the armpits and twirled as a laugh bubbled out of her. "Mo-more!" she cried.

Lily spun and spun until she fell to the ground, dizzy, clutching the little girl to her chest.

A shadow neared. It was their mother, transfixed by the ordinary miracle of her two children at play. She kneeled and offered a helping hand.

Lily grabbed it and held on tight.

ACKNOWLEDGMENTS

MY VERY FIRST thank you is to you, my reader. Thank you for spending your precious time in the world I've created. There's nothing more gratifying for a writer than being read.

The spark for this story came out of a class I took around 2013–2014 in grad school at Columbia University's bioethics program, which was not only a fantastic education but also an incredible source of ideas for a novelist. There, I first learned about IVG and the so-called "celebrity scenario." I knew it would wind up in a future book. Thank you to Robert Klitzman, the program director, and to all the instructors who opened my eyes to many thought-provoking new biotechnologies.

I am grateful to Professor Hank Greely of Stanford, an expert on the legal and ethical implications of IVG and author of *The End of Sex: The Future of Human Reproduction*. Thank you, Hank, for taking my call and answering my wacky questions about how to pull off The Vault—and for reaching out to fellow colleagues for insights into some scientific details.

This book languished for well over a year during Covid, which admittedly sapped me of all creativity. I don't know if it ever would have returned had it not been for the persistent encouragement of my agent, Erica Silverman, of Trident Media Group. Erica, you reignited my inspiration to pick up this story again in 2021 after having started it in 2019. This book would simply not exist without you. I am forever grateful for your support and for our friendship of almost fifteen years. Thank you also to everyone at Trident who has worked to get this book out into the world across foreign markets, on social media, and beyond.

I owe a debt of gratitude to Matt Martz, my publisher at Crooked Lane, for taking on my last book, *Mother Knows Best*, and for the exploratory conversations that helped solidify the plot of *Baby X*. Matt, you asked me all the right questions at the beginning, when the possibilities felt overwhelming. You freed me from writer's block and made all the difference.

My editor, Holly Ingraham, is a gem. Thank you for spotting the promise of my book when it was just an outline and a few pages, and for trusting me to deliver something worthy of you. Your notes undoubtedly strengthened the story and deepened the characters. Thank you also to everyone behind the scenes at Crooked Lane whose contributions are invaluable—the jacket designer, marketing and publicity team, copy editor, production editor, proofreader, page layout designer, and sales reps. My book would not be in anyone's hands (or screens) without them.

Publicity powerhouse Meryl Moss and her stellar team, including Tracy Goldblatt, have worked hard to help spread the word about the book far and wide. I am immensely grateful for their efforts and enthusiasm every step of the way.

I'm grateful for my trusted circle of beta readers, including my dear friends Lisa VanDamme, Julie Shaver, and Amy Odell; and my parents, Leonard and Cynthia Peikoff, who have nurtured my love of writing since childhood.

Rosalie, Alan, Brandon, Molly, and Ashlea Beilis: thank you for being the cozy village we can always count on (with great bagels to boot).

My dog, Wally, has sat next to me during the writing of every single book. My favorite spot to work is where he is.

To my first reader, always: Matt, thank you for proving that a charming, handsome, and wildly talented good guy isn't just fictional.

And finally, to Zach and Leo, my hearts outside my body. Thank you to nature for Selecting my boys just as they are. I wouldn't have it any other way.